REPLAYED

AVA
WIXX

First Edition: May 2023
Published in the United States of America by
Wicked Wixx Press.
The Wicked Wixx Press Logo is a trademark of
Wicked Wixx Press.

Cover Art, Ava Wixx Logo, Wicked Wixx Logo, & Interior Book
Graphics by Lindsay Tiry of LT Arts
Edited by Melissa Ringsted of There For You Editing

Print ISBN: 978-1-955950-06-0
Kindle ISBN: 978-1-955950-07-7
EPUB ISBN: 978-1-955950-08-4

For more information visit: avawixx.com

For my fellow W.W.s~
9/24/1997
Forbes Quad
12am
Ask for Prince Tobias
Bring chocolate

Prologue

As it turns out, time travel is disappointing. Although, no less complicated than it seems.

But I'm getting ahead of myself. I should start at the beginning of this twisted tale, which is technically the end. Or quite possibly the middle ... depending on how you look at it.

I suppose labels don't matter at this point.

I'll simply begin by posing a question: Have you ever wished for a do-over in your life?

Most people would answer with a resounding yes. I am not different than most in that respect. Of course, I never thought I'd actually get such an opportunity. But here I am ... or was ... or ... yeah, it's easier not to think about the tenses part in depth to avoid an aneurism. That's my only tip for time travel. Don't overthink the process because it's a waste of valuable brain resources better spent on things that aren't impossible to outsmart.

For time itself continues to tick with or without a clock, no matter if we hold the power to go backwards or not since we are still inevitably thrust forward once again.

I found that out the hard way.

So don't fight it.

Just go with the flow.

There really is no way around it.

Chapter 1

"Tomorrow's the big day!" Sera's jubilant face appeared over the top of my computer, her golden-brown skin flushed, and her dark eyes glinting with excitement. Even her curls seemingly bounced with an energy all their own. "I don't think I'm going to be able to sleep at all tonight!"

"Tomorrow's the big day for what?" Tapping my chin, I cast my gaze downward, pretending to think. "Oh, that's right." Snapping my fingers, I jerked my head up. "I completely forgot. Thanks for reminding me." I barely managed to wrangle my features into a serious expression before my lips mutinied by stretching to their limit.

"Please, like I believed that for even a zeptosecond."

"Mmm ..." I grunted, turning my attention briefly back to my computer to start the shutdown process. The fluorescent office lights buzzed loudly with Sera's temporary silence, causing me to grit my teeth.

She clicked her nails demonstratively along the top of the monitor. "How are you so calm? After all this time, it's finally happening!" She let loose a squeal. "We're going to make history!"

"Or things could go horribly wrong, and yes, history will be made by us, but as a cautionary tale of what not to do when it comes to time travel." My gut roiled, my overachieving stomach acid bubbling up my esophagus.

"Can you please not with your pessimism right now?" She sighed heavily. "The fact that we even have this opportunity is ... I still don't have words after all this time."

She was right, of course. We were about to embark on an unprecedented experiment. Both quantum physics and quantum mechanics had been used to both prove and disprove the possibility of time travel. The controversial subject a hot topic far longer than either of us had been alive; the best and brightest minds in science unable to settle on a definitive answer. But I'd homed in on a possibility few bothered to explore since it was so restrictive, and yet, in the end, I'd stumbled upon the key to unlocking the enigma of time and space. Even if it wasn't as dramatic as people were hoping for.

Standing abruptly, I slapped my open palms down on my desk. "I'm letting my nerves get the best of me. As usual."

Sera clapped rapidly, her excitement renewed. "Damn straight. None of this would even be happening if it wasn't for you and your brilliant theory. You need to let go and enjoy this."

I barely resisted the urge to roll my eyes. "Once again, I'm going to remind you that the theory of time being a manmade construct, meaning that technically all of one's life exists in one moment, is not something I came up with. I—"

"No, but you were the one who took that idle musing and ran with it."

I frowned, even as I nodded. "True, but I still refuse to take credit for an idea that's not entirely mine. Sure, most of science borrows and builds from previous theories and discoveries, but—"

"But nothing. Jumping from the idea that time is a manmade construct to considering the viability of being able to travel back in one's own timeline—leaping into your younger self—well, nobody but you thought of that possibility, at least not in the way we're doing it. This project is your baby, one I'm lucky as hell to be a part of. I mean, who would have thought when I met my weird roommate freshman year of college—"

"Hey!" My face twisted into mock outrage. "I wasn't weird. Merely misunderstood."

Sera snorted. "Okay, Ms. Misunderstood Harper Davis, whatever you say."

Gathering my purse and empty travel coffee mug, I muttered, "At least my side of the room didn't look like a *Tiger Beat* magazine exploded on the walls."

Trailing along beside me, Sera threw her hands up in the air. "Excuse me for appreciating the male form."

"I appreciate the male form just as much as you, but I didn't feel the need to plaster every inch of my available wall space with pictures of it." I shuddered. "I always felt like they were watching me."

Sera chuckled. "Yeah, that was part of the appeal."

"Does Derek know about your little exhibitionist streak?"

She snorted. "Of course."

My heart cinched, shoving the burn of jealousy through my blood, igniting a familiar longing. I was happy for Sera, yet I couldn't help but desire the same kind of relationship she shared with her husband ... although I'd given up on the hope of actually having one over a decade ago.

Arriving at the elevator, I hit the down button, trying to ignore the lingering tightness in my chest. I sighed. "Thanks for trying to get my mind off my anxiety. It actually worked there for a minute."

Sera's head dropped back as she stared at the ceiling. "You're hopeless, absolutely hopeless." She playfully punched my arm. "But I still love you."

The tips of my ears heated. I loved Sera, too. She was my best friend, and the closest thing to a sister I would ever have. But no matter how hard I tried, I found it difficult to express those emotions as easily as she did. Usually, I went with the good ole' subject change if I could get away with it. "By the way, don't forget that even though this whole thing was my idea, you were the one who built the machines that I dreamt up. Without you, none of this would have been possible, just as much as it wouldn't be without me. We're a team on this."

Sera's perfectly sculpted eyebrows shot up. "Oh, I didn't forget. I'm simply not the one who requires constant reminders of their brilliance to keep anxieties at bay." She grinned. "I'm the stable one in this relationship."

"And I'm the neurotic one."

The elevator pinged open, and we stepped inside.

As the brightly lit numbers indicated our descent, my nerves ratcheted up with each passing floor. It wasn't just the experiment looming over my head any longer, it was the prospect of going home. As if something would prevent me from showing up tomorrow and keep me from the biggest moment of my entire life. Or maybe I should say someone.

If I was lucky, he'd be out with his friends, not even aware of what day it was, or what it meant to me. I considered staying at a hotel, but then he'd probably track me down, thus guaranteeing the activation of his sabotaging tendencies when it came to anything I cared about. If I had any hope of pulling tomorrow off without a hitch, I had to pretend nothing out of the ordinary was going on. I'd been playing things close to the vest for almost a year now, praying he wouldn't discover how near success I was.

Sera squeezed my free hand, pulling my gaze to hers. "It'll be fine."

Squeezing her hand back, I nodded numbly. Sera knew a little about what was going on at home, but I kept how bad it was to myself. Mostly because I was embarrassed. I didn't want anyone, especially her, to know how I let him treat me. Somehow it felt like it was my fault, and exposing the situation would only highlight my own flaws.

"Yeah, it will be." I mustered a brittle smile. "And tomorrow we're going to—"

"Make history!" she exclaimed, dropping my hand to do a little dance.

Or at the very least escape reality for a bit.

Chapter 2

Seconds slip to hours, hours to years, and eventually, you're forced to live with your mistakes, or die trying. I knew I'd fallen into a highly functioning type of depression, quite possibly a trauma response. I wasn't exactly sure why though. My husband didn't beat me or threaten my life. Although what he did felt worse in an unexplainable way. His sabotage, his hateful words … it got under my skin and spread like a disease, infecting my self-worth in unspeakably insidious ways. And yet, at the end of the day, when I found myself sleeplessly staring at the ceiling, wondering how exactly I'd gotten to the lowest point in my personal life, I always placed the blame squarely on my own shoulders.

If only I was strong enough to walk away, if only I made different choices all those years ago. *If only, if only, if only* … My head was filled to the brim with ways the present could be different if only I'd been smarter in the past.

And now, with the possibility of getting a second chance ... well, hope had sprung to life in me. The elusive emotion not one I'd felt in years. I'd almost forgotten what it was like to have that special kind of fragile optimism. Just the mere taste of it had me clawing for more, striving to grab on and never let go. I maybe, just maybe, could fix my life.

I would have to wait though. We all would. Today was merely the first full-fledged trial. Although, that fact didn't stop me from imagining the possibilities that could lie ahead for me, and all of us, if we were successful.

Adrenaline surged through my system, alighting my nerve endings. Everything was riding on today. *Everything.* I shared Sera's expectations that we would make history with our project ... and yet ...

And yet ...

"I think you forgot to hit the button." A familiar high-pitched voice drew me from my inner panic spiral, and I glanced over to meet Glorita's hazel eyes.

"Ah ... right. Guess I got lost in my thoughts there for a minute."

Glorita tucked her silky, jet-black hair behind her ears and flashed me a bright smile, her naturally bronzed complexion glowing with excitement. "I mean, I don't blame you. I'm not even going on a trip through time and I-I don't know, this whole thing seems surreal. Sometimes I think I fell and hit my head on the way to probably a completely boring job years ago and this whole thing is a coma-driven dream. I mean, I'm a neuroscientist. Who would have thought I'd ever get to be a part of a project like this? And yet here I am one part of the girl-powered trifecta on this project just lucky to be participating and monitoring everything you and Sera set out for us ..."

Leaning forward, I hit the up button for the elevator, Glorita's words humming in the back of my brain as they transformed into meaningless babble. I couldn't help it. Glorita was my closest friend besides Sera. I loved and respected her, but the girl had a gift for gab. Something that was impossible to focus on at the moment.

She continued to talk as we headed up to the tenth floor, and I smiled blankly, hoping she didn't notice my lack of interest. My entire body was vibrating with a combination of coffee, nerves, and excitement. I simultaneously wanted to go for a run and crumple to the floor with a weird kind of exhaustion. Everything was dull around me, fading into the background, and yet my mind was crystal clear and on high alert. I focused on breathing properly, hoping I didn't forget entirely, or worse, hyperventilate.

The elevator doors pinged open, triggering a startled gasp from me. Before I could even attempt to center myself, Sera appeared seemingly out of thin air. She grabbed my arm, hurrying me along. "Of all the days for the two of you to be on time instead of early." She glanced at my clothes, crinkling her nose. "Did you sleep in those?"

"You're assuming I slept."

"Fair enough. I didn't sleep either, but I at least don't look like it."

"Harper looks comfy," Glorita chimed in.

I grunted. I knew Glorita was simply attempting to smooth any possible friction between Sera and myself, no matter how small. The girl was seriously averse to any kind of tension. The first time I raised my voice in front of her I thought she was going to curl into herself so hard that she would actually disappear. And I wasn't even directing my anger at her, she was merely present for the interaction.

"Today is not the day for comfy," Sera snapped, continuing to drag me along. "This is going to be documented. The whole thing on video. If things go down the way we hope, then future generations are all going to remember you in your *comfy clothes*."

"I mean, it's not that bad." But she was right. I knew today was going to be recorded, and yet I hadn't stopped to consider the ramifications of that fact if things went according to plan.

Shit. The entire scientific community could become familiar with me in my wrinkly lounge attire. That was just the tip of the iceberg though. I hadn't bothered to wash my chin-length, dark brown bob. It hung limply around my face, my pale complexion blotchy and red from my ratcheting anxiety. I didn't even want to contemplate how red my green eyes were. At this point, they could probably double as Christmas décor. *Shit, shit,*

shit, shit, shit. I wasn't vain, but I also didn't want to be forever remembered as the dumpy scientist of our trio.

Yanking away from Sera, I glanced around in a panic, my hands trembling as I clutched my bag tighter. "Maybe I have time to grab a quick shower?"

Sera crossed her arms over her chest, her foot tapping rapidly against the floor. "And where exactly do you plan on doing that?"

"Umm … well, maybe I could wash my hair in one of the bathroom sinks?"

I was growing desperate, the need to change this, to have some kind of control over my situation when I felt like I was failing in other areas of my life. Work was where I excelled. How had I let such an important detail such as how to present myself in this experiment slip through the cracks? The clothes I could live with, the less-than-perfect complexion I was stuck with, but my hair— my hair I could fix. I needed to appear polished and professional, not like a grad student on their way to class after a bender. First impressions mattered, and mine was about to be digitalized.

"I'm sure we can spare the time for her to make herself feel presentable," Glorita said, the bright smile plastered across her face no longer reaching her eyes. "After all, we want people to pay attention to our findings, not focus on —well …" She cleared her throat, not wanting to say what I already knew. That I wasn't a hot mess, I was just a mess.

Covering my face with my hand, I groaned. I didn't

even need help to sabotage my life anymore, I'd taken over the job completely today.

No. Unacceptable. I can— will make this work. I haven't done anything unsalvageable ... yet.

Renewed determination surged through my system, and I snapped my head up. "I'm going to make a quick run to the pharmacy across the street to grab some shampoo and conditioner. Or—" An idea was forming. "Better yet, I'm going to see if I can rent a room at that hotel two blocks over. I'll use their shower and come back fresh." I glanced down the line of my body to take in my black pants and shirt, smoothing my hands over them. "Or I'll be fresher than I am now."

Sera scowled, even as she nodded slowly, concluding that I wasn't asking her permission, and in this, I wouldn't bend. I'd fucked up, but if we started our experiment slightly later than planned it wouldn't be the end of the world. Getting the entirety of our project just right was paramount. And presentation mattered, plain and simple.

"Okay then." I pivoted on my heels and dashed back the way I came, but skipped the elevator, opting for the stairs instead. If I got a little sweaty it would be fine since I was about to take a shower anyway. Besides, I could use a way to burn off a bit of my anxious energy.

My short trip was a blur, my thoughts centered on repeating my own set of encouraging mantras. *I will not let the slightly less-than-perfect start to this momentous day derail me. I am course-correcting, and all will be fine.*

Suddenly I was stumbling through a surprisingly posh hotel lobby, almost confused by my presence there, even though my feet had brought me by my choice. When I finally reached the front desk, the elderly woman with white hair behind it eyed me with mirth in her sharp-witted gaze.

"Can I help you?"

"Please tell me that you have a room I can rent for an hourly rate. Although I won't need it for that long."

The woman's eyes widened slightly before narrowing. "We're not that kind of establishment. And before you start any kind of protest, we are privately owned, therefore not restricted by laws applied to chain businesses. We can do what we want here."

Realization dawned, and I waved my hands in the air, my face heating with embarrassment. "No, no, no. I don't want it for any kind of … well, you know. I work not too far from here and I forgot— okay, not forgot, but I'm going to be recorded and I didn't even wash my hair. I merely wanted to do that. Wash my hair, take a shower … by myself, in case that wasn't clear."

Wincing, I stopped to replay in my mind what I'd just said, coming to the conclusion that it had been barely coherent, at best. Sighing heavily, I made a second attempt. "I just want to take a quick shower. Not, you know, or I mean, I'm not meeting anyone here for any reason." I tugged on my matted bob for effect. "I mean, would you want to be remembered on potentially the most important day of your career with hair like this?"

"Mary, she can borrow my room," a deep baritone rumbled from behind me.

I froze, something familiar about the tone and cadence of the voice, and yet I was too frazzled to delve deeper into the subject. The entirety of my scientific brand, my entire reputation, rested on the greasy mop of hair plastered along my skull, and whether or not I could wash it.

Am I being too dramatic? Probably. But the world of science is filled with drama. Hell ... magic itself is merely science not yet explained. And what is magic without the drama that surrounds it? Completely boring, that's what.

The front desk lady, Mary, apparently, raised her eyebrows in surprise. "Mr. Sh—"

"Mr. Smith. Yes, that's who I am. Thank you for remembering, Mary." There was a pregnant pause before he continued. "It's fine, Mary, she can borrow my room, as I said."

Mr. Smith stepped forward, moving to stand in front of me, somehow managing to obscure his face completely, and only giving me a view of his broad back. His tall stature was adorned in a grey suit, and his nearly black hair, at least the back of it, was a bit long, curling over the top of his collar. "Just give her a key to my room and I'll wait down here in the lobby for about an hour."

"But, Mr. Smith, you can't trust a stranger in your—"

"It'll be fine." He leaned forward, murmuring something I couldn't quite make out.

I wasn't sure what to think about any of this. It was my

experience that people rarely do things out of the kindness of their hearts for complete strangers. But what could this man have to gain from allowing me to use his shower? He'd already stated that he would remain in the lobby while I was making use of his accommodations. Maybe he had a camera set up in his room? Or quite possibly he was angling for a guilt trip of some sort once I'd already taken him up on his offer. Kind of like when a guy buys you an expensive dinner on a first date. Perhaps …

I shook my head. "No, I'm sorry. I really appreciate the offer, but I would much rather rent my own room, if that's at all possible." Leaning to the side, I attempted to snag Mary's gaze, but she was staring up at Mr. Smith, a pensive expression etched into her weathered visage.

Mary cleared her throat. "We don't have any rooms available at the moment."

I blinked several times, processing. "You mean to tell me the hotel is completely booked?"

I found that hard to believe since we were the only ones in the lobby, and I hadn't seen anyone else besides Mary and Mr. Smith since I'd entered the hotel either. Unless there was an event such as a convention nearby, in which case the guests could be occupied at the moment. It wasn't implausible, simply highly unlikely. Not to mention that this whole thing with Mr. Smith felt … off.

Mary glanced at Mr. Smith and then cleared her throat again. "Yes, that's exactly what I'm saying. There are no rooms available for you to rent. Your only option for a shower here is to take Mr. Smith up on his offer."

"I, well, what I mean is …" *This is insane! There has to be a way other than showering in some strange man's hotel room.* "Hold on," I snapped, fishing around in my bag for my cell phone.

After doing a quick Google search, my head hit my chest, a frustrated growl trickling from my throat on its own accord. Sera and Glorita had no choice but to wait for me, but I didn't want to be any more of an asshat by running all over town, possibly taking hours, in order to fix a problem I created myself. At that rate I would be better off heading back to my house—

But I can't. He might be there. And then he'd ask questions. Shit. I can't risk any more delays or sabotage, from me or anyone else.

"I need a minute to think about this," I blurted. Or quite possibly shouted. It was hard to tell in my current emotional state. "Is there a restroom I can use? Please." I wrung my hands to keep her from seeing them shake.

Mary pointed behind me. "At the end of the hallway just past the elevators."

I scurried off without another word, my gut twisting with indecision. *What should I do?* I wanted to put my best foot forward in all ways when it came to the experiment, but I suddenly didn't know what that meant anymore. I was driving myself insane over a bit of greasy hair. *Maybe it's not that bad. Maybe I should just head back now, forget about this nonsense, and get this show on the road. I'm afraid of failure, so I'm delaying this whole thing over something ridiculous. That has to be it. So no more excuses.*

Stumbling into the bathroom, I beelined for the oversized sinks, gripping the edge of the one closest to the door. I stared into the mirror, one of the lights above me flickering slightly. My eyes ran over my reflection, specifically the mess on my head. *Fuckity, fuck, fuck, fuck. It is that bad. Seriously, I don't remember dumping a bottle of olive oil over my head this morning. So gross! I can't be the genius, but disgusting scientist in this video with Sera. It would be an embarrassment for us both.*

All right. Let's get this over with. Desperate times call for desperate measures.

I marched back into the lobby, loudly proclaiming, "I'll do it! I'll borrow Mr. Smith's room!"

The man in question was no longer anywhere in sight. *Did I miss my opportunity?* My stomach gurgled at the thought.

Mary smiled, some unknown emotion glinting in her gaze. "Mr. Smith thought you'd say that and left his key for you." She pushed it across the counter at me. "Just bring it back here when you're done so I can promptly return it to him."

I guess I didn't have to worry about where he was for that matter either if I had the only available key to his room. "Okay." I nodded resolutely before snatching up the bit of plastic. "I'll be as fast as I can." I paused, shifting from foot to foot awkwardly. "I hate to be any more trouble, but do you have any shampoo and conditioner I can buy?"

"Mr. Smith said you can use whatever is in his room."

I nodded again, silently praying that he wasn't one of those guys who used all-in-one shampoo and conditioners. Although, even if he did, I would have to make do because beggars can't be choosers. And I was definitely the beggar in this situation.

Chapter 3

Some days can be classified as odd or weird, then some days are downright surreal. Today for instance. It went beyond the pending time travel experiment, that in itself would have been enough to make anyone feel a bit off-kilter ... no, it was more than just that. It was me standing in the room of a stranger—a man who appeared in my hour of neurotic desperation—to offer exactly what I needed, only to disappear again without me so much as getting a glimpse of his face. I'd awakened in reality, and somewhere along the line stumbled into fiction. The type of fiction where the main character is missing something completely obvious, and yet they can't seem to grasp what the audience is undoubtedly shouting at them to see.

"How in the world does Mr. Smith have all of my favorite products?" I asked the universe out loud, half expecting the answer to suddenly appear in front of me.

Because ... why not? That was the kind of day I was having. Perhaps I merely needed to ask the right questions —or ask any questions at all to get a response.

But the lush hotel room remained silent as my gaze flitted over the products lined up along the counter in the bathroom. There was also a note, appearing to be hastily scratched out on hotel stationery:

IT ENDS WHEN I SAY IT ENDS, SNOW.

Weird. Even weirder still was how my heart knotted itself in my chest as my eyes traveled over the words. *But whatever. It's not for me and none of my business.*

I snatched up my favorite shampoo and conditioner, the same pairing I'd been using for years, despite people telling me I should switch it up periodically for the health of my hair. I couldn't help it, though. If I found something that worked, I used it until it ... well, didn't work. Plus, there was no scientific proof that—

Aaah, why is my mind grasping at such mundane things to fixate on today? I'm about to make history. If I can get my shit together and focus on the actual experiment, that is. Is this avoidance behavior? Am I so emotionally unstable that I can't even let myself be successful?

Determined to ignore my neurotic impulses, I made quick work of my shower, making sure to leave things as neat as they were when I entered Mr. Smith's room. I even resisted the urge to snoop, which for me was practically a miracle. It was the least I owed the man who helped me in my time of need. Besides, I was afraid of what I'd find, and I didn't need any more distractions as an excuse to delay the experiment.

You won't fail. Even if today doesn't go exactly as planned. You will dust yourself off and try again. Science isn't about getting things right the first time, it's about never giving up until you find the right answer. Sera, Glorita, and I will make history. If not today, then tomorrow, and if not tomorrow, then the next day. Rinse and repeat until we succeed.

Filled with renewed confidence, and clean hair with just the right amount of shine and bounce, I quickly dropped the key off with Mary before heading back to the office. The place I should have been all along.

ON MY SHORT walk to the office, I decided the detour to get myself into a presentable state was not a complete waste of time since it not only served the obvious purpose, but also gave me enough space to get into the mind frame I needed to be in for the experiment.

"We've been waiting for you." Sera spun around in her chair, like some 80's movie villain, her right eyebrow slanting up dramatically.

I sputtered on a laugh. "How long were you waiting to do that?"

Sera shrugged, her shoulders tense despite her attempt to act nonchalant. She was probably just as anxious in her own way, simply a lot better at coping with it. That's what made her the stable one in our relationship. It's not if you get anxiety or not, it's how you deal with it that makes the difference. Sera used humor, I spun out of control. One was the obvious winner out of the two strategies.

Glorita bustled into the room carrying her iPad, her manic energy wafting off of her in palpable waves. "Yay! We can get started now!"

All the equipment, from the cameras to the highly experimental machinery, was in place and cued up. I expected no less, positive the two of them would react exactly as they were the moment I arrived. I couldn't blame either of them. If I wasn't a neurotic, self-sabotaging mess, I would do the same in their position.

Shoving the last of my trepidations aside, along with the roiling nausea bubbling through my middle, I forced a grin onto my face. *Fake it until you make it and focus on the positive.* "I'm feeling much better now." I flipped my hair away from my face for emphasis. "Let's get this show on the road."

Glorita raced around the room, a blur of jerky movements as she checked over her aspects of the experiment. She would be monitoring me and Sera while we got to do the fun part.

Flopping into the huge, leather recliner positioned beside Sera, who was already reclining in a matching chair, I hooked myself up to what we'd dubbed our time machine. In actuality, our bodies wouldn't be going anywhere though. Only our consciousness.

Finally, my mind snapped into work mode, the

familiar calm settling over me. *This is where I excel. This is where I'm successful.* "I'm ready." Turning my head, I met Sera's gaze.

"Me, too," she said, a tad more white ringing her irises than normal.

My lips curled up, causing hers to do the same. "I'll see you on the other side."

Her nostrils flared as she forced herself to take in a deep breath. "I still can't believe we're doing this. We're actually doing this."

"Yeahhh," I drawled. "You and me are doing this."

"Okay, I'm going to start recording now," Glorita said.

"Ready," Sera and I chimed in unison.

A sudden wave of nostalgia washed over me, and my thoughts flittered back to when Sera and I met in our freshman year of college. Mismatched personalities paired as roomies and destined to be oddball friends that somehow just worked. Best friends, partners ... hopefully the world's first documented time travelers.

Glorita moved over to her station, giving us a thumbs up. "Everything looks good over here. Whenever you two are ready."

I glanced down at my controls. "Everything looks good here, too."

"Things are looking good here as well," Sera stated, her tone all business. "Double-check the date set for us, Glorita."

She leaned forward, eyes narrowed on one of the

screens. "Mmm-hmm ... it's set for thirty days ago for both of you."

I gulped. "Okay."

Sera and I were about to jump back into our own bodies from a month ago. We would then leave evidence of our trip, in the form of future facts, inside the safe that was time-sealed twenty-nine days ago and set to open two days from now. Once done, we'd use the same machines to push us back into the present, which was why we could only go as far back as our equipment existed. Again, it was nothing grand, the limitations currently extensive. But it was merely the first step—the first step in many more to come. The main purpose of this particular checkpoint was to hopefully draw attention to what we were doing. Positive attention meant more money. More money meant everything when it came to science. Especially for us since the funding from our singular investor was about to run out.

I flicked back the clear protective cover, my thumb hovering over the obnoxiously large red button. The one Sera thought amusing to install as the activation device on our machines. Hopefully, it wasn't an ironic sign of things to come.

I gulped again, my throat suddenly the Sahara. "Okay, here I go. Right now." My thumb trembled, and I squeezed my eyes shut. "Three, two—"

A loud thud sounded from Glorita's direction. "Oh, shit. Wait. Stop. I tripped and my elbow bumped the—"

"One." I hit the button, and a jolt of electricity zinged

through my system. It was expected, and not exactly unpleasant, kind of like mainlining a pot of coffee. My eyes shot open in time to witness Glorita dashing in my direction, waving her hands frantically.

"Harper, take the headset off no—"

My surroundings disappeared in a rush, a flash of white encompassing everything.

Chapter 4

"**T**urn it *off*!" Something slammed into the side of my face, soft and yet nonetheless jarring.

"What?" I muttered, my brain scrambling to make sense of—anything.

"I said to *turn it off!*"

It was then I registered the annoyingly loud and consistent ringing, the sound pulsating through my skull.

"What's going on?" The last thing I remembered was—

Dim light flooded my vision as a pillow was ripped from my face, Sera's angry visage inches away. She let loose a snarl before spinning to slap her hand down on my alarm clock, the two small bells on top clanging as they came to an abrupt halt.

"I will seriously murder you if you reset that thing one more time. It obviously isn't working ... on you." Huffing dramatically, she stomped to her bed with the reclaimed pillow under her arm and flopped down with her back to me.

Sitting up, I blinked dazedly at my surroundings. No less than a hundred pairs of paper eyes stared at me from across the room from all available angles. "Oh my God!" I clapped my hand over my mouth.

"Go to class," Sera growled. "You know I love you, but I seriously hate you right now."

My mind whirled, finally coming back online, so to speak. I'd been in our office with Sera and Glorita, I'd hit the red button to send me back in my timeline a month. One single month.

And then ...

Glorita waved her hands frantically. "Harper, take the headset off no—"

Realization hit. *Something went wrong. Glorita was telling me to take my headset off before it was too late.* A brick of anxiety dropped into my stomach, stirring up the already bubbling acid. *It's already too late.*

I'd traveled too far back. I knew exactly when and where I was. It was the very same freshman year I'd been lamenting directly before our experiment had spun out of control. And to narrow it down further, judging by the lack of blankets on my bed, along with Sera's familiarity with me, it was the second semester of the 1997 school year—the spring of 1998—at The University of Pittsburgh. The following year we'd moved off campus together and had our own rooms.

Holy shit! I have no way back! I'm not the one who built

those machines. Sera did! And even though she's here, she doesn't have the education to build them yet. My vision wavered, and a handful of black spots decided to do a little dance number.

I'm stuck. My adult self is stuck in my eighteen-year-old body.

But wait ...

Maybe I'd gone farther back than I'd planned on going, this trip anyway, and quite possibly at all. But, in the end, isn't this what I truly wanted? To get a do-over in my life? To alter the bad decisions I once made?

Although when I consider the other side because it would be irresponsible if I didn't ...

This situation left me wide open to a gamut of temporal paradoxes and issues that I wasn't prepared for. I wouldn't need to worry about The Grandfather Paradox since I was still in my own timeline, but I remained vulnerable to causal loops. Those were a kind of time travel entanglement that I especially didn't want to mess with, the complications potentially arising from them unmanageable. Basically, I'd been thrust into a seemingly dream scenario that would most likely turn out to be a nightmare.

Fighting the sudden and nearly overwhelming urge to hide under the covers, I forced my legs to move, and I stumbled awkwardly out of bed. My gaze scanned my side of the room, uncertainty not allowing me to take another step.

My thoughts were now locked onto the possible

ramifications of causal loops. There was a higher than fifty percent chance that I was already snared in one. But the truth was that I couldn't do a damn thing about it at this point. I was trapped in my younger self without a way out. There were certain choices I should, and probably would change, now that I could, but I also needed to be careful not to alter the big things for me or those around me. The best plan of action would be to stick to my old life as much as possible ... in most ways.

The most pressing question was: What were considered the big things? Some might say that one's love life would be at the top of the list of non-negotiables. Walking away from the man who was supposed to be my husband before we even kissed would change a lot, but there was no way I couldn't abandon those horrible choices, aka him.

However, by simply being here, in my past, things would be different. I didn't remember every little thing I did and exactly how I did them. For example, seemingly minuscule decisions like what I picked to wear, or what words I used in a conversation, faded into memory quickly, and according to the well-known butterfly effect, small things weren't insignificant either. Even if the fate of the universe depended on it, I wouldn't be able to move through my past identically to the first time I'd experienced it.

Okay, okay, okay. You can't become a statue in the middle of your room. Indecision is as bad as the wrong decision in this case. Of course, everything is a bad decision merely by being here. No! Stop. You're here. Make the best of it. Live your life ... whatever that means now.

I needed to turn the overanalyzing part of my brain off. To sink into my old self and let go of where I came from, since technically none of that existed anymore. At least to me.

Awareness of my body returned, and I shivered, goosebumps lining my flesh.

My body! What would happen to the one I left behind if I never went back? Would it die? For me to be in my past, I had to come from my future, but as I moved forward again, the original timeline would no longer exist. But it had to exist for me to be standing here, now, in my past with future knowledge. Also ...

Shit. Causal loop. Don't think about that. Or multiverses ... or any of it. It's pointless and an exercise in futility. Plus, I'm bound to give myself a headache.

"Why are you still here?" Sera grumbled. "You're the one who scheduled an eight a.m. chem lab. Learn to live with your poor choices."

A demented laugh bubbled up my esophagus, and I swallowed it down. That was the thing, wasn't it? I didn't have to learn to live with my bad choices anymore. This was my second chance, and I was about to waste it by overthinking ... well, everything. Fortunately, it wasn't too late, not even close. In fact, it suddenly felt like I had all the time in the world to figure my life out.

Without another word I rushed around my side of the room, fumbling through drawers. It would take me some time to remember my normal patterns and schedule. For the moment, I'd settle for knowing where I stashed my toiletries.

I SHUFFLED out into the crisp morning, tugging the collar of my paper-thin jacket up. In the span of an hour, I'd proven that a person's attitude towards the weather did make a difference. Who would have thought that tiny tidbit was more than joke fodder? You see, my youthful body, once upon a time, hadn't been bothered by the cold. Now my aged brain was informing me that I should be freezing, and justifiably indignant that I didn't own any warmer clothes. Apparently, mind over matter wasn't necessarily a good thing.

I'd also discovered that just because I had the knowledge to figure out and be the driving force in the development of time travel didn't mean I remembered how to do basic, freshman-level chemistry. If I continued on my current path, I was sure to fail out of college instead of graduating early like I'd previously done.

"Hey, Harper!" a masculine voice echoed across Forbes Quad. "Wait up!"

I turned stiffly, swallowing back a grimace as my gaze caught on the tall, lanky boy jogging towards me. Of course, in jeans and a T-shirt with no jacket in sight. His face was familiar, but I struggled to conjure his name or how I knew him.

"Hey," I managed when he drew to a stop in front of me. He was kind of cute if not a bit young. Or I supposed not any younger than I currently was ... again. Even though that was the case it would take a while before I could let go enough to accept that. My whole situation kept making me think of different storylines from books with vampires. I wasn't immortal, but I suddenly had an intimate awareness of what it felt like to have a mind chronologically older than my body.

The boy ran his slender fingers through his floppy, auburn hair. "My friend's band is playing at Graffiti's tonight. You should come." He produced a small, rectangular flyer, offering it to me. "Bring your friends."

Taking the bright blue paper from him gingerly, I stared at it a moment before responding. "Oh, uh, I mean ..."

"Come on, it'll be fun. Plus, it's kind of a big deal that they got a showcase there. It would really help if we filled the place up."

I had to re-immerse myself in my life. It was essential to my survival and my future. I just couldn't seem to get past the acceptance part of the process. The problem was the surrealism of my time-traveling dilemma. I couldn't make myself forget what I already experienced, even with a young body and the willingness to do so. Basically, my brain had seen some shit, and I simply wasn't the same person I once was.

And maybe that's okay. If I was the same, then I couldn't make different— better choices than I did before. Ahhh, stop overthinking. How many times do I need to remind myself to stop friggin' overthinking?

Forcing a smile, I said, "Sounds great."

The boy grinned at me, showcasing a crooked front tooth. That, combined with the smattering of freckles on every visible inch of pale skin, made him seem endearing, in a younger brother sort of way. "All right, I'll see you there."

Waving at him feebly, I watched him retreat the way he came. As soon as he was out of sight, I returned my attention to the flyer crumpled between my popsicle fingers. *Nameless*, which was apparently the band's name, was plastered across the top in a questionable font. Followed by Graffiti's logo, the address, along with the date and time. That was it. No pictures, no links, no anything else I'd grown accustomed to in my adult life.

I blinked repeatedly, reading and rereading the scant information presented to me on that scrap of paper. And finally, between one blink and the next, it all sunk in.

I wasn't visiting my old self. I wasn't in a simulation. I was eighteen years old again, wholly and completely. And with that came the opportunity to not only get the option to make different choices with my life but the chance to enjoy all the things I missed about being in the nineties. Simplicity, for one.

My mood suddenly buoyed, and a smile tugged at the corners of my mouth.

Tonight, I will officially start over. Fuck worrying about causal loops and butterfly effects and any of that nonsense. I'm here. That's all that matters. I'm here and I will make the best out of round two.

Chapter 5

"What is up with you today?" Sera tilted her head, snagging my attention, and my reflection's gaze with her abrupt appearance in the bathroom doorway.

Standing frozen in front of the mirror, I was currently contemplating the merits of performing an impromptu haircut with sewing shears. My dark, glossy strands hung in long waves, hitting the middle of my back. And even though I wasn't technically with the man—my future, and past, husband—yet, or hopefully at all, he'd been the one to inspire me to passively-aggressively choose my signature bob. He did adore my long hair, which meant I'd grown to hate it. Not the long tresses in themselves, but the idea that he had the power to influence how I decided to cut them. It was about asserting control over my life, even in such a small way.

But he's not your husband now. And never will be.

Grimacing, I lowered the shears slowly. Impulse control about such things was never my strong suit to begin with. Add in the factor that I was only eighteen years old with a prefrontal cortex that wasn't fully developed ... and yep, I should drop the scissors and run.

"I was just thinking that I wanted a change. Maybe." Even though I'd cut my hair short for the wrong reason to start with, I did look good with short hair, and it was easier to manage. *Ugh. When did my latest hyper fixation become my hair? Hair, hair, hair, hair, hair. My life revolves around it now. Maybe I should shave it off and be done with it. Then I would be forced to focus on things that really matter instead of irrelevant shit. Or at least it would in theory. Because it certainly doesn't feel irrelevant to me right now.*

Sera nibbled her bottom lip, studying me in silence. It was borderline unnerving.

Turning to face her fully, I demanded, "Why are you looking at me like that?"

She lifted her shoulders slowly and dropped them. "There's something different about you today. It's like you woke up with completely different energy or something."

Oh, yeah, my energy was definitely more chaotic than it used to be, that was for sure. Leave it up to Sera to notice something that practically no one else ever would.

"Well, um ..."

"And you know, anytime someone is contemplating a dramatic hair change, it's about more than just the hair." She narrowed her eyes at me. "So what's going on?"

That was true. Hair was definitely about more than the

hair itself. It had recently become my obsession for more than the vanity of it. I knew that deep down, but didn't want to face the fact that I was again using a poor coping mechanism to slap a Band-Aid on my issues of control. That was something I'd have to deal with later though. For now, I needed to focus on what exactly to say to Sera.

She crossed her arms, her eyes narrowing farther to become slits as she waited for me to spit it out.

I sighed. I was never good at sharing on my best days. The truth was, sometimes I couldn't shake the lingering feeling that no one, not even Sera, knew the real me. I hid parts of myself, worried that I'd be rejected if I wasn't what people wanted or expected. I'd often wished to lay it all out in the open, to bare my soul, but I held back bits and pieces, leaving me to continue wondering. Even in the future, when Sera and I were as close as sisters, I didn't tell her how bad my marriage truly was. I just couldn't, positive that at some point she'd have enough of my neurotics and decide to abandon me for good. It was probably another reason I never developed the guts to leave my husband … I was afraid of being alone.

"Spill, Harper. It's written all over your face that something is bothering you."

Lifting my hair to study it in the mirror again, I wrestled internally with myself on what to say. I knew better than to reveal the complete truth since I genuinely might end up in a padded room if I mentioned time travel of any kind in seriousness.

I shot my reflection a death glare. This was my second

chance, the whole thing kind of like when you replayed a movie or show, and you caught things you didn't notice before. The painfully obvious fact that I never admitted to myself at this age was that I needed to adjust my attitude. I always had and always would get in my own way if I didn't finally come to terms with it. My bad choices had been my bad choices, no one else's. To change my life for the better I had to stop overthinking every little thing. I'd already told myself that same tidbit at least a dozen times since waking up in my younger body, and yet my follow-through was nonexistent. Until this point.

"Fuck it." I snatched the shears off the sink and cut off a chunk of hair, the dark strands fluttering to the floor. It was time to stop questioning every motivation. It was what it was, and I am who I am now. I wanted to cut my hair, so I would. The rest didn't matter anymore.

Sera clapped a hand over her mouth, her eyes widening to the size of saucers. "Oh, my God, I can't believe you just did that."

My lips twisted into a cross between a grimace and a grin, the expression fully demented. "I know."

In a sort of daze, I continued lopping off my hair, only finishing when it sat in uneven rows around my shoulders.

"It looks— I can't believe— Well—" Sera, who was rarely at a loss for words, stumbled over what to say, her mouth hanging open like a fish.

I giggled as I reached up to fluff my butchered bob. "I wanted to go shorter anyways. I'll just go to that salon down on Fifth that takes walk-ins and they can clean it up."

Brushing past Sera, I grabbed my coat from the back of my desk chair. "You coming or not?"

"Y-Yeah," she sputtered, eliciting a grin from me.

It was kind of fun being spontaneous. *Maybe I should make a plan to do so more often. Oh, ugh. There is no fixing you, is there? You can't plan to be spontaneous, that's the exact opposite of what I'm going for.*

Regardless, I was all about riding the new wave of freedom I'd discovered. Freedom from the old overthinking me. Freedom to redefine myself as I saw fit. Freedom from the mistakes I technically hadn't made yet, and hopefully wouldn't again.

Yep, I think I'm going to like Harper version 2.0.

"I GOTTA ADMIT," Sera said around the straw jutting out of her milkshake, "the short hair does suit you better." She took another long pull on the straw, pausing to clutch the bridge of her nose while mumbling something about brain freeze. She then cleared her throat and eyed me intently. "Although how you started the transformation was kind of shocking."

Shocking? Ha! You better get used to it, my friend, because future me has a lot more where that came from.

Popping a fry in my mouth, I glanced around C.J. Barney's. It was surreal being back within those walls. The campus favorite was smaller and dirtier than I remembered, though, my memory previously distorted by my age and novelty of such a place. At the moment, it was a ghost town. But later in the day the tables and booths would fill up with students for twenty-five cent drafts. The restaurant slash bar was notorious for being lax on underage drinkers, the level of fake ID only needing to be that you simply had one. Despite its long history, it would be shut down, eventually. Not for many years though, fortunately.

Grinning, I fluffed my hair. "Thankfully, Red was able to fix my hack job."

Sera quirked an eyebrow. "Yeah, thankfully."

I popped a few more fries in my mouth, enjoying the knowledge that at this age I didn't need to worry about what kind of junk I ate. That in itself was an added perk of being back in my younger body. I never fully appreciated my high metabolism until it abandoned me later in life.

Grabbing the menu again, I contemplated another order of food. My stomach would gladly accept the offer, but I wasn't so sure my college-aged budget would. "We should go to Graffiti's to see that band play. You know—"

"Evan got to you, too?" Sera reached into her pocket and produced a crumbled blue flyer just like the one I had.

Evan? Yes! Evan! That's his name! We had ... have a couple of classes together and he lives a few floors down from us in The Towers. "Yeah, he invited me—us this morning."

Sera nodded as she smoothed out the small scrap of

paper. "I was thinking of going, but we could always stay in and watch—"

Unbidden, a flash of memory played across my mind.

Sera burst through the door to our dorm room, her face glowing with excitement. "Oh, my God, Harper! I met the hottest guy I've ever seen tonight! I mean, seriously, hard swoon!"

I glanced up at her from my book, grinning in response. "Yeah?"

She flopped down beside me on our futon, fanning herself as she tipped her head back to stare at the ceiling. "Yeah. You should have come, by the way. Anyways, this guy—total hottie. Like I had to stop myself from drooling." She sighed. "He does seem a bit arrogant though, but I don't care. It's not like I have to get into a relationship with him. I just want to fuck his brains out."

"Sera!" I giggled. "I wasn't aware you were into that kind of thing outside of a relationship. Not that there's anything wrong if you are."

"I'm normally not, but this guy—Derek is his name—I think I could step outside of my comfort zone for a little taste of what he has."

"No!" I blurted out. "We have to go!"

The showcase at Graffiti's for Nameless was the night Sera met Derek, her future husband, and the love of her life. And I'd almost forgotten. These were the kind of stupid little mistakes that I couldn't afford to make. At least not when it came to my best friend.

"Okaaaay," Sera drawled. "You're acting weird again."

You better get used to it. "Yeah, I know I am a bit—"

Sera's eyebrows lifted. "A bit? You—"

I waved her off. "Yeah, yeah, yeah. I'm acting weirder than normal." Because I already knew she thought I was weird as it was at this age, which she never missed an opportunity to tease me about in the future. "But I'm running off of like no sleep and probably too much caffeine."

She nodded sagely. "The over-caffeinated, no-sleep combo is not a good look on anyone. But if that's the case, then we definitely should stay in so you can get some rest."

"No," I ground out, realizing that my excuse wasn't the optimal one of choice and that I was going to have to strong arm her into it now. "We need to go to the showcase. Beginning and end of story." Narrowing my eyes, I delivered her my best resolved face, projecting my determination at her. Either that or I appeared constipated.

Our gazes clashed, a silent battle of wills over the scared faux wood table. Finally, Sera sighed, acknowledging the fact that I was the most stubborn of the two of us. "Okay, fine. We'll go to the show ... for a little while."

Stuffing a fry in my mouth, I grinned. "You'll thank me later."

Sera merely smiled as she stole the last fry off my plate.

Chapter 6

"IDs," The supersized man who was posing as a human bouncer demanded.

I stared in wonderment, questioning the possibility that his size was proof of supernatural creatures such as trolls and ogres. I'd seen big, burly men before, but this guy was just large—absolutely massive. His hands would probably be able to palm my entire skull.

Sera elbowed me in the ribs. "Earth to Harper."

The tips of my ears heated. "Oh, yeah, right." After fishing around in my pocket, I produced my license, offering it to the bouncer with a slight tremble. *Sera's right. I am being weird.*

The surrealness along with the reality of time travel was intermingling to form a sort of levity within my mood. As if my mind thought that since time travel, which had previously been a thing out of science fiction only, could be real, then why not anything and everything from fiction as well?

God, I hope hot male fae kings really exist and one is on his way to Harper-nap me right now.

I shook my head, to dislodge the building fantasy, focusing back on my current situation.

The possible troll bouncer's eyes darted over the bit of plastic in his palm. "Give me your right hand."

Grabbing my wrist with more gentleness than I expected, he drew a large black X across the top of my hand that went from knuckle to wrist. "If you get caught with an alcoholic drink in there, you'll get yourself kicked out and banned. You hear me?"

Sera and I nodded in unison.

He unhooked the rope and handed me back my ID. "Go on in."

Scurrying into the venue, the sound of the bouncer's curt, "*Next!*" was swallowed by a wall of music.

My nose, eyes, and throat caught fire, the burning sensation causing me to gasp for air as I swiped at my eyes.

Sera halted abruptly, peering at me with concern. "What's wrong?"

I waved my hand around in an attempt to clear the cloud of smoke that was threatening to suffocate me. "I forgot that everyone is allowed to smoke at these places. I wasn't mentally prepared."

"What do you mean you forgot everyone is allowed? As opposed to what?"

"Umm ... well ..." *There I go again, spouting off about stuff I shouldn't.* If Sera thought I was weird before, then she was in for a treat now that her roommate was a time traveler. "Never mind," I mumbled as I forced myself to move farther inside. At least I could rest easy with the knowledge that I'd been exposed regularly to places like Graffiti's for many years in my youth and I somehow never developed lung cancer.

Linking arms with Sera, I forced a smile and swiped at my eyes quickly with my free hand. "Let's see what kind of non-alcoholic drinks they have."

"Orrrr," my friend drawled, "we could convince someone who doesn't have one of these monstrous X's on their hands to get us something with alcohol."

I mock gasped. "Underage drinking? How could you suggest such a thing?"

"I know, how could I? I don't know what I was thinking. Temporary insanity maybe?" She winked.

I laughed, enjoying the way my mood had buoyed yet again. *I can do this. I can let go and have fun without worrying about a future that doesn't exist for me anymore. Live in the moment. Revel in your second chance.*

Of course, like some kind of cosmic joke, it was precisely at that moment that my gaze snagged on none other than Logan Sharpe leaning against the bar in all of his 90s brooding, grudge, pretty-boy glory, before my eyes bounced to the other end of the bar to land on Ben Wickham with his classic boy-next-door good looks. One had blond hair, and the other dark, like out of some kind of romance novel, the biggest difference being that they were both my worst nightmare, and this was reality. *Or at least I think it is.*

My vision wavered for a brief moment, and my heart jumped into my throat, pushing a demented laugh from me. Because I swear, I heard Taylor Swift's song "I Knew You Were Trouble" suddenly replace the music that was actually being played. The lyrics ricocheted through my skull, a warning and a taunt from my subconscious rolled into one.

The two biggest mistakes of my life, both here at the same time. And the symbolism, holy shit. Maybe my psyche got fried on its trip through time because it's simply too perfect. Logan on one side of the bar, and Ben on the other. Either that or this is a sign that the universe does not want me to get a true second chance. Maybe it's against rules that exist somewhere that I have no idea about. Or—

No, I can't. No. I can't let this happen. I'm not going through all of this again to get the same exact results. The universe can try to stop me—if it can.

"Harper?" Sera's own gaze tracked the path of mine as it danced back and forth between both guys. "Something you want to tell me?"

"Umm … no," I squeaked, breaking away from her and darting into the crowd. How could I explain to her that the two guys who had just turned my world upside down were from a future that I wouldn't allow to happen again, but also from a past that didn't technically exist anymore?

Don't think about it. Restroom, restroom, restroom. I won't run into either of them in there. It's the only safe space where I can regroup and figure out a new plan.

I scurried around to the back wall, following it until I spotted a sign pointing me in the right direction. There was already a handful of girls waiting their turn outside of my would-be sanctuary, but I wasn't about to let that deter me. Dashing around the line, I blurted, "Don't have to pee, just need a sink."

"You better not be lying!" someone shouted as I burst into the restroom. "Because if I pee my pants, I will find you!"

The several girls next up for a stall eyed me with a mix of annoyance and hostility until they saw I did indeed head straight for the sink farthest from the door.

One of them called out, "She's cool! Just using the sink like she said!"

I pretended to fuss with my hair and makeup while my mind raced wildly. I couldn't abandon ship just yet because that would mean Sera would inevitably join me, which I couldn't have her do. She had to meet Derek tonight. If they didn't end up together, I would forever blame myself and I simply couldn't live with potentially denying my best friend the love of her life. But I also could not face either Ben or Logan … ever again.

Gritting my teeth, I stared my reflection down. *You will ignore those two asshats and focus on the Sera and Derek situation. Nothing else matters tonight. Sera and Derek. Sera and Derek are the end game for tonight. Sera and Derek. Focus on them and don't let anything else get in the way.*

Logan's ice-blue eyes flashed across my mind, followed by Ben's baby blues. *No! They do not exist. Ignore them. And damn, I never noticed that I seem to have a type. Blue eyes, no matter the shade, seems to be my ruination. Which is why you must ignore them. Focus.* I shook my head—hard —in an attempt to dislodge them completely from my brain.

Steeling myself once more, I hesitantly made my way back out to the crowd congregated in front of the bar on the main floor. A quick scan revealed both guys had disappeared. Which was simultaneously a relief and a concern because now I didn't know where they were. *It's like when a spider disappears under the couch.*

Doesn't matter. Sera and Derek. That's all that matters tonight.

I inhaled a deep breath, instantly regretting it as the burn of cigarette smoke renewed its torture of my lungs. *Ugh. Why didn't I remember any of this being as traumatic as it seems now? It has to be my perception of it, which means I can overcome it. Yep, that's right. Make mind over matter work for you. Focus. You have titanium lungs that aren't bothered in the least by any kind of smoke.*

It absolutely didn't work, so I instead decided to take shallow breaths to avoid suffocating.

"Hey! There you are!" Sera grinned at me, her eyes sparkling. "I just spotted the hottest guy I've ever seen. I need you to be my wing woman."

"Yes, of course!" I nodded eagerly. "What do you want me to do?"

She jerked her head slightly to the right. "He's over there talking to a couple other guys."

I pivoted on my heel in the direction she'd indicated. Sera snatched my forearm, digging her nails into my skin as she spun me back around. "Don't look!" she hissed through a forced toothy grin.

"Sorry!" I yanked my arm back, rubbing the indentations left behind by her talons. "It was a gut reaction."

"Be subtle this time."

"Okay, okay." I wasn't even sure why I'd had such a reaction since I already knew what Derek looked like. Not that I could explain any of that to Sera. So I supposed it was necessary to play along.

"He's wearing the blue checkered flannel over in the corner."

Casting my gaze around the room, pretending to check out my surroundings, I paused when I spotted Derek in the corner talking to two other guys. My heart fluttered in my chest. "No," I muttered, unable to stop the words from escaping my mouth. "Why is this happening?"

Sera's eyes widened. "What? Do you know him? Is it bad? Talk to me!"

I didn't understand. Derek and Logan were never friends. They could barely stand to be in the same room. So why were they suddenly all buddy-buddy? Had I landed in some sort of alternate timeline? Was that even a possibility? Although not concretely proven … yet, I was convinced a multiverse existed. But I hadn't considered being thrown into a slightly different version of my life, one that existed in another me's past. If that even was what was happening now. Of course, Occam's razor would imply that it was. And if that was indeed the case, then I had no idea what I was working with. How could I avoid potential pitfalls of my past if this wasn't my past?

Although, there was also a more than fifty percent chance that I wanted to be in an alternate timeline ... for reasons I wasn't ready to admit to myself.

"Harper, come on, spill it! What do you know about him?"

You don't have any concrete facts about what's going on yet. Stick to the plan. Focus on Sera and Derek. "It's ... it's not the guy you're scoping out, it's his friend."

Relief sagged Sera's shoulders briefly before she leaned into me, her expression intrigued. "Oh? What about his friend?"

How did I explain anything about Logan without mentioning the whole traveling through time thing? I had to say something though, but what? "Um ... well, I kind of know him."

Sera's eyebrows raised. "Aaaand?"

"He's just ... He's the ... Umm—" I swallowed around the sudden boulder in my throat. "His name is Logan and he—" Is—or was—my kryptonite. Even now, knowing what I did about him, the pull of his charisma was tangible. It's why I had to avoid him. *But now I can't.*

I supposed I simply had to take one for the team. *Wait. What? Take what for the team? Logan? And what am I giving myself permission to do with him exactly?* I cringed. "It doesn't matter. He's just a jerk I know. What's important is being your wing woman for his hot-as-hell friend."

A swarm of wasps had found their way into my stomach, and my gut clenched with the dueling sensations of foreboding and excitement. It was then I came to the conclusion that youth was not wasted on the young, because here I was young in body once more, with all of my older self's knowledge, and yet my hormones seemed to have the deciding vote in how I would react to Logan. I knew better—*I knew*—but the idea of getting to interact with him from the beginning ... the potential to have those sexual firsts with him all over again ... Yep, my hormones wanted it, even if my heart and brain didn't.

What is wrong with me? Is it the prefrontal cortex? It has to be! Because you are not this dumb, Harper!

"Should we just go over there since you know Logan? How much of a jerk are we talking? Like second-hand stories or has he done something to you that's unforgivable?" Sera mused while gnawing on her bottom lip. "Because the friends you keep and all of that could be applied here."

Snapped from my inner scrutiny of the situation, I shook my head demonstratively. "No, it's fine. It's just some stuff I heard. He hasn't done anything unforgivable to me." *Yet.*

"I guess I don't care all that much if your jerk's hot friend is also a jerk since I'm not interested in him for his relationship potential." She waggled her eyebrows while stifling a laugh.

"Yeah, okay." I'd heard this song and dance before about Derek, but in the end, he put a ring on it.

"I'm serious. He's so hot that just hooking up with him will be enough for me. I mean, he is complete and utter perfection. I don't want to fly too close to the sun." Fanning herself, she sighed.

After Sera and Derek had become official, he'd quickly become the brother I never wanted, but even I could appreciate the fact that he was an attractive guy. If Tyson Beckford and Jason Momoa had a male lovechild, he would look exactly like Derek.

"Mmm … hmmm …" I curled my lips in over my teeth to keep from laughing in her face. Sera and Derek's relationship hadn't been smooth sailing in the beginning, but once they overcame Sera's hesitancy to trust … well, then they'd quickly morphed into couple goals for me. And probably anyone else who was around them long enough to see how they were together. It was one of the reasons I couldn't risk my best friend not meeting Derek tonight. The two of them were meant to be together, and if I had to throw all caution to the wind to become their own personal cupid, I would.

Sera glared at me. "Enough. We need to make a move before we miss the chance. How do you think we should do this?"

I shrugged. "Let's just go over there, I guess."

"That's it?" Sera squeaked. "Just go over there? Are you

going to use the knowing his friend connection oooorr
…" She then waved her hands in front of my face. "Come
on, you can do better than that. Do not half-ass your wing
woman duties."

Grabbing her arm, I moved us through the crowd with
a surprising amount of resistance from her. After all, this
whole thing, including going over to talk to Derek, was
her idea. "Sometimes the best plans are the simple plans," I
called over my shoulder.

"Wait, wait … wait!" she hissed. "How's my hair? And
my makeup? And my—"

"You are absolutely gorgeous, as always. Now stop
worrying because this is what you want."

Sera attempted to dig her heels into the floor, literally,
like some kind of oversized toddler. Fortunately, I had the
leverage to keep us going. "I changed my mind. We can't
go over there and—"

Coming to an abrupt halt directly behind Derek, I
tapped him on the back of his elbow, all the while Sera
was attempting to break free from my death grip so she
could make a run for it. As soon as Derek turned in our
direction, Sera stilled, donning a mask of calm
indifference.

I dropped Sera's arm and plastered on the brightest
smile I could conjure, despite the fact that I was closer to
Logan than I ever hoped to be again. "Are you in my
chemistry class?" He wasn't, but it was the best I could
come up with at the moment.

Derek flashed a perfect smile, and his dark gaze flicked up to lock on Sera. "No, I don't think so. Why?"

"Oh, um, I missed the last class so I was wondering if I could get your notes."

"Sorry," he muttered, his attention riveted to Sera, who was twirling a curl around her finger coyly. "Must have me confused with someone else."

"My bad," I said, scooting away to make room for Sera. "By the way, this is my friend, Sera. We both missed the class."

She shot me a silent question before I saw recognition of what I was doing flare to life in her eyes. "Our alarm clock didn't go off."

Derek took a step in Sera's direction, still completely riveted. "I really wish I could help you out. I'm so sorry I can't, Sera." He practically purred her name, his voice dropping an octave.

No doubt causing her to think about dropping something else if her expression was anything to go by.

I stifled a laugh. The two of them were ridiculous even from day one apparently. I wasn't there the first time they'd met, and I had to admit the scene in front of me was an adorable meet-cute.

"Can I get you a drink?" Derek took another step closer to Sera, causing subtle color to bloom in her cheeks.

"Sure. I am underage though." She lifted her hand to show off the gigantic X on her hand.

"That's okay, we don't need alcohol to have fun." He winked, and her cheeks darkened.

I fought the urge to roll my eyes. *Cheesy much?* Guess it didn't feel that way when it was you on the inside of the situation. "Go ahead. Don't worry about me."

Internally I screamed at her to take me with them. I didn't know what would happen the moment I was truly faced with Logan. His presence had been steadily burning in my awareness, a bright spot off to my side, the entire time I'd been standing there.

Derek offered Sera his hand, and she glanced at me before taking it. I gave her another encouraging nod, which was all it took before the two of them were floating away towards the bar on a cloud of lust.

"Hey."

Logan's husky greeting sent panic surging through my veins. Without lifting my gaze to meet his, I muttered, "Hey," in return, before scurrying in the opposite direction.

Strong fingers snagged my forearm, halting me in place. "You seriously not even going to look at me?"

My heart thrashed against my ribcage, threatening to break free.

Trapped. I was trapped. And when trapped there were only two options to choose from: run or fight.

I, of course, chose the sane option. I ran.

Chapter 7

My rapid heartbeat pulsed against my eardrums, the sound a familiar theme song for my anxiety. Logan's voice, low and gravelly, and not quite fully matured yet, was a siren's song to my teenaged body's libido. It conjured memories that didn't technically exist, and I needed to keep it that way, even if my hormones strongly disagreed.

Flashes of our sweaty limbs entangled, my body arching under his, threatened to break my resolve. Logan was many things, but unfortunately, one of them was a fast learner, which had quickly turned him into a skilled lover shortly after we'd slept together.

The cacophony of bar sounds only served to rachet up my nerves as I searched for a black hole to disappear into. At the very least a tear in the fabric of reality that I could slip into to escape my current predicament. Perhaps if I clicked my heels three times and wished really hard, I could send myself back to the future. Or maybe I needed a DeLorean for that?

No. And give up just like that? I was the Queen of Self-sabotage in the future, but it was time to change that. How many times would I let myself buckle under the weight of my emotional baggage? Baggage that hadn't been packed full of my issues, at least all of them yet. If anything, a second chance meant throwing caution to the wind. I needed to not only learn from my mistakes but take actions to reinforce behaviors that would enable me to make the choices I needed to this time around.

I stumbled up to the bar, careful to avoid Sera and Derek, who were on the other side because they needed time alone to … to do whatever it is they were supposed to do at this point in their relationship. I'd done my job by making sure they met. Crisis averted.

Blinking down at the X on my hand, I smiled to myself. I did it. I'd been so worried about escaping Logan that I almost forgot to pat myself on the back for a job well done. Too bad I couldn't have a glass of beer or wine to celebrate.

"Harper. Hey. I didn't recognize you at first."

I spun towards the familiar masculine voice, my mouth agape. *Out of the fire and into the frying pan. I've become a human pinball, bouncing from Logan right over to Ben. Why, universe, whyyyy?*

Ben ran a hand through his dark blond hair, gaze sliding over my new shorter do with uncertainty. "I guess it looks good on you. It would be kind of difficult to make someone as pretty as you look bad, though. Even if you shaved it all off."

Annoyance shot through me, and I narrowed my eyes. "Thank you so much for the *compliment.*" I emphasized the last word, knowing full well that it wasn't meant as one. Ben didn't like my hair short, and I didn't give a shit what he thought. "I don't remember asking for your opinion on my appearance though."

He raised his hands in the air, giving me a self-deprecating smile as his pale skin flushed. "My bad. Sometimes things come out wrong. I was just trying to show you that I noticed." He tilted his head and chuckled. "Don't girls like it when guys notice when they change their hair?"

"Some do. But this one doesn't care what anyone but herself thinks."

Ben fought a scowl as he backed away from me. "Okay. Obviously, you have something going on and you're in a bad mood. Pretend like I wasn't here. I'll talk to you some other time when you're feeling better."

I stabbed an angry finger in his direction. "No, you don't get to put this on me. I wasn't in a bad mood. I simply didn't like what you had to say. Which I don't have to."

Shaking his head slowly, as if I was an escaped mental patient, Ben shared a conspiratorial glance with a nearby guy before walking away.

Inhaling a shaky breath, I gave myself a second pat on the back for managing to run Ben off. *For now. You ran him off for now. If the universe has anything to say about it, Ben and Logan will both show up at your door by the end of the night.*

"Men, or should I say boys? Am I right?"

I turned to my right where another familiar face awaited me. But just like earlier in the Quad, I couldn't quite remember who she was.

"Yeah." I forced a laugh. "Exactly."

She set her drink on the bar and used both hands to fluff her shoulder-length, strawberry-blonde hair. There was no X adorning her pale, freckled hand so she either had an awesome fake ID or she was older than me. "You here for Nameless or—" She glanced at me in question.

"Yep, yeah. I mean, I guess I'm here to see Nameless. A friend of theirs, Evan, was handing out flyers."

"Ah, yes, sounds like my brother got to you as well. It's not even his band." She laughed. "But the drummer has been one of his best friends since the first grade, so ..." She finished up with another laugh.

Evan's sister! I possibly didn't know her, and she only seemed familiar because of the family resemblance, which I could see once it was pointed out. Both had shades of red hair, both were pale and covered in freckles, and both were tall and thin. And both were extremely friendly and outgoing. Although the overall aesthetic worked better on a female because Evan's sister was drop-dead gorgeous.

"I'm Harper, by the way." I gave Evan's sister a little wave.

"Jesse," she muttered, her attention having gone from

our conversation to the stage. "They should be going on soon, I hope. I'm over whoever is playing now. Their sound isn't bad, but their lyrics ..." She rolled her eyes as she continued to stare straight ahead.

I noticed movement behind her as a lanky, pale guy with a dark buzz-cut dropped some powder into Jesse's drink. I felt my face go slack, the shock of what I was witnessing temporarily short-circuiting my motor functions. But I guess this was the 90s, a time before awareness and extra caution surrounding roofies was widespread.

As if nothing untoward had gone down, Mr. Buzz Cut sidled up to Jesse and bumped her shoulder. "Jesse, hey."

"Craig," she grated between clenched teeth. "I thought I told you I didn't want to see you again."

"You gotta give me another chance." He reached for her arm, and she slapped it away.

"I don't even know why I agreed to go on a date with you to begin with. Just please, leave me alone."

He glowered. "Fine, all right. Have it your way." He skulked out of view, but I had a feeling he wouldn't be too far off.

Grimacing, Jesse turned to grab her drink. Jolting out of whatever stupor I'd fallen into, I hit the glass out of her hand, knocking it to the floor. The bright pink liquid and shattered glass caused a cluster of people to jump back, a few glaring at us.

A male voice declared, "Party foul!" and a few people sniggered.

"What the hell?" Jesse snapped.

I grabbed her arm and leaned in close. "That guy you were just talking to put something in it."

Her eyes widened as comprehension flitted across her face. "Oh my God!"

"I guess I could have just told you, but—" I sucked on my teeth. "Sorry for the dramatics."

"No, I— Thank you," she said, her eyes welling with tears. "I only said yes to a date because I thought he would leave me alone if I gave him a chance, but it was bad. I mean, really bad. And now he's doing the opposite. He pops up everywhere. And now this." She swiped at her cheeks where a few rogue tears mixed with dark eyeshadow and liner had settled.

Even in modern times, calling the cops, getting a restraining order, all of the things people advised girls to do in Jesse's situation, didn't often work. But in the 90s, things were a lot worse, especially when it came to victim blaming. "If there's anything I can do ..." I said the words, and I meant them, but they weren't much more than an empty platitude. Because what I could I do?

Unless ...

I swear an actual lightbulb blazed to life over my head.

"Maybe he doesn't know that I put a kibosh on his plan." I waved frantically at Jesse. "Quick, order another drink of whatever you had."

Her forehead furrowed. "But—"

"Just do it before he sees, and then I'll explain."

Jesse nodded hesitantly, turning to flag down the

bartender. While she gave him her order, I scanned the bar for our target. Chances were, if I couldn't see him, he might not have witnessed me spilling the contents of Jesse's drugged drink. He was hopefully lurking and waiting to make a reappearance once he felt he gave Jesse enough time to ingest said drink.

"So, what's your plan?" Jesse white-knuckled the glass, her hand trembling slightly.

"You need to pretend like you're drugged."

Her eyebrows shot up. "You've got to be joking."

I shook my head slowly. "No, I'm dead serious. We can lay a trap. Once he shows up, we can record him confessing what he did and then—" *Oh, shit.* Smartphones didn't exist yet. There would be no catching Mr. Buzz Cut, aka Craig, on video to show the police, or if that didn't work to publicly post his misdeeds online to demand action.

I pinched the bridge of my nose, struggling for a plausible explanation for my little time faux pas. "Sorry, my parents have a camcorder at home, but yeah, I can't use it, not here … since I don't have it."

"Oh, then I don't think—"

"No, wait. We can't let this asshole get away with harassing you and trying to do who knows what once you were drugged. He put drugs in that drink with nefarious intentions. We can't ignore that fact."

"Who did what to you?" Logan's angry voice slammed into me from behind, and I stifled a shiver despite the situation. I'd read one too many romance novels later in my life to not reflexively respond, like one of Pavlov's dogs, to anything even vaguely resembling the line "Who did this to you?" from a guy I was attracted to.

Fighting the urge to whirl in his direction and swoon in his arms, I hung my head, and whispered, "None of your business."

Logan spun me around, his fingers digging almost painfully into my shoulders. "The fuck it isn't."

Carefully keeping my gaze leveled at his chest, I sucked in a shallow breath, just enough to push out my response. "It really is none of your business. You barely know me."

His grip on me tightened. "I know you enough to want to protect you."

My heart took off at a gallop, taking all sense of rational thought with it. I was left with raw emotions, and vivid memories of the pain he'd caused me. The thing was, none of it had happened ... yet. I couldn't condemn his betrayal or explain my reaction to it. It simply did not exist to this version of Logan. *And I have to keep it that way.*

"None of this is relevant right now," I grated. "Someone put a roofie in Jesse's drink and I'm trying to help her come up with a plan or retaliation ... or something."

Logan peeled his fingers off of me and eased back a step. I let loose the breath I didn't realize I was holding, something that my anxiety caused frequently. It was a wonder I hadn't passed out at some point. I was sure I would eventually though. Either from forgetting to breathe or from hyperventilating. If only I could get the whole balance between oxygen in and carbon dioxide out under control ...

"Tell me who the guy is, and I'll take care of it."

Jesse's arm shot out, her index finger sighting Craig, who had emerged from his hiding spot to hover at the other end of the bar. "He's right over there. White guy, buzz cut."

I shoved at her arm with all of my strength, but it magically stayed aloft. "No, we don't need his help. We can take care of it—"

Logan nodded resolutely. "Got it." His jaw muscles twitching, he stalked over to Craig. The would-be predator scowled when Logan forced his attention away from Jesse, confusion replacing his displeasure when he noticed who was interrupting him. Clearly, he'd just seen him talking to us.

Logan's upper lip curled into a snarl, and his fist connected with the underside of Craig's jaw. Chaos erupted as fists began to fly.

When a barstool clattered to the floor, and someone yelled, "Fight!" the bartender threw down his bar rag in annoyance and started ringing a bell hanging near the register. Several big buys all wearing Graffiti's security shirts appeared on the scene moments later. They dragged Logan off of Craig whose nose was gushing blood down his face.

Whoever declared the scene a fight had been a bit off since it seemed more like a beatdown from what I could tell. And I definitely wasn't enthralled by the way Logan moved with quick, precise movements like he possibly might have trained in the ring a bit at some point, which would have been news to me. Nope, I was not the type of girl turned on by a guy who defended a girl with violence. Not even a little bit. It was barbaric, not sexy. Logan was not sexy with his disheveled hair, and eyes flashing with—

"We should say something!" Jesse grabbed my arm and swept me along with her towards the commotion.

I was relieved Jesse had pulled me from my thoughts because I was not a fan of the direction they'd been going. "It's not like Logan's going to be arrested or anything! He's just going to get kicked out!"

"Excuse me! Excuse me!" Jesse pulled at the shirt of the bigger of the two security guards. "Logan, the guy who hit the other guy, Craig, he did it because Craig roofied my drink."

Dark eyes in an alarmingly handsome face turned to regard Jesse, even as he continued to drag a still extremely pissed off Logan away from the bar.

"Please!" She steepled her hands together in front of her face, her eyes welling with tears again. "He was just trying to help me. That guy—" She raised an accusatory index finger to point at Craig. "He's been harassing me."

"Take them to the back," security guard one commanded. "We need to get to the bottom of this." He returned his attention to Jesse. "You willing to come with us? Tell us what happened?"

Jesse nodded quickly and pointed at me. "She saw what happened. She needs to come, too."

"Well, someone needs to tell me what happened!" Sera demanded, having made her way to my side at some point.

I gave her a wan smile. "Oh, you know, just me finding trouble."

Concern pulled the corners of her lips down. "You okay? You need me to do something?"

"Psssht ... I'm fine. Go back to Derek. I'll find you whenever I'm done here."

"Thank you," Jesse said, grabbing my hand and tugging me along with her again.

Sera nodded, the concern only deepening on her face. "You better tell me everything when we get home."

"I will." *Ha! If only I could.*

Chapter 8

The best-made plans, at least my plans, seemed to go to complete shit lately. I set out to make sure Sera and Derek met like they were supposed to at Graffiti's tonight, so that part had gone smoothly, but the rest—avoiding Logan and Ben, not causing any huge deviations in the past—yep, that part of my plan had gone horribly awry.

Now I was sitting in a small, musty office with two security guards, a would-be predator, a girl I just met, and Logan. The scientist in me knew getting involved in the Jesse-Craig situation was a huge mistake if I wanted to cause minimal ripples with my presence. But the humanity in me couldn't walk away without doing something. What if I'd just prevented a rape? Or a murder. Or—

What's done is done. You can't rewind time, Harper. Or you can't again.

Security guard two, a muscular, dark-skinned guy with short-cropped hair, hovered by the door, as if one of us would try to make a break for it. Security guard one, a muscular model reject with bronzed skin, and long, dark hair pulled into a low ponytail, was conducting the interview slash interrogation.

Security guard one leaned on the scarred wooden desk, massive arms crossed over his chest. "Who saw the drink get roofied?"

Jesse elbowed me, and I jerked away from her into the arm of the dingy, green couch. Slowly, I raised my hand like I was in elementary school. "Oh, yeah, that was me." I cleared my throat as all eyes turned in my direction.

Craig spat, "This is bullshit. I didn't roofie anybody's drink, especially Jesse's. Why would I? I don't need to do something like that to get her naked. Everyone knows she's easy. She—"

Security guard one lunged at Craig, lifting him out of his seat by the collar of his shirt. Craig flailed his arms but didn't even attempt to fight back. "I thought I told you to shut the hell up." Held aloft for a minute, Craig was dropped back into his chair, and security guard one returned to lean on the desk.

Craig's outburst served to confirm his ulterior motive. His grand plan was going to be sexual assault. I kind of figured—had hoped for him aiming to embarrass her only —but I was obviously kidding myself.

My blood heated with feminine rage. Leaning forward, I hissed, "I saw him put powder in her drink, clear as day. If there was a bible, I'd swear on it right now. I have zero doubts about it—about what I saw. The only thing I'm not one hundred percent sure about is if it was a roofie." I shrugged. "Could have been poison. We could have an actual serial killer wanna-be on our hands right here. I mean, are there any missing persons in the area fitting—"

Craig's face turned red and splotchy. "It wasn't poison! I just wanted to get what I deserved from her! I spent all that money on our date, and she wouldn't put out! It's—"

I jumped to my feet. "She doesn't owe you anything! No woman does! But thanks for admitting you put something in her drink! I'm sure the police will be happy to hear that!" My chest heaved as I struggled to breathe.

Craig's gaze shot to me, and then to security guard one. "Police? Wait. No. That's not what I meant."

"Save it for the cops!" I slashed my hand through the air. "Case closed!"

Security guard one's lips twitched. "All right, Matlock, we're not in court." He sobered completely as he regarded Jesse, who remained on the couch, hands clutched in her lap. "Do you want me to call the police?"

"Of course she does!" I snapped.

"Let her answer for herself," security guard one said calmly, gaze not wavering from Jesse.

Dropping back down to the couch, I took her hands in mine. "You want to report this to the cops, right?" I leaned closer, imploring her with my eyes. She couldn't just let this go, especially if some of the desire to drop the issue was from what Craig said. I wasn't about to let him slut shame Jesse into submission.

"Or we could take him out back and beat him within an inch of his life," Logan chimed in, speaking for the first time since we entered the office.

I'd almost convinced myself I could ignore him.

My nostrils flared as I struggled to continue ignoring his existence by not acknowledging his comment in any way. "Jesse, if you don't do it for yourself, then do it for the next girl."

Indecision swam through her eyes, causing her forehead to furrow. "There's no proof though. It's going to be he said, she said. And we all know how well that turns out for the she."

I opened my mouth to protest, then shut it with an audible click. I'd lost track of the current technology in the 90s once again. Surveillance cameras in nearly every bar were a thing of the future. Currently, there was no security footage to review. There was no possible video catching Craig in the act in the background of someone's TikTok or Instagram Reel. There were upsides and downsides to being able to live anonymously, and this was one of the downsides. People were able to get away with being predators without any real repercussions. Not that the same didn't happen in all eras, but the lack of concrete proof did make it exponentially more difficult. At least for the victim.

As much as I hated to admit it, the police wouldn't be able, even if they were so inclined, to do anything legally about what Craig had pulled. Logan's plan to take him out back and beat him within an inch of his life suddenly became appealing.

"This isn't fair," I hissed, frustration surging through me once more. I withdrew my hands from Jesse's and balled them into fists, my entire body trembling.

Over the course of my life, I'd developed a pattern of lacking the conviction of being able to stand up for myself in tense situations. But the same couldn't be said when it came to defending other people. Some might say I had a bit of a hero complex. I would not back down when it came to protecting those I viewed as vulnerable. And Jesse was vulnerable with or without drugs coursing through her system.

I lifted my gaze to security guard one since he seemed to be in charge. "What would you tell her to do if she were your sister or girlfriend?" I wasn't a fan of attempting to manipulate him into feeling some kind of empathy since he should have been chest deep in it already, but sometimes a girl had to use the tools at her disposal.

He cleared his throat. "I'd tell her to be more careful next time. To watch her drink, her surroundings, and who she associates with." He shoved off the desk, looming over Craig. "With that being said, I kind of like the idea of taking him out back and giving him a little talking to." He smiled and winked at me.

Security guard two grinned. "I could be down for that."

Violence wasn't something I usually condoned, buuut

...

"Sounds like the best option we have, I guess."

"Wh-Whaaat?" Craig sputtered. "You can't be serious."

Security guard two crossed the office in a burst of speed, taking hold of Craig. He flashed perfect, white teeth in a feral grin. "Oh, you don't like someone taking advantage of you when you're more vulnerable than them? Can't imagine why."

A kind of jittery excitement pushed me to my feet once more. "I guess we can go then." I wasn't opposed to the turn of events, but I didn't necessarily want to witness the eminent beatdown. I was a bit squeamish when it came to blood. It took more resolve than I wanted to admit to ignore the reddish-brown crud already dried on Craig's face and shirt.

"You three wait here," security guard one commanded.

I froze. "But why?"

"We'll escort you out when we ... get done with this him," security guard two responded, grin widening as he stared down a Craig.

Not that I particularly wanted to hang around any longer, but the injustice of the situation riled me up again. "We're still getting kicked out? How is that fair?"

Without another word, the two of them hauled Craig out of the room, our little would-be predator kicking and screaming to no avail. Good thing the music was loud.

As soon as they were gone, doubts assaulted my system. I wanted Craig to get his just deserts, to learn his lesson, but how would violence do any of that? Maybe it would make him think twice about bothering Jesse or anyone else again. One could hope. But there was also a possibility that it could make things worse—make him vindictive.

"I think I'm going to be sick." Jesse dropped her head into her lap.

I patted her back gingerly. "It'll be fine, you'll see. Maybe they'll knock some sense into him, literally." I chuckled, the sound lacking any humor. A beatdown like Craig was being served would never happen in the future. Bygone eras, such as the 90s, held a brand of brutality that most, even myself, usually forgot about when reminiscing.

"Harper," Logan rumbled, having made his way to stand directly in front of us without me noticing. "We need to talk."

I chuckled again, this one just as mirthless. "No, we don't."

"Why won't you talk to me, or even look at me? What did I do? Or rather what do you think I did?"

Unable to resist any longer, my head snapped up, gaze locking with his. It was the first time since being back in my younger body that I'd allowed myself to look at him— really look at him. And the sight made my chest tighten, the familiar urge to touch him when I was this close almost undeniable. I could almost feel the abrasion his light stubble would cause under my fingertips, the way his sun-kissed skin was softer than it appeared. How his full lips pressed against mine would be firm and unyielding ...

Memories of us in rumpled sheets, limbs entwined, took center stage in my mind. Words of worship, of love, replayed as if I heard them being said right at that moment. He said forever and claimed that he would never hurt me, or betray me.

All of it had been lies.

Logan's icy gaze scanned my features, searching for clues as to what I was thinking, but there was no way he could know. What was between us now was nothing compared to what ... what would never be.

He cupped the back of his neck with his hand, frustration marring his sculpted face. "Come on, Harper. What do you want from me? Is it because I didn't call you yesterday like I said I would? I got busy, and I wasn't aware that after meeting you just last week that—"

My jaw slackened. "Last week? I—" If he thought we met last week, which I guess to him we had, then I completely understood why me giving him the cold shoulder would seem weird. And it wasn't unreasonable to expect some kind of explanation from me either. "I-It has nothing to do with you not calling me."

Standing, I paced to the corner of the room. I needed to think of a plausible excuse for my actions and put some much-needed space between us before my hormones decided to stage a mutiny and take control of my body. There were already whispers of an uprising below deck.

Logan followed me, closing the scant amount of distance I'd managed to put between us. He leaned his hands against the wall above my head, caging me in with his large body. "If it were anybody else, I'd write you off as some over-expectant psycho, but—" He dragged his teeth over his bottom lip. "There's something about you."

"Thanks?" I squeaked.

Being so close to him scrambled my senses, his unique scent intermingled with cigarette smoke, which should have been disgusting ... but it wasn't. I wanted to grab him and smash my lips against his. To wrap my legs around his waist as I—

Stop it right now, Harper Davis. You are a grown woman on the inside of this dumbass eighteen-year-old body. You get your hormone-addled, underdeveloped prefrontal cortex brain under control. Now.

"Harper," Logan's voice dropped an octave, his eyes sucking me into their fathomless pools, "talk to me."

In no scenario did I want to talk to Logan Sharpe. I could jump his bones right now, on the spot, audience be damned, or I could make another attempt at fleeing from him. Words most certainly did not enter into the equation of either option.

"I have nothing to say to you."

His nostrils flared, and his jaw muscles jumped. He was clearly beyond annoyed with me, and maybe that was a good thing. *Secret option number three for the win!* I could possibly run him off by using this method. He was only two years older than me, and what twenty-year-old guy who just met a girl was going to put up with a ton of bullshit?

Crossing my arms over my chest, I smirked. "Why don't you do the talking?"

He blinked at me, confusion replacing the annoyance on his visage. "About what?"

"Well …" I tilted my head, pretending to study him. "You could start by telling me why you think I was ignoring you. And don't forget I already said it wasn't because you didn't call me when you said you would."

He pushed off the wall, still regarding me with confusion as he pulled both of his hands through his hair. "Are you serious right now?"

"As a heart attack." I could feel my smirk morphing into a smug smile against my will. I tried to fight it into submission, to don some kind of unaffected expression to mirror my supposed pissed-off slash unreasonable attitude, but it was way more difficult than I thought it would be.

I knew the moment he recognized what I was trying to do. Logan pursed his lips, a knowing glint warming his eyes with mirth. "Ah. I see."

"You see nothing," I snapped. "That's the whole point."

"Mmm hmm … yep. I see exactly what you're trying to do."

"No, you don't." Manipulating a twenty-year-old guy should have been child's play when I had years of experience under my belt mentally. *Why is nothing going the way it should?*

He was back in my personal space in the blink of an eye, mouth brushing my ear. "I see right through you, Harper."

A raspy breath rattled my chest, my heart taking off at a gallop. "You wish you did."

Logan stayed where he was, his breath warm against my cheek. His hands found mine, and he slowly raised my arms above my head. My entire body lit up like a live wire, electricity zinging through every molecule.

Would he let me go if I asked him to? Did I want to risk finding out? Because I couldn't remember the last time I had something physically feel this good in my adult body.

"Harper, I know you're trying to purposely push me away. And I know it's because you're afraid after what happened last week between us."

My mind reeled. *Hold up ... wait.* We didn't have sex until we'd gone on several dates. And after one week of knowing him, we had not gone on any dates yet. Either this was proof positive that I was in another version of my life in the multiverse, or my brain was stuck in the gutter.

"I don't know what you're talking about, Logan."

He nipped at my earlobe, and I stifled a moan, internally cursing my reaction. *It's just an ear. Just a friggin' ear, Harper. What the hell is wrong with you?*

"Our all-night conversation. We touched on some pretty deep and intimate stuff ... and now you're scared. Now you're pushing me away." He chuckled. "Usually that would be my move in the situation, so I know it when I see it."

"You're right, I am afraid," I murmured, causing him to pull away enough to meet my gaze.

His lips turned up slightly at the corners, triumph alighting his face.

Yanking my hands out of his grasp, I shoved him in the chest. He stumbled backwards, surprise working on my behalf. "I'm afraid of making the same mistakes with you twice."

I darted around him and snatched Jesse's arm. "Come on! Let's get out of here!"

Chapter 9

Eyes wide, Jesse followed me back into the main part of Graffiti's. The booming music dropped on us as soon as we were outside of the soundproofed office, making it seem as if we'd stepped into an entirely different world.

I didn't exactly have a plan or a next step, my immediate goal of escaping Logan and my body's desire to give in to him accomplished, at least for the moment. In the meantime, I kept moving, hoping an idea or option would present itself. Unfortunately, Jesse was along for the ride whether she liked it or not.

Sera jumped into our path, and we narrowly avoided a collision. "What the hell happened?" she bellowed over the music, which definitely was louder than before we'd entered the office. "People are saying someone was drugged!"

I coughed, the smoke worse than before as well. My

interaction with Logan had left me overwhelmed and overstimulated. The world was too bright, too loud, too crowded ... basically too much for me to deal with. I wanted to go home and curl into a ball with a blanket pulled over my head. I was angry at myself about how I was handling ... well, everything since I'd traveled back through time. I'd gotten a second chance at my life, and all I'd done was find new ways to screw things up along with barely sidestepping the same exact mistakes. I was making things worse not better.

"Harper!" Logan marched up to me, his chiseled features pinched with frustration. "Stop running away from me!" He tugged at his hair, glowering down at me. "We need to talk."

Whirling to face him, I poked my right index finger into his chest. "You keep saying we need to talk, but that wasn't talking in there. You were trying to seduce me into compliance."

Logan snorted. "Seduce you into compliance? You're making it sound like you're a spy and I'm trying to get information out of you."

I poked him in the chest again. "You might as well be."

His lips pressed into a flat line. "That doesn't even make sense. Almost nothing you've said or done tonight makes sense. You're acting like a completely different person than the one I stayed up all night talking to last week."

He had no idea how accurate he was. I was not the same Harper he thought he was getting to know. The years had changed me, and not for the better. I was jaded and bitter, and in a lot of ways broken. This was my chance to put myself back together, to heal my inner wounded goddess—or whatever cliché line I could use to describe the fact that I wanted to give myself a better life and to be happy.

Tipping my chin up, I leaned closer and narrowed my eyes. "You think I'm acting like a completely different person? That's because I am one!" *And I'm too old for this shit! I may bodily be eighteen again, but with every passing second, it's becoming clearer that I am dangerously close to a 'get off my lawn' mentality. When did that happen?* It was like when people in their forties thought they could still hang with the twenty-year-olds until they actually tried ...

Pivoting away from him, I grabbed Sera with one hand, and Jesse with the other, propelling the three of us towards the exit sign. I'd introduced Sera to Derek, saved Jesse from being roofied, and now I was getting us all the hell out of Dodge.

The side door slammed open, the alarm miraculously not going off, which I only considered after the fact, and I halted, lungs burning as I inhaled several deep breaths. I bent over, hands on knees, Sera and Jesse hovering on either side of me, both silent.

"I-I'm sorry. For dragging you both out of there." I kept inhaling and exhaling, still feeling like I wasn't getting enough oxygen, like I was going to suffocate at any second.

Sera dipped down to crouch in front of me. "What happened? And who was the hottie you were yelling at?"

"I— He—"

"What happened in the office between you two was intense. I felt like I was watching a movie," Jesse added.

I groaned. "Now is not the time to rehash that or what just happened with him either. We need to get you home, Jesse. You just went through something traumatic." I unfurled myself, tugging Sera up with me.

Jesse shrugged, all signs of her earlier anxiety from the office gone. "I'm fine now." She glanced longingly at the door. "I kind of wish I could just go back in there, enjoy the Nameless show, and pretend none of this happened." She twirled a piece of strawberry-blonde hair around her finger. "Why should I be made to suffer when I was the victim?"

My eyebrows crept up my forehead. I forgot how people her age—or our age—liked to sweep traumatic things under the rug in an attempt to ignore them. Was that why red flags and other warning signs were ignored until it was too late? Or was it merely my generation—Gen X—who thought nothing could or would affect us?

I shook my head. "Yeah, I get it. You came here to have fun, and Craig had to go and ruin it not just for you but for all of us."

"It's not too late." Sera motioned to the door. "We could go back in."

Jesse nodded enthusiastically. "We could. Those

security guards aren't going to waste their time tracking us down since we weren't the ones in the wrong."

"But Logan's still in there," I grumbled.

Sera crossed her arms over her chest, her indignant glare burning into the side of my face. "And why exactly have I heard exactly zero about this guy, Logan? Huh? Not even a mention of his name in passing at this point."

"I don't know." Suddenly my shoes were extremely interesting. "Not much to say, I guess."

"Really?" Sera scoffed. "That didn't seem like not much to me from what little I saw in there."

"Yeah," Jesse added. "And that was nothing compared to what happened between them in the office. Seriously, I couldn't look away even though I knew I should. Logan was all growly and had her pinned up against the wall. And Harper was all breathy and moany." She grinned. "Yep, right out of a movie with all the sexual tension."

Sera stared at me with outrage. "You better start talking now."

I threw my arms up in the air. "Why does everyone want to have complicated conversations with me all of a sudden? I thought the beauty of youth was being blissfully, emotionally ignorant."

"Harper?" Ben said my name hesitantly, his head poking out of the exit door. "You okay?"

"Ben! Great! Exactly who I wanted to see!" The universe wasn't even trying to hide its intentions to screw up my second chance.

"Ben, well at least I've heard that name before." Sera

continued to glare at me. "Guess that's a step in the right direction."

Ben slid out of the back door, shuffling towards us. "What's going on? Everything all right? You guys need any help? I heard someone was drugged."

"No one was drugged!" I shouted, exasperation winding its way through my system.

Ben shoved his hands in his pockets. "Yeah, all right. Just wanted to see if everything was okay."

"How did you even know we were out here?" I demanded. Was the universe sending Ben and Logan messages and or signals of my whereabouts? I wouldn't even be the tiniest bit surprised.

Averting his gaze, Ben shrugged, the move meant to make him seem nonchalant. But I knew better. He was a master manipulator. "The three of you weren't invisible when you ran out here shoving people out of the way."

"And you just had to follow?" I bit the insides of my cheeks to keep from saying anything else. It would only make me seem mean and irrational, especially when factoring in the rest of the situation.

"Yeah, to see if you were okay, like I said." He glanced from me, to Sera, to Jesse, and back again, turning to them for support. "But if I interjected myself into something that I wasn't meant to, then I—"

Sera shot me another glare before giving Ben a tight-lipped smile. "No, it's fine, Ben. Harper is a bit stressed and flustered from everything that went down tonight."

Ben gave her a relieved smile in return. "Oh, yeah, I get that. Stress can make people act insane sometimes."

I ground my teeth together. It might have sounded innocent enough, like a slip of the tongue, or a thoughtless choice of a word, but Ben was too calculated for that kind of mistake. The use of insane was meant to undermine me and garner sympathy for him. He always wanted people on his side, no matter how trivial the situation. It only served to give him call-backs later for something bigger with more on the line.

"Okay, well, time for us to go back inside." I motioned with my thumbs to the door. "Come on, before we miss Nameless."

That got Jesse in motion, as I'd intended. She strode for the door with determination. "I don't want to miss them. And I don't want to let Craig win."

I turned to follow her, Sera trailing me, but before we could disappear inside, Ben said, "You maybe want a ride home after the show? I drove."

Sera's face lit up. "We'd love to not have to take the campus shuttle or walk."

Ben smiled again, making me want to punch his handsome face. "Meet you out front after this is over?"

Freezing in place, I scrambled to find an excuse, but nothing came to mind. Even still, I wouldn't verbally agree. I refused to give him that satisfaction.

"Sounds great!" Sera responded.

I elbowed her in the ribs as soon as Ben was out of sight. "Sounds great!" I mock sing-songed. "Why did you have to agree to a ride with him? Huh? For someone who is so perceptive you certainly whiffed on that one."

Rubbing her side, she frowned. "What do you mean?"

"How did you miss the fact, the very obvious fact, that I don't want to be around Ben, and then you just went and said we'd grab a ride with him? Why would you do that?"

"Okay, what is going on with you? First the hair, and then this Logan character, and now Ben. I thought you said Ben was a friend—a nice guy."

"That's what he wanted me to believe. That's what they all want me to believe." Okay, yeah, now I did sound a bit insane. I needed to rein myself in a bit before someone decided to code fiftyone fifty me.

"Are you sure you weren't drugged?"

Cracking a smile, I shook my head slowly. "No. No, I'm not."

Sera laughed, the tension bursting between us. "Guess we all have days like that."

"Don't we ever." I sighed, scanning the crowd for Jesse or hostile security guards. Unfortunately, the only person who caught my attention was Logan, who was leaning against a pillar, arms crossed, gaze riveted to me. Didn't he have anyone else to bother?

Hooking her arm in mine, Sera steered me away from Logan and closer to the stage. "I've had a good night so far though." She fanned herself with her free hand. "Derek. That's all I'm going to say. All I need to say is just … Derek."

We settled to the right of the stage along the wall,

waiting for the next band to go on. I was hoping it was Nameless so we could leave soon. I was done with my night out and one hundred percent ready to become one with my bed and a pint of ice cream. I wouldn't have to twist Sera's arm to stop by the 7-11 down on Forbes Avenue. It always had the best array of snack foods for late-night revelers on campus.

Despite some of the unpleasantries of the venue, it was nice to see people not all mesmerized by their phones. There was no worry of being caught in an embarrassing photo or video either. I never realized how lucky we were at the time … how free. Sure, I'd come face-to-face with some of the downsides of the 90's technological deficiencies, but overall, maybe it was worth it.

Glancing down the line of my body, I scrunched up my nose at my wide-legged jeans and cropped baby doll tee. My generation's fashion choices weren't always on point, but at least most of them were largely forgotten, or at least not memorialized in the same manner the kids of the future did with everything. My shoulders sagged with relief. Maybe the 90s weren't the best of times, but they were home. I was comfortable here, and here I was going to stay. Until the years rolled on by again, that is. *Well, nothing is perfect. Not that I would want to stay here indefinitely. Because that would actually be insane.*

"Hey, check it out." Sera pointed towards the stage, where I could see Jesse having a serious discussion with some guy. I noted that he held a set of drumsticks in one hand. With the other, he put his arm around Jesse, who sunk into the embrace for a moment before jerking away. She then whipped her head around warily, as if embarrassed by the interaction. The guy frowned, annoyance flitting across his features.

"Must be the childhood friend of her and Evan's she mentioned before. He's the drummer for Nameless apparently."

Sera nodded, her attention rapt. "Hmmm … I don't know him, but I've seen him before. He's in one of my engineering classes. Super smart guy. Didn't peg him for someone who might be in a band. Can't judge a book by its cover and all of that."

"So he's younger than Jesse?"

"Seems so."

We watched as Jesse hurried away, the drummer staring after her wistfully. He had a thing for Jesse, but it was unclear if Jesse had a thing for him or—

A conversation between me and Sera skittered across my brain, triggered by the scene.

Sera sat on her couch, elbows on her knees and face cradled in her hands. "It's a shame you didn't go with me the night I met Derek because love was in the air." She leaned forward to grab her glass off the coffee table.

Giggling, I took another sip of my red wine and propped my feet up on the ottoman across from the chair I was in. "Love was in the air? Really?"

"Yeah, maybe you could have met someone better than—"

"Stop. I'm not playing the what-if game about my love life

again. It's depressing and I'm not here to be depressed. I'm here to get drunk with my best friend."

"Pfft." She squinted at me, her cheeks flushed from all the wine she'd consumed. "I met Derek, who is the love of my life, and Tommy, Derek's friend, finally got together with his long-term crush." She paused to take a sip from her own glass. "Well, not together that night, but like, he took care of her after someone drugged her or something equally heinous, and she finally realized ... that age is just a number, baby! Or their age difference was anyways since, you know, it's only two years. Because a really big age gap ... eww ..."

"Tommy? I don't know any friend of Derek's who's a Tommy. And who'd he get together with? Do I know her?"

As if I didn't say anything at all she continued, "And now Tommy and Jesse have the most adorable baby. They are so happy." She hiccupped. "Do you think I need a baby with Derek to be happy? I want one eventually, but maybe I need one now? And maybe you could have had a baby with someone you met that night and we could all be happy. But now you won't be happy because you didn't go that night and you married a sometimes jerk. And everyone knows you can't have a baby with a sometimes jerk." She lifted her glass in the air, the red liquid nearly sloshing over the sides. "But whatevs. I still love you though! And wine can make us both happy!"

Focusing on the present, I dug my nails into Sera's arm, a feeling of foreboding washing over me. "Do you know the drummer's name?"

Wincing, she flicked my hand away. "No, why? We

could ask Jesse." Spotting our new friend heading our way, Sera waved her over.

"Hey." Jesse slid up to lean against the wall beside us. "Nameless is getting ready to go on. Finally."

"Oh, yeah? We saw you with that guy just now. Is he the family friend—you and Evan's—you were telling me about before?"

Color settled in her cheeks, spreading quickly to her neck and ears. "Yeah, that's him. Tommy."

My heart dropped into my stomach.

And just like that, I have another couple's future relationship to mend.

Chapter 10

Despite the discovery of yet another romantic butterfly effect catastrophe, I found myself lost in the music when Nameless finally took the stage. They weren't anything groundbreaking, but they embodied the sound and aesthetic I'd sorely missed. There was just something about 90's music that got inside of my blood to get it pumping. It made me feel alive, like I was small and infinite simultaneously, like the world was full of possibilities just waiting for me to take. And perhaps everyone felt that way about their generation's music. It was the theme song of our childhoods and teenage years. It held memories we both wanted to lose and cling to …

This is exactly what I needed tonight after all. To remember what it feels like to be real. To exist in this moment, this time. Forget about the future and what will never be, and focus on what could be.

I nibbled my thumbnail as I swayed to the music. *Or*

forget about it after I fix what I broke between Jesse and Tommy. And then after that no more interfering. Whatever happens, happens.

The crowd erupted into applause after the final chord was plucked, and the lead singer of Nameless mumbled a thanks into the microphone. With a bow and a wave, he exited the stage, followed by his bandmates.

Shaking myself from my music-induced stupor, I grabbed Jesse's arm. "Come on, you know the band, introduce us!" It was the best way I could come up with to work some cupid magic between Tommy and Jesse. But then again, my plan didn't go beyond getting them next to each other in my presence. Hopefully, the patch for their fledgling relationship could be applied as easily as it had been for Sera and Derek.

Startled, Jesse glanced uncomfortably towards the stage. "Really? I didn't peg you for the groupie type."

"Groupie? What? No! I just wanted to tell them how awesome I thought they were. You know, give the artists some compliments and ..." I grimaced, knowing I sounded exactly like a groupie trying to convince someone I wasn't one. "I'm really not a groupie though."

Sera raised her eyebrows and mouthed, 'What are you doing now?' behind Jesse's back.

'I don't know,' I mouthed back. Widening my eyes, I tried to ocularly communicate to Sera my desire to get Jesse and Tommy together. She just blinked at me with confusion.

"I think we should just let them do their thing," Jesse grumbled, annoyance interlaced in her tone.

Following her gaze with mine, I spied the source of her sudden attitude. Tommy was currently smiling down at an attractive blonde girl who kept touching his arm as she talked.

No, no, no, no, no. Tommy should not be flirting with anyone but Jesse. For all I know, the blonde girl is ruining her own happily-ever-after that she's supposed to have with someone else by having this one interaction.

Rushing the pair, I waved my arms around like an insane person. Which, at this point, it wouldn't be completely unfair to consider me one anymore. After all, the definition of insanity was doing the same thing over and over and expecting a different result. Wasn't that precisely what I was doing by getting involved in situations that I'd inadvertently caused by traveling back into my younger self's body?

"Tommy! Hey, Tommy! Jesse needs you ASAP! It's important. Extremely important!"

At the mention of Jesse's name, Tommy's gaze sharpened on me, the blonde instantly forgotten. "What's wrong? Where is she?" He flipped his sweaty, long, dark hair out of his eyes, pale complexion flushed from the set he'd just finished.

I pointed to Jesse, who was frozen in place beside Sera, still leaning against the wall. "That guy, Craig—"

"Yeah, I know the douche canoe." He crossed his arms over his chest, nostrils flaring.

"He tried to drug Jesse and she—"

"He what? When? While we were on stage?"

"No, before, but—"

"And she didn't tell me?" Zeroing in on Jesse, he stalked across the room. I kept pace beside him, trying not to grin maniacally about how easy he was to ramp up.

Chest heaving, Tommy stopped in front of Jesse, and she stared up at him defiantly. "You weren't going to tell me about Craig trying to drug you?"

She dropped her chin and averted her gaze. "It was taken care of, and I didn't want to mess up your set. I know how important this gig was for you guys. I—"

He grabbed her shoulders roughly. "Nothing is more important to me than you. Do you hear me? Nothing."

Jesse blinked rapidly at him, staying silent.

"Were you going to tell me at all?" he hissed low.

Jesse remained mute.

"I know you think of me as your brother's stupid little friend, but you have to know ... I would do anything for you."

Sera inched towards me, not taking her attention off of the scene in front of us. I had to admit it was quite compelling. When she bumped shoulders with me, Sera whispered, "This is seriously hot. If she doesn't kiss him right now, I might just do it for her."

I snorted.

Maybe Jesse heard Sera's comment, or quite possibly it was because of what Tommy had just confessed. Either way, I barely contained the urge to clap with glee when Jesse smashed her lips against Tommy's.

"So hot," Sera whispered again.

"Okay, Paris Hilton."

"Who?"

Wait. When did Paris Hilton start overusing the hell out of that phrase again? Oops. Obviously not yet. "Oh, um, never mind."

"We should probably let them … do whatever."

Tommy was now pressed into Jesse, her hands tangled in his hair, the two of them having an intense make out session right there in the middle of Graffiti's.

Sera laughed. "That escalated quickly, didn't it?"

Some of the pressure lifted from my chest, and I sucked in a deep breath, miraculously not coughing this time. "I'm happy for her, for them. Bet they'll make a really cute baby one day." I smiled to myself, amused by my own inside joke.

"Baby? They're making out, not reproducing. At least not on purpose."

"Yep, mmm hmmm." Yet. They were making out not reproducing … yet.

Slowly the lights in Graffiti's went up another increment, the sign that the show was officially over and the staff was giving the crowd the not-so-subtle hint to get the hell out.

Warily, I glanced around, half expecting Logan and or Ben to jump out at me from any direction. If I could manage to get home without another interaction with either of them, then possibly I could avoid them completely as I'd originally planned.

"Oh! We should go wait out front for Ben."

Shit. Somehow, I'd forgotten. Or I'd purposely blocked it out of my mind. Most likely the latter. "It's fine. We don't need to trouble Ben. Let's just call an Uber."

Sera tilted her head quizzically. "What's an Uber? You sure someone didn't put something in one of your drinks tonight? Because you've been spouting all kinds of nonsense lately."

Holy hell, I'd done it again. I take back everything I'd ever said about time travel movies and books when the main character can't seem to get the simplest things right. Things that were no-brainers from the outsider's perspective. But here I was, bumbling all over the place. I would be lucky if I didn't butterfly effect the world out of existence at the rate I was going.

"What?" When in doubt, play dumb. "What's an Uber?"

Sera narrowed her eyes at me, and I batted my lashes at her innocently. "What do you mean, what's an Uber? You're the one that said that word, and I asked you what it was."

I blinked at her. "What are you talking about?"

She stabbed a finger at me. "Don't you dare try that with me. I know what you said."

"I think Derek scrambled your brain. Did he kiss you yet?"

"No, not yet. But it wasn't for my lack of trying. He's

trying to be respectful or something." She stuck out her bottom lip in a pout.

Ah, the young mind, so easily distracted. "Maybe you should have made the first move then?"

"Please! He's too hot. I got nervous. If he doesn't make the first move, then nothing beyond what already dwells in my imagination will ever happen between us."

"For shame." I laughed at her outraged expression. "I thought you went after what you wanted when it—"

"Stop!" She ushered me out the front door, which was kind of a shock since I didn't notice we'd started walking again. "He's like a work of art. He's too pretty to touch."

"That's kind of a problem."

She sighed dramatically. "You're telling me. But I gave him our phone number and subtlety not so subtlety told him where we live. And he seemed interested. Very interested. But who knows with guys like that, he might have been in it just to prove he could get those things from me. Maybe it's all a game for him."

I rolled my eyes. "He's not like that, trust me."

"And how would you know?"

Yeah, how did I know? It wasn't like I could tell her that I also considered him a friend in the future. That I'd spent many hours in forced proximity at first, thanks to her. "Just trust me."

"Harper. Sera. Over here."

"Damn it." I swung my gaze around, searching for an escape route, but short of literally sprinting off into the night, I was stuck.

Sera elbowed me. Hard. "Stop it. I don't want to wait for the shuttle, or worse, walk."

"I think I'll brave the shuttle."

She yanked on my arm, spinning me in Ben's direction as he closed the last bit of distance between us and him. "No, you will not," she hissed out of the side of her mouth.

Ben fidgeted with his keys, his smile faltering. "You guys ready?"

"Yep!" Sera said brightly. "Thanks so much for giving us a ride, by the way. We really appreciate it."

Gnawing on the insides of my cheeks, I remained silent. I was done faking politeness for anyone. Especially for Ben. It didn't matter that he was doing this for my benefit, and I was being a brat. It was impossible to scrub his future bad behavior towards me from my brain. I just wanted him to go away, but obviously the universe had other plans.

"Okay, well, this way." Ben's keys jingled as he walked, the sound putting me on edge.

I slipped into the backseat of Ben's blue Mustang before Sera could, leaving her with no other choice but shotgun. She glared at me for the move, but I pretended not to notice.

The silence in the car was oppressive. A minute or so into the drive, Ben finally spoke. "What did you think about Nameless?"

I knew he was asking us both, or really me, but since I was in the backseat, I decided to ignore him, too.

Sera cleared her throat, answering Ben with forced

cheer. "Nameless was great! I'm so glad Evan let us know about their show." She twisted in her seat, addressing me. "And did you see Jesse and Tommy before we left? They were all over each other!"

I snorted. "Yeah, just friends my ass." It was a relief that fixing their connection had been as easy as righting the trajectory of Sera and Derek's budding relationship.

"What made you cut your hair?" Ben blurted out.

Of course he wanted to know, but I wouldn't give him the satisfaction of answering that question either. I merely met his gaze in the rear-view mirror with cold detachment.

Sera cleared her throat again, this time more dramatically. "Every now and again a girl just needs a change. Right, Harper?"

Normally, Sera wasn't bothered by tense silences or even a bit of conflict, so for her to currently be uncomfortable was a sign of the magnitude of the bad energy in the car. I wouldn't bend to placate Ben though. Not ever again.

Ben drummed his fingers along the steering wheel. "You feeling okay, Harper? You look a little flushed."

I narrowed my eyes at the back of Ben's head. Yep, that sounded about right. Ben couldn't fathom anyone he wanted to talk to not being receptive to his efforts on purpose, so therefore the only plausible explanation, according to him, must be that I was unwell in some way.

Sera twisted farther in her seat, eyeing me with concern. "You do look a little flushed." She widened her eyes demonstratively as if to say, 'And you've been acting off all night.' Thankfully, she didn't say the latter part out loud, although she communicated it loud and clear, no words necessary.

"I'm fine," I muttered, turning to stare out the window as dark buildings slid by in the brisk Pittsburgh night.

Chapter 11

A repetitive ringing sound beat against my eardrums, reverberating through my skull.

"Not again!" Sera whined, followed by a crash a bit too close to my head for comfort.

Blissful silence descended upon me, lasting for all of two minutes.

"You need to get up, Harper!" Sera whisper-shouted. "Your alarm clock is dead. I killed it, and I'm about to go back to sleep."

Good. It's dead, and now I can sleep in peace.

"I said to get up!"

I groaned. "Why do I have to get up?"

"You have class. How many times are we going to do this?"

Rolling over, I was greeted by grey light filtering in through the blinds. I laid there another few minutes, gathering the strength to rise. I had not considered the mental torment of going back to school on repeat. Of course, I hadn't needed to since I never planned on traveling this far back in time. *But you're here now so you need to suck it up and not fail out.*

"Harper," Sera growled. "This is a part of our friendship that I don't enjoy. I am not your wake-up service. I didn't schedule a ridiculously early class and shouldn't be made to suffer for your poor decision."

Groaning again, I stumbled out of bed. "Fiiiine. I'm up."

Sera grunted and pulled her comforter over her head. I scowled, jealous that she got to sleep in. *Poor decision, indeed.*

My heart pulsated in my head, the dull thump signaling an imminent headache. Shuffling towards the bathroom, and rubbing my temples, my gaze snagged on a piece of notebook paper sitting in the middle of my desk. On it in black Sharpie was written:

LOST DAYS??? DRUGGED? CONCUSSION? MENTAL ILLNESS?

Confusion nettled. When did I write that? It was then I noticed the date on my tear-away calendar sitting directly above the notebook paper. It was nearly a week to the day since my night at Graffiti's.

I stumbled back, covering my mouth with my hand. I had no memories whatsoever of anything beyond the car ride home with Ben and Sera. In fact, I didn't remember getting back to my dorm at all, not even hazy images or impressions.

Panic sizzled through my blood, burning away any traces of lethargy. I struggled to breathe as my thoughts bounced around to possible explanations, coming up with none beyond the potentially catastrophic. Did I break something in my brain when I jumped back into my younger self's body? Destroy some neural connection needed for short-term and or long-term memories? Was I doomed to be like that guy in *Memento*, having to piece together my past every single day with whatever notes I left for myself?

Did the movie *Memento* even exist yet?

Slumping into my desk's wooden chair, I rifled through my belongings for any other clues I'd left myself, finding none.

What do I do? Think, Harper, think. What do you know? Okay, you can't be like the guy in Memento since you still have some memories—most of them actually. You remember your future adult self, the time traveling, who you are ... You just lost the past week.

A possible answer pushed through my panic. Something that I never considered before. If a person jumped into their past self and took control of their younger self's brain and body, where did the younger self's consciousness end up? Going on the assumption all of time and space technically existed at once, therefore a person is all the same being throughout time, living in the same moment, that wouldn't be an issue. But if I had jumped into a different me from the multiverse ... or if my hypothesis was wrong ...

I slapped a hand over my mouth, stifling a horrified scream. Could I have two versions of me battling for control of my eighteen-year-old body? What would that mean long term for my—and her—sanity? And where was my consciousness during the past week?

But then again—if time and space didn't exist in the manner that I thought they did, then how did I travel back in time at all to begin with?

I rubbed my temples, a migraine blooming. *This is why we were testing short jumps, to avoid this type of thing. Now I'm free-falling into oblivion. And what can I do about it? Neuroscience was Glorita's field of expertise, and tracking down the younger version of her won't do me a damn bit of good. So what do I do other than try to live this life and hope for the best?*

Under the circumstances, I had no other options. I would simply have to push forward and hope for the best. Quite possibly the blackout was an anomaly and I didn't have to worry about it. *Yeah, right.*

I NEEDED to get my shit together before I failed out of college. Not only was I behind my peers to start with since it'd been years since I'd studied the curriculum in my classes, but now I was also spacing out, my mind wandering to my time-traveling dilemma. I might as well have stayed in bed instead of trudging out into the frigid morning with all the good attending my early morning lab did. *Okay, maybe frigid is a bit of an exaggeration, chilly is perhaps a better description. Even still—*

"Harper." Logan's voice startled me out of the beginnings of my internal whining session. Yanked against a hard chest, I abruptly found my back pressed into the cold stone wall of the nearest building. "I missed you."

Logan's lips descended onto mine before I had a chance to comprehend let alone react. I opened my mouth to protest, or question … or something, when his tongue slid past my lips, entangling with mine. My body disregarded any burgeoning mental protests, sinking into the kiss with fervor.

Logan's hands skated down to my ass, squeezing firmly as he ground against me. I groaned, wanting closer, wanting more, my hands fisting in his hair.

He pulled away from me long enough to say, "I know you said you'd come over tonight, but I can't wait that long. Let's go somewhere now. I need you, Harper."

Alarm bells sounded. *Wait. What?* I shoved at Logan's shoulders, and he reluctantly stopped kissing me, his gaze lust-laden as he stared down at me with question. "When did I— What are you doing?"

He smirked. "It's so adorable when you get flustered around me."

My ears heated, and I shoved at him harder, my mind beginning to clear. "I'm not coming over tonight or any other night. And I don't know what made you think you could just grab and kiss me like that."

He brought one of his fingers up to boop my nose. "Did you have a bad morning? Don't worry, I can fix that." He leaned into me again, smoldering gaze intent on my lips.

I smacked at his shoulders. "No! Stop! No means no."

Raising his hands, he backed away slowly. "Okay, so you're not in the mood now. I get it."

"Now? I'm not ever going to be in the mood for you." I didn't understand what was going on. After what happened at Graffiti's I fully expected him to show up again in some capacity, but to just grab and kiss me before openly propositioning me ... I wasn't prepared for those moves.

Logan ran a hand through his hair, confusion pinching his features. "What are you talking about? I thought—"

"Well, you thought wrong." Pivoting on my heels, I stalked off in the opposite direction, muttering curse words under my breath. The worst part was, I totally wanted to turn around and pick up right where we left off. The taste of his lips lingered, the ghost of our kiss haunting me down to my molten lava center. My nerve endings were like live wires, crackling with the need to—

Logan dashed in front of me, heading me off. "What the hell happened? I don't understand ..." He tugged at his hair, frustration wafting off of him in palpable waves. "What's wrong? Talk to me."

I adjusted my shoulder bag and crossed my arms over

my chest. "Talk to you? This again? I thought I told you at Graffiti's that I didn't want to talk to you. Period. Not sure how that translated to you thinking I'm going to sleep with you."

Logan's mouth went slack, and he stared at me for several heartbeats. "Yeah, I know. But that was before … before you slept with me. A-And all the rest."

Shock swept through me, freezing me in place. "I—What?"

And then it dawned on me. The lost week. One entire week for my younger self to get herself back on track—back on track and into bed with Logan. Somehow seven measly days lost me the progress I made in turning my life around.

A wave of dizziness slammed into me, and I swayed on my feet. "This can't be happening."

Logan lunged forward, catching me before I could fall. "I've got you."

I clutched his jacket, wanting to push him away, but seemingly unable. "I don't need you or anyone else to get me. I'm fine on my own."

"I'm taking you to one of the campus clinics. There's something wrong with you."

I sucked in a sharp breath. "How dare you? There's nothing wrong with me!"

"Did you hit your head or take something you shouldn't have? You on any new medications you shouldn't have mixed or with side effects? What about food? Did you eat enough this morning?" With a grunt,

Logan scooped me into his arms. "Tell me what's going on with you, damn it!"

"Last time I heard you were pre-law, not pre-med, so stop acting like—"

He pierced me with a stormy glare, nostrils flaring. "Yeah, I know, which is why I'm taking you to see a doctor."

Warmth bloomed inside of me, another unavoidable gut reaction to his overprotectiveness. If I wasn't careful, I would choose to have sex with him being fully aware of the future consequences and not caring one bit.

My fingertips trailed along the back of his neck as he trudged down the sidewalk with me in his arms. Maybe I should have said yes to his invite to get naked with him. It would have saved me from a needless trip to the clinic, and avoided the stares from practically everyone we passed by. Plus, I gave in to him already, and now the craving for him went beyond my mind—beyond memories that would never come to pass. My body was screaming at me to let it happen, to take the pleasure Logan could give me.

I pressed my face into his neck, inhaling deeply. He smelled a bit of sweat and whatever soap he used, but underneath that was his unique scent, the part that was all him … and the fact that it was like coming home rattled me to my core.

Logan groaned, the sound felt more than heard. "Can you please not do that? Walking around in public with a hard-on is not something I want to be doing today."

I snorted against his warm skin. "Not today, got it. How about tomorrow? Or next week?" I bit my tongue, hard, tasting the slight tang of copper. It was just so easy— too easy—to be comfortable around Logan.

His grip tightened on my shoulder and under my leg as he pulled me impossibly close. "You ready to tell me what happened? You don't need to be embarrassed, whatever it is. It's me. You can trust me."

My heart swooped down into my stomach. One week, after only one week he was saying stuff like "it's me" and "you can trust me". I didn't remember us moving so fast in our relationship the first time around. Did I make things worse by trying to ignore him, therefore forcing the younger-me to push to be even closer to compensate for what she ... I would have seen as a mistake? Or did things merely seem different from my new perspective? We were both young—in body anyways—and the young moved through life with supersonic speed, especially when it came to love. Later in life, people became more cautious after years of experience and most likely getting burned more than a few times.

I bit my lower lip, considering what way to play this. I thought I'd broken the connection between me and Logan by how I treated him at Graffiti's, but obviously it was repaired easily enough. To truly boot Logan from my life I would need to do something unfixable. But what?

"Nothing is wrong with me. I just don't want to see you anymore. What happened between us was a mistake and I finally realized it."

Logan halted abruptly and dropped me to my feet. He kept his hands on my shoulders, drawing my gaze up to his by sheer force of will alone. "Bullshit. What happened between us was not a mistake."

"Yes, it was. And you would realize it as well if you searched deep down inside of you."

His full lips twisted into a sneer. "You think I'm going to buy that you think we're a mistake? Because I'm not."

"I know with your massive ego it's hard to comprehend that anyone would willingly walk away from you like this, but it's the truth. We're not compatible. If you choose not to listen or believe what I'm saying ... well, that's not my problem."

He flashed his teeth before growling low, "Massive ego? Is that what you think? Or is it someone got in your head about me again?"

Again? Okay, I'd just roll with that one since I didn't have a choice. "These thoughts are one hundred percent mine, and I arrived at this conclusion all on my own. Like I said, I know it's hard to believe, but—"

He shook me slightly, his eyes flashing with anger. "You're going to look me dead in the eyes right now, and tell me after this past week, and what happened before that—you're going to tell me that you don't think what's between us is real?"

"One week? How can anything be real after only a week? You certainly don't love me after a week. You barely know me after a week. Great sex is lust, not real feelings ..."

His expression shifted to something akin to smug, and I knew I made yet another mistake.

"Great sex. Yeah, we have great sex because we have a connection. I've never felt anything like what's between us before. You're right, I don't love you. Yet." His voice dropped an octave, and he leaned in to whisper in my ear, "But I know I could fall in love with you. I can feel myself falling already."

I jerked away from him, hands trembling. Logan wasn't some romance hero from one of my favorite reads, he wasn't an older guy with practiced lines and speeches, he wasn't even someone who knew me long enough to be able to push my buttons. His words and actions were awkward and unpolished … But I wanted him anyways, and I always had.

It doesn't matter, it doesn't change anything. I want him, but he's not what I need. He's not good for me.

"Logan, please. I can't be with you. Just accept it, please."

He ground his teeth together, a muscle in his jaw feathering as he took a step back from me. "I'm not giving up, Harper. You can keep pushing me away, but I'm not giving up. No. Something spooked you again, and I'll figure out what it is" He moved past me, stalking down the sidewalk, people moving out of his way as if they could sense his tumultuous mood.

I watched him go, heart cinched tight, making it hard to breathe. "You will eventually because I'll make you."

Thunder clapped overhead, causing me to jump. There

wasn't a cloud in the sky even though the day was mirky. As I walked back to my dorm, I couldn't shake the feeling of foreboding, like the universe had just announced its plans to keep me on my old life's path despite my best efforts.

"Challenge accepted," I muttered, giving the sky one last glance before heading into the safety of the Towers.

It wasn't the universe I was worried about, though. It was the younger version of myself who could be just as stubborn—after all, we were the same person.

Chapter 12

I picked up the battered copy of *Wuthering Heights* from the corner of my desk and chucked it across the room. It hit the wall with a dull thud before falling onto my bed in a fluttering heap.

Once upon a time, I'd thought the book romantic, the story churning up feelings of longing—and deeply misguided ideas about what was acceptable in a relationship. I didn't blame the book or the long-dead author for that matter, it was my own misgivings from lack of experience and the inability to see truths right in front of my eyes. I thought butterflies were a sign of a spark with someone, but it turned out they only signified the gut's early warning system. It was basically your body putting you on notice to be wary of whoever was giving them to you.

Heathcliff from *Wuthering Heights*, Mr. Big from *Sex and the City*, Edward from *Twilight* ... the list of trash fictional characters that I'd always consumed like crack was nearly unending and problematic for me.

I sighed loudly, my forehead thumping against the top of my desk. It wasn't the fiction I consumed. I was smarter than that, even if my track record with men said otherwise. I was merely looking to point a finger at something so I could avoid responsibility for my own actions. Panting after dark heroes and even villains from books and movies was not the same as going after them in real life. I knew better.

Perhaps if I could pinpoint the allure of Logan Sharpe, I could figure out how to resist it. What was it about Logan that drew me to him? All it took was a smoldering glance from his ice-blue eyes and I was putty in his hands. Sure, he was attractive, with his pretty-boy, chiseled face, contrasting dark hair, blue eyes, and full, sensual lips ... and his body ... his sinewy, sun-kissed muscles ... And daaamn, did he know how to use that body.

A flash of him gazing up at me from between my thighs had me pressing my legs together.

No, nuh-uh, this took a turn in the wrong direction.

I tapped my forehead against my desk, groaning. Instead of daydreaming about Logan Sharpe, or guys like him, I needed to find myself a nice guy. Sure, Logan didn't seem like an asshat yet, but I knew what the future would bring if I didn't get away from him ASAP. Or maybe the only true solution was to remain single for the rest of my life.

Sera burst into our room, and flopped onto her bed, splaying out dramatically. "I'm so over this semester!"

I turned my head in her direction, not bothering to lift it off my desk. "Tell me about it."

She propped herself up on her elbows, staring at me curiously. "What's going on with you? More headaches? I told you after what happened last week that you should go to the doctor."

I wasn't sure what the younger version of me had experienced or what her explanation had been for the time she'd lost and her actions during that period, but unless I wanted people to keep telling me to go to a doctor, I needed to figure out a feasible plan.

"No headache. Just a bad day."

"I'm surprised to see you here. You've been spending every spare second with Logan since last week."

Okay, great. How would I explain the Logan thing? The sudden urge to tell her the truth—to come clean about everything—nearly overwhelmed me. But I knew even Sera wouldn't be that open-minded. I'd definitely end up in a padded room for my efforts.

"Logan and I ... I broke it off with him."

Sera jerked up, her eyes resembling a baby owl. "What? Why? You were so happy."

"I don't wanna talk about it," I grumbled. "But it's over. For good."

"You can't not talk about it! You have to tell me what happened! And down to every last detail!" Sera was on her feet and in my face faster than I thought humanly possible.

I fisted my hands in my lap. "What do you want me to say? The sex was great, but he's not boyfriend material." It was best to stick to the truth as much as I could. It would be easier to remember and left me with plausible deniability for the rest.

"Except you said the exact opposite two days ago. What did he do to change your mind so fast? It must have been pretty big."

Two days ago, I'd been a younger naïve version of myself, unable to see the writing on the wall with Logan. But now I was older and wiser, or at least my brain was. But of course, I couldn't say any of that.

"Red flags. Lots of red flags." I pushed myself up to a full sitting position. "If I let myself sink any further into the relationship, it would have been harder later on. It was just best to break it off now before my heart got totally crushed." Accept that it was already crushed, and I was merely attempting to prevent an encore performance of my romantic death knell.

Sera pursed her lips as her eyebrows crept up her forehead. "Red flags? Okaaay. But what did he do exactly?"

Shit. Red flags was not a commonly used term yet. I really needed to remember where—or *when* I was. It was exponentially more difficult than I'd ever thought it would be to try to unlearn the things I knew. Hmmm ... but what if I could use that knowledge for good? Like, warn people about 9/11? I could save lives. Why hadn't I considered that before? Maybe I could—

Sera snapped her fingers in front of my face, forcing me to focus on her. "Hello? You completely spaced out … again."

"I know this whole thing with Logan is giving you whiplash, but it's hard to explain. Sometimes you just know one way or the other with people. Kind of like how you know with Derek."

She scrunched her nose up. "Yeah, Derek."

"Umm … what was that?"

Her gaze flicked away. "What was what?"

"Oh, no. Nuh-huh. You're getting all up in my business about Logan but you're not telling me something about Derek."

"No, there's nothing to tell."

"You said his name weird. Tell me."

Sera shuffled back to her bed and sat, her shoulders sagging. Looking up at me, she blew a curl out of her face. "I think he's seeing someone else. Total player, like I said."

It had to be her imagination. Derek and her were meant to be together. Unless I hadn't fixed things all the way between them. There were a lot of possibilities, and I had to get more information before jumping to any conclusions. "Okaaay, but you said you basically just wanted to hook up with him. So it doesn't matter if he's seeing someone else. Or, you know, you guys just met, maybe he needs time to break things off. You're not exclusive, right?"

She scowled. "No, we're not exclusive. We haven't talked at all about any of that type of stuff."

I was almost afraid to ask, but I did anyways. "What do you talk about then?"

Her cheeks flushed, and she gave me a sheepish grin. "We haven't done much talking yet."

My lips twitched. "You don't say."

"Well, you know how it is. You and Logan—"

"Can we not bring him up again? Thank you."

"But I kind of hoped ..." She stuck out her lower lip in the most pathetic pout. "You know ..."

I tried to remember if this was how it'd gone down before between them. I did remember that they hooked up pretty quickly, but the rest in between the beginning and when they'd gotten serious was a bit of a blur. I still needed more information.

"What makes you think he's seeing someone else?"

She shrugged. "He just seems secretive."

I quirked an eyebrow. "You've known him a little over a week. There are probably truckloads of stuff he hasn't told you, and you can't really fault him for it either. That's not exactly secretive, just cautious."

"But you and Logan already had the talk ... you know, the all-night conversation at the beginning of a relationship where you both reveal your soul to the other person."

I snorted. "There was no soul-bearing from Logan, that's for sure."

Sera huffed. "You know what I mean."

She certainly was assuming that I knew a lot since she kept saying that. Unfortunately, it seemed that the older I got the less I knew. "What are you going to do?"

She curled up on her bed, hugging her pillow. "I don't know, probably break it off with him."

"You can't do that!" *Oh, no, not good.* That definitely didn't happen before. But why now? What changed?

"If he's going to be all closed off and continue to see other people, then I got what I wanted. I got a hot hookup, and it's time to move on."

Shit, shit, shittity shit. It was because of what she perceived was going on between me and Logan. She was comparing where she thought she should be and thinking her relationship was falling short. I'd messed things up again, and again I needed to fix it.

"Would it make a difference if he wasn't seeing anyone else? If he was just being slow with opening up to you?"

Sera hugged her pillow tighter. "I don't know, maybe."

Jumping to my feet, I grabbed my coat. "That settles it then, we have a guy to get intel on."

Sera remained where she was, her eyes glazed over. "I'm not in the mood for whatever—"

I yanked her up and shoved her to the door. "We're going."

"Wait. My coat!" She snatched it off the back of her desk chair as I continued to shove her forward.

It had been a while since I'd been on an old-fashioned fact-finding mission, and I was hoping I remembered how to do it without the use of the modern internet.

Chapter 13

"And what facts have we discovered exactly?" Sera side-eyed me, her face twisted with displeasure.

"Give it time."

We were stationed across the street from Derek's apartment on a little park bench. We'd donned disguises that consisted of hats and sunglasses, which—with the distance—would hopefully fool Derek if he spotted us. The key was to act inconspicuously. Regrettably, the best activity I could come up with was holding coffee cups, like we were two friends, sitting on a bench, drinking coffee.

I sighed. "This would have been easier with smartphones," I mumbled to myself.

"What?"

"Nothing."

"You know," Sera fiddled with the lid on her to-go cup, "even if he comes home soon, and he is seeing someone else, what are the chances that he's going to parade her right past us at this particular moment in time?"

"I don't know." Again, my mind went to how easy getting information on someone was with the future version of the internet. Cheaters definitely got away with a lot more before it existed. Hell, everyone got away with a lot more before it existed. "We could always break in."

Sera glanced at her ordinary wristwatch. "I think I made a mistake. I think he has class for another half hour." She slowly stood, shaking out her stiff limbs. "I say let's do it. Let's break in and snoop around."

I blinked at her. "I was joking."

"And I'm not."

"We can't break into his apartment. I don't know how we'd do it even if I thought it was a good idea."

"I'm sure we can figure it out." Sera was already striding across the street before I could get a word in edgewise.

Dashing to catch up, I fell into step beside her. "Let me repeat, I was joking. Breaking in is a horrible idea. We could literally go to jail."

"We'll be in and out fast, his apartment is an efficacy."

I pulled on her arm, tugging her back as she struggled to open the entrance door to the lobby. "Sera, no."

She stopped, considering. "You're right. We should go up the fire escape and check his window first. There are bars on it, but one of them is loose and I bet we could wiggle it off."

She darted around the back of the building, leaving me

no choice but to follow. "Sera!" I hissed. "Please, you've lost your damn mind."

Or maybe I had. Literally. Maybe I wasn't from the future in any way shape or form and the delusion was the first sign of something like a brain tumor. The second being the blackout. The thing was, I couldn't share any of it with anyone to find out. Or rather, I could tell the entire world, but I didn't have any real proof. Sure, I had knowledge of the future, potentially, but surprisingly most of it was useless until it wasn't.

No. Don't doubt yourself. There's no point in doing so.

"Harper! Get up here now!"

I blinked rapidly as I tilted my head back and spotted Sera three flours up. Damn, she was fast when she wanted to be. "I can't let you do this!"

"Shhhh … quiet before someone hears you!"

"Yeah, because you're being so stealthy." I made my ascent up the rusty fire escape, the whole thing rattling with every step I took. By the time I got up all three flights, Sera had already set to work.

Face flushed with exertion, she was yanking on the window bar. "See this is the loose one. Help me pull it out."

"And then what? How do you know the window is even unlocked?"

She smirked, pointing at the widely open window. "Just a hunch."

Damn it, Derek. Why would you go out and leave your window open, with or without bars? What if it rained?

"I'm going to say it again—this is a horrible idea. Please, stop."

The bar popped off, taking with it a piece of brick. Closing my eyes, I sighed heavily. There would be no stopping her now. Why did I ever even joke about this? Clearly, she had lost her mind over Derek. Which I should have known. I mean, I did know, and yet I guess I didn't take it seriously because of their future.

Wiggling through the scant space, Sera grunted as she pushed the window open. "Come on, before someone sees us."

I glanced around nervously. I didn't want to go in, but she was right. If I stayed out on the fire escape, I could be spotted. "I'm going to say one last time that this is a bad idea, but I guess it's too late now."

Clambering through the bars and then the window, I spilled onto the worn linoleum floor. Sera was riffling through drawers and papers before I made it to my feet.

I dusted myself off. "Well, this is great." I surveyed the tiny apartment from the kitchen slash living room slash bedroom, to the ... well, that was about it. There were two doors, counting the front door. I assumed the other was the bathroom. There wasn't even a closet. Thankfully, there wasn't much ground to cover in our investigation, so we'd be able to leave quickly.

"What do you think you're going to find? A manifesto or list detailing all the girls Derek has ever slept with along with the dates and times?"

Sera paused with her hand on a pile of haphazardly stacked books. "This was your idea."

I threw my hands up in the air. "It. Was. A. Joke."

"Ah-ha!" Sera pulled a magazine out from under one of the books, waving it at me. "A dirty magazine!"

I rolled my eyes. "Every guy in the world has that." At least until free internet porn became a thing.

As if I hadn't said anything, she flipped through it with dawning horror on her face. "None of these girls look like me."

For crying out loud, were all young people this ridiculous? I don't remember being this bad before. But then again, I wouldn't be here determined to make different choices if I hadn't been just as much of a disaster. I decided to play along. "What do you mean none of them look like you?"

She choked back a sob. "They're all blonde, all of them no matter their skin color, and with ginormous boobs." She dropped the magazine and clutched at her chest. "I'm like a C at best. And I'm definitely not blonde either."

"You know guys, they take what they can get with porn. It's not like they can search specific types online or something." *Yet.*

"No." She slashed her hand through the air, face twisting with anger. "I'm not his type and he's just using me for sex. The other girl he's seeing probably looks like these girls."

"He's not using you for sex. Derek lov— Derek— Well, he …" How could I tell her anything reassuring without having to explain how I knew? "Please, trust me. Just don't break it off with him and everything will end up good in the end."

Sera picked up the magazine again, grumbling insults under breath as she stared at the contents.

"Okay, that's enough." I marched over to her and forcefully removed the offending periodical from her hands, letting it drop back to the desk. "It's time to go." I steered her to the front door, and she continued to mutter things under her breath, some of them nonsensical.

Digging her heels in, she turned watery eyes to me. "What do I do?"

I took her by the shoulders. "It's too soon to be like this. Please, just keep seeing him. Let things happen the way they're supposed to happen. You and Derek ... you're meant to be together. Trust me on this. Even if he is seeing someone else right now—"

She gasped.

"He won't be later. Give him some time before you drive yourself crazy for nothing. He's not cheating on you no matter how you look at it. You've only known him a week."

I wouldn't add that she shouldn't have slept with him so soon if she couldn't handle whatever went with that decision. It was irrelevant in her situation. But the truth was, all too often women caught feelings once sex was involved whether they wanted to or not. It happened a lot less often with men. Having a purely sexual situationship was perfectly fine if you could cope with all it entailed.

Knowing that Sera married Derek, in the end, made everything different from my perspective, unless...

Again, I wondered if something was different between Sera and Derek because of some minor detail I'd missed. I'd introduced them on the night they'd previously met, but what if something had shifted because it didn't happen in exactly the same way?

I'll just have to keep an eye on things and act accordingly. I would not let Sera's happy marriage slip away because I traveled too far back in time.

"Okay. Out, out, out. I don't think either one of us would do well in jail."

"You'd post bail easily enough, but you'd have to go to court. I wouldn't take my word for it, though, since I'm only pre-law and B and E isn't something we've gone over yet."

Sera and I screamed in chorus, whirling towards the sound of the male voice coming from the fire escape. It took me a few seconds of panic to register the familiar blue eyes and dark hair.

"Logan? Wh-What the hell are you doing here?"

He was leaning casually against the railing, arms crossed. I supposed he was too big to fit into the space we'd made by removing the window bar. "I saw you two climb up here, and yeah, my curiosity got the best of me."

I blinked, slow to process his response. "You followed us?"

"Yeah. The two of you were acting extremely suspicious, and I was curious about what you were up to."

I blinked several more times. "I don't understand."

"It's not complicated."

He was acting so nonchalant about following us, about finding us illegally inside of someone's apartment—about all of it. Especially after the last time I'd seen him when I told him I wanted nothing to do with him. What was his plan exactly?

"I thought you said you broke things off with him," Sera whispered out of the side of her mouth.

She might as well have shouted it though. Her words echoed inside of the tiny apartment, hanging awkwardly between all of us.

Logan's jaw muscles flexed. "She did. But I also told her I wasn't letting her off the hook that easily." His gaze flicked to mine, some unreadable emotion dancing within the icy depths.

"So you followed me?" Like I had room to criticize when Sera and I had been staking out Derek's apartment before the decision to break into it. Men made just as many ridiculous and rash decisions as women, they just rarely admitted it.

"You two planning on waiting in there until whoever's place this is comes back and decides to call the cops, or are you going to get out of there?"

I scowled at him. "We were just about to leave before you showed up out of nowhere."

"Were you going to walk out the front door and risk more people seeing you?"

Sera's eyes got wide. "Someone might tell him they

saw people coming out of his place. I didn't think of that at all."

"It's not like he's got security cameras or a camera doorbell. And none of his neighbors do either, so ..."

I was met with silence as both Logan and Sera stared at me blankly. *Shit. I did it again.* I waved my hand through the air. "You know, like in that sci-fi movie about big brother ..." I chuckled nervously. "Cameras everywhere."

Grabbing Sera's arm, I propelled her towards the window. Whether I liked it or not, Logan was right. Leaving through the front door was risky. Not as risky as it would be in the future, but risky nonetheless.

Logan waited where he was, watching us with mirth glittering in his eyes as we struggled to get out the way we came in. Once we were safely on the fire escape, Sera and I clanged down the metal stairs to the street, Logan not far behind us.

"Whose place is it? Ex-boyfriend or current boyfriend?" Logan asked as we exited the alley behind the building.

Sera's head was on a swivel as she scanned the street for any signs of Derek approaching.

"Well?"

I ground my teeth together, refusing to meet his gaze. "We don't owe you any explanations. You just showed up outside after admittedly following us."

"Coast is clear," Sera exclaimed with relief. "Now let's go home to debrief."

Logan's laugh rumbled low, the sound tickling things

on my insides, making it impossible to ignore him. "The two of you are trouble."

"Nobody asked you," I snapped.

"Don't care if you did," he retorted.

Sera grabbed my hand and squeezed. "Logan." She smiled at him sweetly. "Can we trust you not to tell anyone about any of this?"

One side of his mouth quirked up. "Don't know. What's in it for me?"

Sera paused, and a second later her elbow met my ribs. "Tell him what's in it for him, Harper."

I stared at my so-called friend, annoyance surging. "You can't be serious right now."

She elbowed me again and gave me a pointed look, letting me know that she was.

Sucking on my teeth, I notched my chin up as I regarded Logan with skepticism. "You won't hang this over our heads. Besides, who will believe you anyways? You have zero proof."

His eyes sparkled. "Ah, but all I need in the court of public opinion is reasonable doubt and suddenly you're the crazy chicks who broke into a guy's apartment. It doesn't even matter who or why."

"I don't wanna be a crazy chick!" Sera exclaimed, panic interlacing her tone. "Please, don't make me into the crazy chick, Harper." She shuffled in front of me with her hands clasped together in supplication.

I glowered at her. "I'm not making you anything, you're doing a pretty good job of it all on your own."

Her lower lip popped out. "Hurtful. That was really hurtful, Harper."

"I'm asking for a conversation," Logan interjected. "Just a conversation where you don't run off until the completion of it."

Narrowing my eyes at him, I said, "Yeah? And who gets to decide when it's come to," I raised my hands to air quote, "*completion*? You, I bet."

He smirked. "Of course."

"Hmmm ..." I quirked an eyebrow.

"He just wants a conversation, Harper. Just give him one, Harper."

"Stop saying my name over and over again like that, *Sera*." It felt like she was trying to use some kind of psychological trick, but I didn't have a clue what it was. Maybe she didn't either.

She blew out a breath, a few stray curls wafting into the air. "Fine. If you want us to be social lepers in the local dating world for the rest of our college careers, then go ahead and be stubborn."

I threw my hands up in the air. "He's not actually going to say a word to anyone. He's manipulating you into manipulating me right now." And the worst part was that it was working. Or quite possibly I wanted an excuse to talk to Logan again—any excuse that would allow it to be beyond my control and therefore not another bad decision made by me.

The longer I stayed in my younger body, the more it seemed like I was merging with my younger self's brain.

Or perhaps it was where my brain was developmentally. Thrusting my future self's consciousness into my younger body was akin to an older computer not being able to support a new browser update. Things weren't going to run smoothly.

"I mean, maybe let's not risk it?" Sera's gaze darted from me to Logan and then back again.

"Fine. But you owe me big time. For this entire debacle in fact."

She grinned, completely unrepentant. "You're the best."

I rolled my eyes.

"Tonight then. Seven o'clock, my place." Logan sauntered off down the street, not even bothering to wait for any kind of response from either of us.

Infuriating, cocky bastard.

Chapter 14

I often felt as though I remembered the time from my youth clearly—people, places, and other miscellaneous things—but in actuality, it's like peering at a faded photograph without your subscription reading glasses on. The reality of it is sharper, and frankly discombobulating after being removed from the harshness of it for such a long period of time.

Sure, nearly everyone wants to relive the point in their lives after high school, when they attended college, or simply when they were out on their own for the first time. The freedom, the possibilities, seemingly endless. But for some of us, how easily things like having to take the bus that reeks like pee, having to sleep on a lumpy futon, or only having enough money to eat Ramen every night, is forgotten. Hardships are discarded, and only fond memories are revisited.

But that isn't all. I, for instance, couldn't remember

exactly where Logan lived. I could picture his front door, and the rest of his cramped apartment, but as far as how to get there ... it was a bit fuzzy. And it wasn't like I could ask Logan for directions since I would have no way of explaining how I forgot after technically just being there last night.

Stuffing my frozen hands into my pockets, I turned to study two apartment complexes in North Oakland that looked nearly identical. After about half an hour, I'd narrowed Logan's building down to one of the two. Unfortunately, there weren't names by the buzzers, and I was over getting yelled at or invited up by people that were not him.

I sighed heavily. I'd caved too quickly to not admit to myself that I wanted to be here, with him. Or rather, in a few-mile block radius of him, as was the current case. Logan Sharpe was my sexual kryptonite and just having him in my general vicinity inevitably sent me crashing to the ground with my legs spread wide open. Not an entirely favorable idea to acknowledge.

But why? He was smart, funny, and his sex appeal was on another level, but he was also a jackass. And his seduction skills were clumsy at best at this stage of his life. An experienced man wouldn't have followed me and then leveraged a conversation from what he'd learned. He would have love-bombed me until I ran into his arms, begging to be with him forever. And yet, in the end, he was getting what he wanted either way, so I supposed I couldn't criticize ... too much. It seemed like both of our bars were set low. His because of age, and mine because, apparently, I was a dumbass.

Crossing the street, I stood between the two buildings on the sidewalk, studying them closely for any kind of detail that might jog my memory.

Eventually, I decided to go with eeny-meeny-miney-moe, my index finger settling on the building to my right. Sighing again, I hesitantly made my way up the cement steps, pausing at the front door. What was my plan? Knock on every single door? It wasn't much better than pushing random buzzers. Plus, it was exponentially more dangerous.

I should just give up. The universe might actually be on my side this time. Otherwise—

"Harper?" Logan's voice called from off to my left.

Nope, definitely not on my side. Thanks for making that crystal clear, universe. I whirled in his direction, like a flower powerless to avoid the warmth of the sun. My breath caught in my throat as his piercing gaze met mine.

Smirking, he motioned to the building—the building that was not his. "You lost? Or are you double booked tonight?"

I narrowed my eyes, annoyance sparking. No explanation or snarky retort was forthcoming, my mind utterly blank. Which obviously made me even more annoyed. Instead, I chose to ignore the entire situation. I was a pro at denial. "Are you that desperate for our talk that you're waiting outside for me? I mean, you already blackmailed me to be here to begin with."

He glowered. "Funny."

I grinned. "I thought so."

Steam streamed from his nostrils as he exhaled heavily. "Well, come on. It's cold out here."

"Eh, it's not that bad."

"If you want to freeze, your choice, I guess." He turned, stalking back into his building, leaving me to wonder if he actually had been out looking for me. Or was he leaving, believing that I'd stood him up? Not that he'd admit the truth at this point.

Forcing my stiff limbs to comply, I hurried after him. As soon as I was past the front entry, a wall of heat enveloped me. "Oh, thank God."

"Thought it wasn't that bad?"

"Shut up."

He chuckled, making me want to punch his smug face. Or kiss it. Or punch it and then kiss it. *Ugh.* Being in my younger body again with the raging hormones and underdeveloped prefrontal cortex was more difficult to manage than I thought it would be. Plus, the longer I was in my younger self's body, the more I slid back into myself, so to speak. It was what I kept telling myself I needed to do, but I was still concerned. What if I followed the same path I did before? What if it was unavoidable? What if fixed points in time were more than a plot device for sci-fi fiction?

"Are you just going to stand there or …" Logan raised his eyebrows in question.

"What do you want from me? Do you think

blackmailing me to come have a conversation with you is going to make me happy to be here? Do you think I'm going to happily skip to your apartment and after a few sentences from you things will be back to the way they were last week?"

A storm rolled through his eyes, darkening them. "We both know I wouldn't have told anyone. I just gave you an excuse to be here, and we both know that, too."

I ground my teeth together. "You are a jackass."

He raised his hands defensively. "Hey now. I think you owe me a bit more of an explanation than what I got in the middle of the street on campus after—"

"After what? A week of having sex? Sex doesn't mean anything, not all by itself." And he'd shown me that truth eventually with his lies and betrayals.

He was in my space before I could blink, crowding me against the wall. "Stop saying what happened between us didn't mean something special." With trembling fingers, he reached up to cup the side of my jaw. "I'm not a sentimental guy. I didn't even want a relationship. But with you ... with you, things are just different for me."

"You'll get over it, in time." I'd believed him once, truly believed that I was special to him. But time proved me wrong and made him into a liar.

He swore under his breath, his clenched fists hitting the wall on either side of my head. I flinched. "I'm not having this conversation out here in the hallway for all of my neighbors to hear."

If he got me into his apartment there was a good

chance I'd succumb to my hormones and let him ravage me before either of us could utter a word. Which I'd known all along, from the moment I stepped out of my dorm room. I wanted Logan Sharpe, this version of him, one last time, even if I knew it was a spectacularly bad idea.

No. Fight it. Walk away now. It's not too late. I am in control. And if I give in, I have no one to blame but myself, contrary to what I want to believe.

Logan gently pulled me off the wall, steering me down the hall to the stairwell by my elbow. And I let him do it. Even with my thoughts swirling in protest, I didn't fight my urges, or so much as resist his touch.

And then there I was, inside of his tiny apartment, the past and present colliding with my future self. I shuddered in revulsion at myself, and delight for what was surely to come. Even still, I was frozen in place, unable to move from the space I was hovering in just inside of his front door.

"Harper." Logan said my name gently, as if somehow sensing my fragility in that moment. "I do want to talk ..." But the way his voice trailed off, breaking low, let me know he wasn't opposed to more, the decision ultimately controlled by me.

Body numb, I shuffled to his miniature couch, the faded leather cracked and peeling in places. Idly, I noted that I'd never noticed the shabby state of his belongings before. I hesitated a few heartbeats, finally slumping down into the corner, boneless and confused.

Things had seemed so simple in the beginning. Avoid Logan and Ben, don't cause any catastrophic ripple effects, and live my life complete with my knowledge of the future giving me that extra edge to succeed the second time around. I'd already failed on all accounts.

Jumping to my feet, I exclaimed, "Bathroom!" then made a mad dash for the small room off to my right. Thankfully, I remembered where that was. After closing and locking the door, I slumped against the flimsy fake wood, sucking in several deep breaths. But I couldn't hide in the bathroom all night, nor was there a window I could crawl out of.

Catching my reflection in the mirror above the sink, I glared at myself. *This is quite the mess you've gotten us into. But no plan on how to get us out?* I scrunched up my nose. *I didn't think so.*

Part of the problem—or the entire problem—was that there were things I would never have taken into consideration with traveling back into my younger self, things I wasn't prepared for on any level. For instance, I had the thoughts, feelings, and memories of a fully-grown adult woman, but every time I saw myself in the mirror, my younger self peering back at me, I lost myself bit by bit to who I used to be. As if time in the past was erasing the future for me, and soon, I'd forget who I'd become. Maybe that's what the blackout was about. The beginning of the erosion of a person I'd never grow to be since I was essentially starting over.

Or perhaps I was losing myself to another version of me from a multiverse as I'd previously considered.

No matter what way I looked at the problem, I should have been able to stay away from Logan for a multitude of reasons, but I was being overridden by my younger self's stupidity.

Admitting to being a dumbass is half the battle. Probably. Hopefully. I grimaced at my reflection one last time before deciding it was time to face the source of my anxiety.

Logan eyed me from his perch on the edge of the couch. "Thought maybe you were planning on hiding in there."

Am I that obvious? "Don't be ridiculous."

Logan motioned in my general direction. "You going to take your coat off? Or you leaving it on so it'll be easier to bolt?"

I knew what he was doing. He was calling me on my bullshit in hopes that I would do the opposite just to prove him wrong. And even knowing what he was doing, the urge to do exactly what he thought I would was nearly overwhelming.

Slowly, and deliberately, my gaze boring into his the entire time, I unbuttoned my coat and tugged it off. My cheeks heated when he licked his lips slowly. The same lips that had—

Nope. You don't remember what happened between you last week, and the other stuff hasn't technically happened at all. And those future-past memories might as well be something you read in a book.

I flung my coat on the back of the couch, refusing to sit beside him in the small space he'd left.

Sighing heavily, he scooched over, and only then did I sit. We stared at each other for several heartbeats.

Why am I even attracted to him? He's a few years older than my eighteen-year-old self, meaning that my adult woman brain should find him too immature. I should be repelled, repulsed. But it's different because I've been here before, and he's Logan. My Logan.

No! Not your Logan. Not ever again!

I cleared my throat. "You said you wanted to talk, and yet you're being awfully quiet."

He ran a hand through his hair, tousling it. "I was giving you a second to center yourself since you seem jumpy ... anxious."

"You can give me all the seconds in the world and I'm not going to be any less anxious right now."

Logan's visage darkened. "What happened to make you do a one-eighty so fast? Yesterday you couldn't get enough of me—we couldn't get enough of each other. And then boom, you don't want to see me ever again." He tensed as he waited for me to respond.

I tried to ignore how loud my heartbeat was. "I can't give you what you want, Logan."

"What? An explanation? Because all I want is an explanation."

My gaze dropped to my bouncing leg, and I forced myself to still. "You want more than an explanation, Logan. You think I'll give you something you can fix, something to fix us." I swallowed several times, my throat tight. "But I can't do that."

He was on his feet, pacing in front of me, his eyes wild. "No. No. I don't accept that. You have to give me something."

I shrugged, my shoulders heavier than normal. "The truth of the matter is that I don't have to give you anything. And in the end, if you don't leave me alone, you'll be no better than a stalker."

Logan froze, his head whipping in my direction. "You've got to be fucking kidding me. You're going to try and say—"

"When one person wants out of a relationship and the other won't accept it, won't leave that person alone, and does things like follow them and threaten them—"

"I didn't threaten you. Not really."

"What do you call blackmail, if not a threat? And you only had that information to begin with because you followed us. I told you it was over, and you won't let it go. I don't owe you anything, not even an explanation if I don't want to give it."

Silence fell over us, the tension of it making it difficult to breathe.

All emotion had leeched from Logan's face, and he slowly trudged to the front door, flinging it open. "You're right. You said it was over."

This is it. This is what I wanted.

And yet …

His gaze was downcast, his shoulders hunched inward,

in a way I never thought I'd see someone like Logan. He seemed crestfallen and defeated.

My heart lurched, pulling me forward, and I staggered into him, my hands curling against his chest. Wanting to touch him, and not willing to hold him—to touch him one last time. "I-I'm sorry. I wish it could have been different." He would never know how much.

He remained silent, his breathing ragged.

I didn't know why I was hesitating, what I was waiting for. I finally got through to him. He would leave me alone. I was free to make my future what I wanted, what I needed to be happy, but I couldn't seem to make my feet move.

Slowly, Logan's eyes lifted to mine, green clashing with blue. He swallowed audibly, his Adam's apple dancing in his throat. "You're giving me some strong contradictory body language right now. If you want me to leave you alone, then plastering yourself to me is what I'd call confusing."

I inhaled sharply. "I know. I'm sorry. Sorry for all of it."

"Stop saying you're sorry. Just leave. If that's what you want." Hope sparked in the curl of his lips, and the tension in his body.

I was officially making things worse. Here was my out. My chance—my second chance delivered to me despite the universe's best efforts. So why did it feel like someone had reached into my chest to fist my heart?

What if ... what if this really is a different version of Logan? What if I'm blowing a whole different type of second chance?

No. Stop. I'm making excuses for wanting something I know with one hundred percent certainty that's bad for me.

Logan's hand pressed against the small of my back, his thumb making small circles. It shouldn't have been erotic or enticing in any way, but it was.

Maybe just one good-bye kiss to remember him by.

My hands unfurled, dancing up to rest on his shoulders.

"Logan," I murmured, "I really am sorry."

"Stop saying sorry."

"Sorry." Lifting onto my tiptoes, I brought my face closer to his, our breath intermingling and syncing.

And then my lips were on his, or his lips were on mine, I couldn't tell at that point. Our tongues clashed ferociously, our kiss brutal in a way I'd never experienced before. My back met the wall as he lifted me to cup my ass, and my legs crossed behind him, resting on his hips.

I was about to combust, my insides burning with need. All reasoning, all logic, the ability to think of anything except wanting to feel Logan moving inside of me lost as he ground his pelvis into mine.

Logan broke the kiss, skimming his lips down the side of my neck to suck, lick, and nip. "Harper, I'm going to need to hear you say yes because I won't have you accuse me of—"

"Yes." I slid my hands into his hair, tugging. "Yes." He ground into me harder. "Yes."

With me still wrapped around him, he kicked the door shut and stumbled to the couch. We fell back onto the worn leather, me on top. Snagging his lips again, I kissed him hard, our teeth clinking.

He shoved my shirt up, cool air pebbling my skin as he latched onto my left nipple through my bra.

"Oh, God, fucking yes." The younger version of me might have gotten down and dirty all last week with Logan, but this was my first post time traveling hook-up in my hormonally supped-up teenaged body. Every little touch sent me higher and higher. I was pretty sure foreplay wasn't even needed, although I wasn't exactly willing to pass on it either.

I pushed at Logan's shoulders, forcing him to lie back. Quickly standing, I started stripping out of my clothes. Gone were any bodily insecurities I'd once harbored, which was going to make this different than what I'd done with him before.

Logan stared at me slack-jawed and wide-eyed, his gaze bouncing all over my body like he didn't know where to look and where to touch. Feeling empowered, I smirked. "Well, are you going to take your clothes off, too? Or should I leave after all?"

"Yeah, no, I'm— Yeah." Logan stripped eagerly, his fingers fumbling at the buttons on his pants.

Maybe this wasn't such a bad idea after all. I am quite liking this new dynamic. It's something I've never experienced.

Once he stood before me completely naked and unabashedly turned on, I dropped to my knees, taking his rock-hard cock between my lips.

His hands shot to my hair, fisting. "Ah, fuck."

Humming a song that probably didn't exist yet, I delighted in his reactions to the hand twist and tongue moves I'd picked up over the years. A girl my body's age generally didn't know how to give head all that great, not that guys the same age were complaining.

But I didn't want Logan to finish in my mouth, as tempting as it was to lord that kind of power over him. I needed him inside of me—wanted it desperately.

Wait. Birth control. I'd been on it since I was sixteen due to an irregular cycle, but I don't think I remembered to take it since I traveled back in time.

With a pop, I released Logan, smiling at his glazed-over expression. "Condom?" I asked.

He blinked. "You said you're—"

"I think I forgot to take it."

"Yeah, okay. Um ... yeah. Beside my bed."

I nodded once and sashayed away, Logan hot on my heels. It was truly a treat to have a guy like him panting after me with such frantic energy.

"Harper," Logan rasped. "I just want you to know—"

Doing my best to crawl onto his bed gracefully, I grinned at him. "I don't care about anything you have to say right now. Just get that condom."

If this was going to be the only time I let myself have Logan before I said good-bye for good, I was going to enjoy it to the fullest. I didn't want any kind of promises or small talk, I wanted action, plain and simple.

Logan stilled, his lithe muscles tensing. "What is this?"

I nibbled my bottom lip. "I'm pretty sure I don't have to explain."

A jaw muscle twitched as he met my gaze, careful not to move down my naked body. "No, what is going on right now? Are we together or ..."

I huffed out an exaggerated sigh. Since when did guys his age want to stop right before sex to ask about the status of a relationship? I mean, seriously ... *This can't be happening right now.*

I had to remind myself that from his perspective, even after last week, we were still learning each other's bodies. To my advantage, I held memories of what he liked and exactly how to make him mindless with lust.

Instead of answering, I slid out of bed, coming to stand directly in front of him. His body's interest in mine hadn't waned at all, even if his gaze was now cautious. One of my hands came up to his chest, the muscles jumping at the contact as I gently scratched my nails downward. With my other hand, I roughly stroked his cock, causing him to groan.

I regarded him closely. His pupils were blown, his expression dazed. He was exactly where I wanted him.

"Logan," I purred, "I don't want to talk right now."

His chin dipped slightly, his full lips parting on a jagged breath.

Leaning into him, I nuzzled and then nipped at his pec. "I just want you to fuck me hard ... rough. Pull my hair, smack my ass like ..." *You used to. Shit. Maybe he didn't hear that, or—*

"Like who, Harper?" Logan pulled away from me, his gaze clouding over with anger and uncertainty. "Because we've never had rough sex like you're describing."

Shit, shit, shit. I couldn't tell him that we would have eventually, that we'd both discovered that although gentle was nice sometimes, rough could be extremely hot under the right circumstances.

"A book," I sputtered. "I read about some characters doing it in a book I read."

He studied me, nostrils flaring and teeth grinding. "Sounds plausible, but I don't believe you. Is this what's going on? Is this what you don't want to tell me? You met someone else? Have been fucking someone else?"

"No! I haven't been fucking anyone but you!"

He yanked at his hair, gaze never wavering from mine. "I want to believe you, I do. But it would make sense. It's the reason why you didn't want to talk. You didn't want to tell me you were with someone else."

"No," I whispered, knowing if he made up his mind there would be no arguing, even if it was the truth. "I haven't been with anyone else since we've been together."

He grabbed my arm, and I gasped. "Who the fuck is it, Harper?" he growled. "Who?"

"I swear to you, it was fiction, all of it was fiction based." Technically not a lie. None of that would happen between us. It was a future for him and my younger body that had dissolved the moment I stepped back in time, leaving it as nothing more than figments of my imagination.

"Then why? Why are you doing this ... any of this? And —" He paused, regarding me with cold calculation. "This wasn't about changing your mind and getting back together with me. This was about having one last time with me."

My eyes burned as I watched the realization sink in, answering pain rising to etch into every fiber of his being.

"I never said we were getting back together."

"No," he grated. "You didn't, did you? Guess I was just a fool to think what was happening meant as much to you as it does me."

"It's just sex, Logan." My heart cinched, slowing and cooling my blood.

"It was never just sex to me," he said harshly, his ice eyes cold fire. He turned, giving me his back. "Get out, Harper. I still don't know what happened—to us, to you. It's like you changed into a different person, but ... but it doesn't matter. I'm done. With you. Just get out."

My vision wavered, dark spots dancing. Pain bloomed in my temples, spreading down my spine as I swayed on my feet.

"Logan?" I heard myself say just as the floor came up to meet me, darkness swallowing me whole.

Chapter 15

Steady mechanical beeping wound its way into my ears as my eyes fluttered open. The first thing I noted was Logan slouched in a chair beside my bed, his hair tousled, and dark smudges under his eyes. My gaze flitted around the small room, snagging on the curtain drawn down the middle, comprehension alighting.

I'm in a hospital room. With Logan. What the hell happened?

Groaning, I registered a dull ache in my head, and nausea roiling my gut.

Logan's eyes slitted open, and then he was on his feet, tightly grasping my hand. "You're awake."

I jiggled my free arm, discovering an IV hampered the movement. I frowned. "What happened?" My throat was like sandpaper, my voice barely above a whisper.

Logan dropped my hand to pour me a cup of water,

which I accepted with delight, chugging it down in a few gulps.

"What happened?" I tried again.

Sera rushed into the room, tears brimming in her eyes. "I'll tell you what happened. You scared the shit out of me."

Logan grunted in agreement.

"How long have I been here? And what's wrong with me?" Panic surged, my heart pounding against my eardrums.

Both Sera and Logan glanced at my heart monitor, the machine outwardly registering my anxiety.

"A nurse will probably be in here soon," Sera said. "You know, to check on you since you woke up."

"What's wrong with me?" Was there some kind of unforeseen side effect from time travel? I'd pondered the possibility before, but lying in a hospital bed for some unknown reason pointed to it being fact instead of theory. Or maybe there was some merit to the brain tumor theory as well. "Someone better tell me before I freak the fuck out."

"They don't know," Sera finally offered. "Which in a lot of ways is way more concerning since you passed out and have just been lying there for days."

"Days?" I squeaked.

"Days," she confirmed.

"Well, shit." *Please don't let them have called my parents. My mom will have a meltdown.* Sera was my local emergency contact, and I'd left it to her discretion whether or not to call in the big guns in a medical situation. Although, their lack of presence was a good sign that they didn't. At least not yet. And now that I was awake, I wouldn't let them.

Sera's lower lip quivered. "Exactly."

Logan cleared his throat. "Mind if I talk to her for a minute?"

Sera shrugged. "Go for it."

"Alone."

Sera lounged on the edge of my bed, picking at her nails. "She's just going to tell me whatever you say anyways. I'd prefer to cut out the middleman."

"Sera," I chastised, even if she was telling the truth.

She shrugged. "It's not like you won't."

Narrowing my eyes at her, I pointed at the door. "Please."

She rolled her eyes. "Fine. I'm going. But I'll be right outside if you need me."

"Thanks."

She shuffled out, glancing back several times on her way.

Once she was gone, Logan shifted his weight from foot to foot and cleared his throat again. "About what happened before you passed out."

Heat bloomed along my cheeks. It was one thing to be confident in the moment, but thinking about what I'd said and done ... yeah, it was a tad disconcerting. "You mean the sex ... stuff?"

"Yeah, and what happened before that." He took my

hand again, interlacing our fingers. "I'm here for you. I'm not just going to cut and run because something may be medically wrong with you."

I blinked. "What?"

He circled his thumb against my palm. "I'm just saying, if whatever's wrong with you made you confused, I'm here to support you. My feelings about us being together haven't changed."

"Confused? The only thing I'm confused about is this conversation."

"The doctor said that certain neurological issues could cause extreme mood changes, confusion—"

I yanked my hand back. "Let me get this straight. It's easier for you to believe something is broken in my brain than to think that maybe I simply just don't want to be with you?"

His lips pressed into a thin line. "That's not what I was trying to say at all."

"It's what it sounds like to me."

"I'm sorry I accused you of wanting someone else, too."

I attempted to cross my arms over my chest, giving up after a few tries with the IV getting in the way. "Just because there isn't anyone doesn't mean it changes anything between us."

"Harper," Logan rasped, "don't do this. Not now. Not with everything."

"I'm probably not even sick. I probably forgot to eat." In actuality, that might be the problem. I couldn't remember the last time I had a decent meal, and in my younger body, I needed to consume a ton more calories than I was used to. Either that or it was another mini-blackout session, this one slightly different than the first. I suspected that both times I was aware, but the first my younger self had taken over. She hadn't this time, but maybe—

Maybe nothing. I had no explanation or way of finding out. I had to just go with the dice I was rolled.

"You've been unconscious for days."

I shrugged.

"You've been acting weird. Even Sera says so."

"Did she now?" So Logan and Sera had been discussing my *weird* behavior while I'd been lying in a hospital bed? *Great. Just fucking great.*

"You're forgetful—"

"I've always been forgetful."

"You're acting out of character—"

"Says the guy who hardly knows me."

"And your best friend says the same thing."

"Obviously, she doesn't know me that well yet then. It's not like she's been my best friend since birth."

"You're having sudden and massive mood swings—"

"When did that supposedly happen?"

"With your hair. At Graffiti's. After Graffiti's. At my place. When you—"

"I'm an eighteen-year-old girl, we all have mood swings."

"You're saying weird shit about things that nobody's heard of."

"I have no idea what you're talking about."

His eyebrows slid up his forehead. "Sera has a whole list of instances. Not to mention how your speech choices and patterns change."

Everyone in Hollywood and the book world makes time travel seem so easy. I thought I'd made a few casual verbal slip-ups, things that were brushed under the rug and forgotten. I also thought that people would let me do a one-eighty without significant protest, but again, apparently not.

"What do you want me to say, Logan? You're right, I made a big mistake because my brain is broken. Please, oh, please don't listen to what I said before. I want to be with you."

He pinched the bridge of his nose. "I just wanted to tell you that I'm here for you. That I'm not going to abandon you."

"You're not abandoning me if I want you to go. I stand by what I said. We can't be together. It's going to end badly. Better to get out now before I get hurt." More, again … however it was described, I was done with it.

He threw his hands up in the air. "You keep saying we're going to end badly. You have no way of knowing something that. I think you're just afraid."

He was right about that part. I was afraid—afraid of experiencing the same heartbreak that nearly killed me. "But I do know. You are going to break me if we stay together. I can't let it happen again. I won't."

He regarded me with some unreadable emotion, his

body tense. "See. This is the kind of thing I was talking about. You can't know how things between us will go. Not unless you traveled through time."

I met his gaze head-on. "Maybe I did." I wasn't sure why I let myself utter those words. They were a mistake, even if he didn't believe them. All it did was support his theory that my brain was broken.

The muscles along his jaw feathered as his eyes narrowed. "You don't believe that. Why are you trying to antagonize me?"

"So you'll leave me alone."

"You don't actually want that."

"I'm really not in the mood for you or anyone else to tell me what I do or do not want."

His glazier gaze slid to mine once more, making me squirm. He stood there, staring at me for what seemed like an eternity, until finally he nodded once, an almost imperceptive motion, and walked silently from the room.

Sera hurried back to my side, confusion and curiosity radiating from her. "He hasn't left your side almost the entire time he's been here. The nurse made him go eat."

Even I was surprised, but things change, and he would eventually grow into the person capable of hurting me. "Yeah, and?"

"Aaaand ... you broke it off with him again?"

Running my hands over the rough blanket covering me, I studied it, refusing to look at her. Sure that if I did, she would see right through me somehow. "Yeah, we just don't work together."

"I wish I didn't work with someone the way he doesn't work with you." Her voice dripped sarcasm and skepticism, a hard combo to nail in my estimation.

"You and Derek work better than us, so I don't want to hear it."

"If not working at all is better, which clearly it is for you, then yeah, I guess you're right."

My heart dropped into my stomach. "You and Derek—"

"Broke it off."

"What?" No. That didn't happen before. I wasn't privy to all the behind-the-scenes drama leading up to their eventual coupledom, but I was positive there was no complete calling off of said fledgling relationship.

"I can't be with someone like him."

"Like him?" *The love of your life? Your perfect half? A man who worships the ground you walk on?* Oh, my God, my best friend was throwing away the best part of her personal life, and she didn't even know it.

But I did. And I had to fix it. No matter the cost.

STEP ONE: Repair whatever I broke in Sera and Derek's relationship.

Step two: Save lives by averting major catastrophes.

Step three: Use my knowledge of the future to win lots of money so when I fail out of college I won't need to worry about it.

Step one was proving to be a bit more tricky than I thought it would be, but I was determined to prevail. It would simply take more work. Steps two and three were going to be the difficult ones since the longer I stayed in my younger body, the more I lost from my future. I was positive it had something to do with the longevity of my trip, combined with the neural pathways used to forge new and old memories. Since, technically, the current brain I was using, didn't possess the pathways to hold my future memories, they were slipping away. It made sense, and yet at the same time it didn't, since if that was the case then how did my brain hold any of my knowledge from my future self at all? That led me down the rabbit hole of trying to define consciousness and other things I didn't have the capacity to do, especially with an underdeveloped prefrontal cortex ... amongst other things.

I tapped my pen on my notebook, scowling at what I'd written so far, which was pretty much nothing. I thought I'd focus on some of the bigger things first, like school shootings and 9/11. The problem was, the dates were slipping away. I couldn't even recall what year 9/11 happened—or would happen. The thought of that was absurd, and yet, there I was, racking my brain for an answer that just wouldn't come.

"You sure you're okay?" I could feel Sera's eyes, along with all her paper boyfriends plastered on her side of the room, on me. "You've been brooding over whatever you're working on for a while now."

"I'm fine. The doctor said nothing is wrong with me. I told you that it was probably low blood sugar. It's happened before." It hadn't. I was moving forward on the assumption that it was a side effect of my journey through time. I just hoped things would settle down eventually. At least this time I didn't lose a week to my other self.

"I'm allowed to be worried about you."

"There's nothing to worry about." I nibbled on the cap of my pen. "Seriously, don't. It's going to make me feel guilty, especially when I start getting grouchy about it."

Her perfectly arched brows rose. "Start being grouchy? Ha!"

Shifting, I folded my legs under me and faced her head-on. "Sooo ... Derek. I think you should give him another chance."

She bared her teeth demonstratively. "If you don't stop bringing him up, I'm going to harass you about Logan."

I rolled my eyes. "It's not the same thing at all. Stop attempting to deflect."

She slammed her textbook shut and shifted to mirror me on her bed. "You stop deflecting."

Sera always did have a way of calling me on my bullshit. But I wasn't about to let her put Logan in the way of her and her happily-ever-after. "Derek isn't going to hurt you. He's a good guy. Please just trust me and give him a real chance. You won't be sorry."

Sera's face scrunched up. "Why is it that you can say that about Derek, but when I say the same thing about Logan, you tell me to shut the hell up? Hmmm?"

Logan, Logan, Logan ... aaaaah! His presence was a constant even when he physically wasn't there. "I never said to shut the hell up."

"I read between the lines."

I ground my teeth together, frustration burning through me. "You and Derek. Please."

She notched her chin up in challenge and smirked. "You and Logan. Please."

Grabbing my pillow, I stuffed my face into it and screamed. *Why is this so hard?* Even the parts that I thought would be easy-peasy have become super complicated. Every teenager thinks the universe is against them at some point in their lives, but I was convinced it actually was against me. Occam's razor said so. And I knew my science. Or I used to. That was another thing slipping away, along with my adult language skills. Was I doomed to truly become my younger self and forget I even came from the future? What if I'd done this thousands of times and simply couldn't remember?

What if ... what if I'm stuck in a time loop and I don't know it? Shit. How can I save lives when I can't even save myself?

"That's it." I hopped out of bed, beelining it straight for my stubborn friend. "You're coming with me."

If I was stuck in a causal loop of some sort, or in a multiverse, in the end, it didn't matter as long as I fixed Sera and Derek's relationship before I forgot everything. I was officially in a race against time.

Yes, because this is going to end well.

Chapter 16

Time is like death ... inevitable. The construct of it, man-made or not, would flow forward because that's what we expected. It's what our brains have been conditioned to experience, it's hard-wired into us as human beings since birth. And even though I'd not only discovered but experienced a way back, a workaround, once here, my brain was attempting to reset me—to push me into the box I'd learned was essential to existence.

"Stop giving me death glares. If you really didn't want to be here, then you would have fought me harder." I glanced at my best friend sitting across from me, face pinched in annoyance.

Her tongue stuck out at me briefly before she went back to her default glare.

Eyeing the offerings of beer in front of me, I sighed, not wanting to handicap myself mentally. But the promise of escaping my thoughts for a bit was extremely appealing, nonetheless.

Still verbally ignoring me, Sera's dark gaze darted around CJ's, the bar already bustling with students for quarter draft night. We were parked at a booth in the corner, the table filled with untouched drinks. There were a few familiar faces, both male and female, that had dropped by to greet us, but Sera's attitude had sent them running.

"How do you know he's going to be here? Not only do I not want to see him, but I think this is a massive waste of time."

Running my finger around the rim of the closest plastic cup filled with frothy goodness, I rolled my eyes. "If you don't want to see him then this isn't a waste of time. Only if you wanted to see him and he doesn't show up is it a waste." I quirked an eyebrow at her and suppressed a smile. "Which is it?"

"Whatever." She crossed her arms over her chest and leaned back in the booth.

Another few seconds ticked by before she spoke again. "And what exactly do you think is going to happen if he does show up? We're over. Done. Fini—"

"I'm going to have a little chat with the two of you to set you straight. That's what." It was pointless to pretend I wasn't involved anymore. I figured I might as well face the problem head-on. The risk of looking like an overinvolved friend was high, but the reward would be priceless. I needed to secure my best friend's future happiness before I didn't have the capacity to do so anymore.

"Yeah, because—" She sucked in a sharp breath. "He's here." Her hands flew to her curls, fluffing and shaping them into place. "And you're never going to guess who's here with him." Her tone was smug, raising the hairs on the back of my neck.

Whipping my head around, I groaned in frustration as I watched none other than Logan swagger in beside Derek and a few other guys. "But they're not even friends," I muttered, slamming my fist against the table. Some of the fuller cups sloshed beer onto my hand, which I hastily wiped on my pants.

Sera threw her head back and laughed. It was my turn to glare at her. "Maybe I should sit you and Logan down for a little chat, too." She rubbed her hands together with glee. "Maybe this won't be a waste after all."

"This isn't about me and Logan. Me and Logan are not in the same situation."

"Well, then, if you don't want me to talk to Logan then you can leave Derek well enough alone." She stared at me in challenge. "Your move."

I ground my teeth together, my jaw aching. She thought she had me, but I would do almost anything for Sera, even face Logan again for her. "Fine. If that's the game you want to play." I tilted my head and gave her a tight-lipped smile. "Then game on."

Jumping to my feet, I quickly adopted the slight sway of someone who was buzzed. Ambling towards my prey, I plastered a crooked grin onto my face. "Derek!" I hollered, making sure my volume matched my faux drunkenness level. "Come sit with us, we have room!"

Derek's gaze immediately pinged to Sera, who was now riveted by her nails, eyes completely downcast. He shifted from one foot to the other nervously as I approached. "Come on, there aren't any more tables, and I know you want to sit with Sera!"

Logan's presence burned in my peripheral vision, but I forced my focus to stay on task.

Frowning, Derek ran a hand over his hair. "I don't think that's such a good idea. Didn't she tell you that we—"

I grabbed his arm, digging in my nails, my mask temporarily slipping. "You listen to me right now, and you listen to me closely. You and Sera are both being dumbasses, and I'm over it. The two of you want to be with each other, and I'm going to make sure it happens because she's my best friend and you're going to make her happy. So deal with it."

Dazed, Derek stared at me blankly.

It took Herculean effort not to smack him upside his head. To him, I was just the roommate of the girl he was into. To me, he was practically my brother-in-law since I considered Sera my sister. But that meant I also knew how to manipulate him, and he wouldn't suspect a thing, unlike his future self.

I lowered my voice and leaned closer to him. "You know, Sera would die if she knew I was telling you this right now, but she's been so depressed since the two of you ended."

Derek's limpid eyes widened slightly. "Depressed? Like how? I didn't think she cared that much."

Ah, Derek, such a softy at heart. "She's hardly been eating, and she's been lying in bed all day. I had to literally drag her out of our room tonight."

Derek's gaze flicked to Sera, his expression turning mulish. "She's the one who ultimately called it quits."

"Because she was feeling insecure. She was convinced you were seeing a ton of other girls and were only going to break her heart."

"Not ... not a ton of other girls." Derek's Adam apple bobbed. "And I—"

"Whaaaat?" I snarled. "You've got to be kidding me? How could you do that to her? You fucking—" I stuffed the rest down. This was Derek. His dating history, previously unknown to me, didn't effect the man he would become.

"We never talked about exclusivity yet. And I—" Derek dipped his head to whisper in my ear, not wanting his friends to hear. "I stopped hooking up with any of the other girls when I met Sera." He pinned me with a pointed look.

"Oh." Whether or not Sera was ever privy to any of this information was none of my business. The only thing that I was worried about was fixing what I'd broken. As long as Derek wasn't currently banging a bevy of girls, then his past was his past alone.

"Yeah," he muttered. "But Sera was crazy jealous."

I shrugged. "Because she cares. That should have been your proof right there. I mean, come on." I flicked Derek on the forehead.

"Hey!" He reared back, eyeing me warily.

"That was for being an idiot." I snatched his arm again, and marched him over to Sera, shoving him down in the booth. I slid in next to Sera, groaning under my breath when Logan and their other friend joined us.

Unable to resist the impulse any longer, I downed a warm beer in two gulps, needing to take the edge off my nerves. I grimaced at the foul taste of cheap beer, burping loudly a minute later.

Swiping at my mouth, I grinned unrepentantly. "Excuse me."

Sera and Derek were both fidgeting in their seats, not acknowledging each other. "You two are so ridiculous. It's a wonder you get ma— It's a wonder you got into college."

Derek muttered something under his breath I chose to ignore, and Sera kicked me under the table. Glaring at her, I picked up another beverage and chugged it.

"Okay," I said. "Let's get down to business. Derek, are you currently having any kind of sexual relations with anyone besides Sera?"

"Technically, I'm not having any with her right now," Derek muttered.

I chugged another beer and then slammed my fist against the table, jostling my current coping aides of choice. "Answer the damn question."

"No." Derek reached for a beer, and I slapped his hand.

"Mine," I growled.

"Let him have one, half are mine." Sera gave Derek a coquettish smile.

Derek's gaze flew to hers, the corners of his mouth slowly curling up.

But I wasn't satisfied yet. I needed to make sure they weren't going to backslide at the slightest provocation. "Are the two of you good?"

Sera pressed a plastic cup to her lips as she shrugged, gaze still locked with Derek's. He jerked his head to the right at her, and she nodded in return.

"We need to talk alone." Sera shoved me to get out of the booth, and I spilled out of it, nearly crashing to the floor in my haste.

With more than a little satisfaction I watched the two of them exit the bar. I had a feeling I wouldn't be seeing my roomie for the rest of the night. I wasn't a fan of her ditching me, especially since I was now with Logan and his friend, but I would gladly make the sacrifice.

I slid back into the booth and took up two cups, one in each hand. "Cheers!" I muttered to myself before pouring both beers down my throat, one after the other.

"This girl can drink!" the unknown friend chirped.

"Yeah, but can she handle what she drinks?" Logan demanded, his tone sour.

A warm and fuzzy glow buffered me from the place in me where common sense was produced. Suddenly, ignoring Logan didn't seem like a big deal anymore. "I can handle my alcohol just fine." With a wink, I downed another pair of drafts.

Beer is good and it makes me feel good. I should drink all the beer and feel really good. Yeah, fabulous plan.

Logan's hand shot out to grab my wrist as I went for another cup. "Harper, if you're this buzzed this fast, then drinking more probably isn't a good idea."

I snorted. "You're not the beer police, sooo ... whatever." I dipped my head and clamped onto a cup with my teeth. When I threw my head back, the beer splashed my face and went up my nose instead of in my mouth like I'd intended.

Sputtering, I said, "Your fault. Let go." I yanked my wrist out of his grip.

"Oh, look, I see Trish," Logan's friend exclaimed, getting up from his seat abruptly.

Whether he wanted away from me or actually did she this Trish person, I didn't care. The result was the same either way ... I was now buzzed and alone with Logan.

"What are you doing?" Logan tried to wrangle the remaining cups onto his side of the table and out of my reach.

"Me? What am I doing? You aren't even friends with Derek and now you're just hanging out with him casually?" I'd forgotten that little tidbit when I'd first spotted them together at Graffiti's, but then here they were together again tonight.

"What do you mean I'm not friends with Derek?"

"You didn't know whose apartment Sera and I broke into ..."

I grabbed a beer and chugged it as he fought to keep them from me.

"We've never hung out at his place, so I didn't know it was his. That doesn't make us not friends."

"No." I waved my hands. "Sera and Derek didn't invite you to their wedding. If you were friends with Derek, you would have been invited to their wedding. And I never once heard him mention you in any of his stories." I waved my hands around some more. "I'm not even married to him, and do you know how many times I've had to listen to his stupid stories? Huh? And never once did he mention you." I managed to steal another cup. "So not friends." I chugged the contents, finishing up with a smug smile.

"You're drunk and uttering complete nonsense."

I burped, the room spinning slightly. "Ugh. Why is my tolerance so low? This is cheap-ass beer, and everything is fuzzy." But I was kind of liking it, the feeling of not caring, not overthinking, just existing in the moment. "You can leave, you know. Me and my beer would like to be alone."

"I'm not leaving you when you're like this," Logan hissed, his dark eyebrows two angry slashes on his face.

I giggled. "You look so intense when you're mad. Do you know that? You remind me of a werewolf, all growly and sexy. Somehow appealing even when I don't want you to be." I scrunched up my nose. "It's not fair."

Tapping my fingers along the table, I considered him

some more. "Although, you're not bulky or scruffy enough to be a werewolf. Vampire, maybe? Ooor … how about a demon? Yeah," I nodded to myself, "definitely a demon."

"And you think you can be left alone right now?" Logan snorted. "Demon? What have you been watching?"

"Reading, not watching. Although I would. I'd watch the hell out of sexy demons, werewolves, and vampires. Hmmm …"

My thoughts were bouncing around, unable to stay on one topic for long. "You know what isn't fair? The fact that I came all this way and I haven't been able to change anything. And I'm forgetting important dates like 9/11. What year does that happen? I need to save all those people … and the Twin Towers."

I struck out for another cup, losing half its contents in the battle with Logan. "Harper, stop," he growled.

Of course I didn't listen and slurped down the now decidedly delicious beer. "Instead of using the gift of future knowledge, the literal gift of time, all I've managed is to fuck up people's lives that weren't previously fucked up and then I had to fix them. At least I hope I fixed them. If I haven't, I'll circle back. The fixing needs to happen."

Yanking on my short hair, I peered at the end of my dark strands. "And I gave myself a hair makeover. Which is really the same cut that I'll have in like two decades. But I guess I become obsessed with hair."

I burped again and then hiccupped. "Did you know the day before I came back here, I was so obsessed with getting my hair washed that I went to that weird hotel a couple of blocks from my office, and then there was this even weirder guy who let me use his room to shower and then I couldn't see his face, but he had all my favorite products? How did he know to have them? Or did he? Maybe it was all just a coincidence."

I threw my hands up in the air and then let them fall, my knuckles hitting the table with a dull thud. "Ouch."

"What hotel and what guy?" Logan demanded.

"What?"

"I knew there was someone else!"

"What?"

"The guy at the hotel that—"

I clicked my tongue. "Really? I said he let me use his shower, not that he was in it. The front desk lady, Mary, made sure he was away."

Logan's face was mottled red, his eyes wild. "Tell me the truth, Harper. Why did you break it off with me? I can handle it. It's the not knowing that's driving me crazy."

I threw my head back and laughed. "You think you can handle it, but you can't."

He grabbed my chin, forcing me to meet his stormy gaze. "Tell me."

"Okay, but don't say I didn't warn you."

His hand fell away from my face, and he waited, his attention riveted.

"Time is a man-made construct. So we live all in one moment." I shook my head. "It's a bit more complicated than that, but—" I shoved my palms into my eyes and rubbed, probably smearing my 90's-style heavy eyeliner all over my face. *Shit.*

Logan snapped his fingers in front of me. "Harper. Focus."

"Yeah, right. Focus. Okay." I frowned slightly as I rubbed at my cheeks, my fingers coming away with black smudges. *I knew it!*

"Harper," Logan said again, "why did you break it off with me? The truth."

The room spun slightly, an old or maybe not so old, song warping. I narrowed my eyes. "The machine can send us back in our own timeline. I was only meant to go back a month or so ... I think. Not very far, but something went wrong, and I woke up here a few days before the Graffiti's showcase. And I'm stuck. So—"

I hiccupped. "Can we get food? I'm hungry."

"You're stuck. And?"

I sighed. "You're like a dog with a bone. I just don't want to make the same mistakes twice. And you, Mr. Super Sexy Logan, are one of the biggest mistakes of my life."

He stared at me, his features blank.

I chortled. "See, told you that you wouldn't believe me."

"You'll say anything to push me away. Do you want me to think you're crazy now? Is that it?"

"I haven't considered the possibility that maybe I am. Does it mean that I am since I haven't questioned it?

Although I am questioning it now, so that counts, right? So not crazy." Grinning, I downed another beer.

"Now, how about some O fries? Can we get some of those?" I smacked my lips. "Oh, my God, it's been so long since I've had those! I need to have some while my metabolism is still this good. If I ate them now—or in the future—the grease would put me into a coma for like a week."

Pushing to my feet, I wobbled. "To the O!"

A sudden sharp pain twisted my gut, and I bent over, a rush of liquid erupting up my esophagus and mouth, splattering onto the floor in front of me. "So gross."

"Get her out of here!" a male voice boomed.

"We're going!" Logan yelled back as he swept me up in his arms.

I groaned. "Oh, no. Put me down. Everything's spinning." At least I think that's what I said. I wasn't sure if most of what I said wasn't a jumble of incoherent words.

An unbidden image of Ben, bearing an unsavory grin, swirled directly in front of me, real or imagined, I wasn't quite sure. "Please, put me down."

"Shhh, I've got you."

"I don't need gotten," I grumbled.

Clutching at Logan, I squeezed my eyes shut, fighting another wave of dizziness and nausea. I slapped at his chest. "Put me down. I'm gonna be sick again!" I slapped at him some more. "Down, down, down!"

I was dropped to my feet, and I lurched to the side, dry heaving several times. "I don't feel good."

Logan gathered my hair and rubbed my back with large, slow circles. "I know."

"I just wanna go home."

The real question was: Where was home now? Here or in the future?

Chapter 17

Someone was tap dancing on my skull, the sound ricocheting into my brain which was nothing more than wet cotton candy. My tongue was desiccated in my mouth, thick, heavy, and unable to move. Groaning, I cracked open sleep-encrusted eyes, only to be blinded by a gamma-ray burst directly in my face.

What the fuck happened?

Clouded images of Logan carrying me back from CJ's swept through my barely functioning consciousness, causing me to cringe into myself, forming a tight ball of pain and regret. I could only hope I didn't say or do something irreversible.

"Drink," Logan's gruff voice commanded, his hand sliding under my head to prop me up enough to bring a glass to my lips.

I complied without attempting to open my eyes again, the ice-cold water soothing my raw throat. When done, I curled up once more, wanting to disappear completely, and yet too much of a mess to do anything but exist.

At some point, I fell back into oblivion, the darkness that swallowed me welcome.

LOGAN'S *icy gaze met mine over the apex of my thighs with a wicked glint.*

My legs trembled with expectation. "Please."

A single lick was all it took to have me falling back into the bed, writhing with need. He paused at my reaction, causing me to arch up in silent demand. "Please," I said again.

Another lick.

Another pause.

I cursed him, thrashing my arms in frustration.

"Logan," I growled, reaching down to grab his hair.

His only reply was a knowing chuckle.

"Just you wait until—"

"You're the one who started this."

I huffed loudly, not able to deny his accusation. I'd started the teasing game, practically begging for retaliation when I'd repeatedly denied him what he wanted when I was on my knees before him last night. When he'd finally spent his release down my throat, I'd seen the promise of payback in his pupil-blown eyes.

"And I'm ending it." Rolling out of bed, I hastily snatched at my clothes. Yeah, I was being a brat, but I found I didn't much like being on the receiving end of sexual torture.

"I don't think so." Logan's arms wrapped around my waist, lifting me off my feet.

I squealed as he tossed me back onto the bed, pinning me down with my hands over my head, and his muscled legs spreading my thighs wide.

He leaned in close, our breath intermingling. "It ends when I end it."

My body melted into the sheets, both loving and hating how quickly he'd learned how to dominate in just the right way. To give me exactly what I needed and craved.

Undulating his hips, he rubbed against me, ripping a moan from my chest. "Is this what you want?"

I didn't answer and instead lifted my hips in a bid to force him to relinquish control. He flashed an almost feral grin, halting my move with a press of his hips.

"I already told you that it ends when I end it."

"Come on, I don't want to play this stupid game anymore. Just fuck me already."

Dark eyebrows lifted on a lust-laden face. "If I can have restraint, so can you."

"I can, but I don't want to."

"Too bad." Logan dipped his head to ensnare the sensitive peak of my nipple, biting down just hard enough to mingle pain and pleasure.

"Logan, please." I squirmed underneath him, loving and hating every minute of his ministrations. "Please."

Flipping me over, he pressed into my entrance from behind as he gripped my hip with one hand and pushed at my back with the other. *"Just so we're clear ... it's only ending because I'm ready for it to end."*

He slammed home, and I moaned, long and loud into the mattress, twisting my hands into the sheets. "Yes—fuck, yes," I choked out. My senses narrowed down to the one point in my body, the bundle of nerves coiling tighter and tighter with each stroke, each expert thrust and roll of Logan's hips.

And then I was screaming his name, my release pulsating deep within. A few more thrusts and Logan joined me with a groan, his hot breath fanning out along my sweaty back.

Still encased within me, he cradled me against his chest as his body relaxed, pushing me into the mattress. He pressed his face into my neck, nipping lightly.

"That was a good ending."

His answer was his lips curling up against my cooling flesh.

"Who said that was the end?" His fingers trailed down my side, pushing up underneath us to find the oversensitive bundle of nerves once more. He lazily rotated his wrist. "I need a little time to rebound, but nope, I'm not nearly close to done making you scream my name."

Jolting up, I blinked bleary eyes at my surroundings, confusion riding me hard. I couldn't place where, and more importantly when, I was. And worse, the dream—or memory—I wasn't sure which, had flustered me to my core. It'd been so real my body still quivered from the release, and craved what was promised next. Logan's scent clung to me, burrowing deeper with each breath.

"Logan?" I whispered, his name more than a question,

but also an answer. I wasn't sure what I'd do if faced with him now, right after that dream.

A door creaked open, more light spilling in to reveal what I remembered to be Logan's small room. I was in his bed, fully clothed and alone. The man in question lingered near the entrance, his tall frame backlit, with his features cast in shadow.

I swallowed, nerves twisting my already roiling gut. "Wh-What am I doing here?"

"What do you remember?"

I didn't like where this was going. Had I blacked out and missed more time while my other self had taken control of my body again? The best plan was to play stupid, and answer any questions vaguely until I could gauge the situation. "Not much. How about you fill me in."

Leaning against the doorframe, I could feel his gaze on me, studying and assessing. "Not much to fill in. You drank too much, babbled utter nonsense, puked, and then passed out. I brought you back to my place to take care of you. You've been sleeping most of the day."

Utter nonsense? That needed further elaboration. "What kind of stuff did I babble about? And where is Sera?" Hopefully, putting her life back on track with Derek.

"Time travel."

My heart quadrupled in time, adrenaline surging through my veins. I forced myself to remain still, calm on the outside, as I nonchalantly said, "Oh? Like *Back to the*

Future type stuff?" I chuckled, the sound off even to my ears. "I do love that movie."

"Mmm ..." Logan grunted, moving several steps farther into the room. "Not exactly."

There was some kind of weird tension hanging in the air between us, and I wasn't sure if I'd said something that made Logan want to call ahead to reserve me a padded room, or if I was being paranoid.

"You hungry?"

I blinked. "What?"

"I asked if you were hungry."

The churning acid inside my stomach was moments away from burning a hole straight through it. Even if I wanted to, I wasn't sure food was something I was capable of consuming at the moment.

"Well?"

"I ... um, no." Sliding out of bed, I scanned the dimly lit room for any of my personal effects, such as my shoes. It was time for me to leave before things got any weirder.

"You're not leaving, Harper."

"Where are my shoes? And coat for that matter?"

Logan crossed his arms over his chest, his frown visible even in the low light. "Didn't you hear me? You're not leaving, so you don't need your coat and shoes right now."

"You can't keep me here."

"I want answers, and you're not leaving until I get them."

I exhaled a long breath, my shoulders sagging as

exhaustion set in anew. "I can't do this again, Logan. We're over. Just accept it."

"No, I want answers about time travel. I need you to tell me what you know."

My gaze shot to his, and I nearly choked on my own spit. "I-I don't know what you're talking about." It was a trick. There was no way he was entertaining believing any of what I'd said about time travel. Clearly, he was probing to see if I was crazy or just a drunken fool.

"Normally, I would have thought you a complete head case after what you've put me through the past few weeks, and then add in what you said to me last night—" He snorted. "Yeah, no matter the perceived connection between us, there's no way I would have stuck around, but …"

I was held hostage by that word, the three small letters dangling from the end of his sentence and in the space between us. They were filled with possibilities both frightening and laden with potential.

"But what?" I pushed.

"But there was a note."

There's no way I heard that right. "A note? You're asking me about time travel and saying that you haven't run for the hills from my crazy ass when you normally would have, all because of a note?" I sucked on my teeth, considering. "Must have been one hell of a note."

Logan ran his hands through his hair. "You have no idea."

"Are you going to share the contents of said note?

Because now I'm beginning to wonder if you're the crazy one."

"Funny," he said drily.

From the moment I'd been thrown back too far in time, the entire situation had been ridiculous. I was at the point, especially with the introduction of this supposed note, that if I didn't laugh, I might cry. Or worse, legitimately go insane. If I wasn't on my way there already.

"Are you going to share the contents of this note at any point, or what?"

"I guess I'm going to have to, even if I'm completely aware that I'm going to sound like the crazy one once I do."

Silence hung heavy between us as we stared at each other, features and gazes partially obscured by the lighting.

I threw my hands up in the air. "Oh, my God! Just spit it out already before I friggin' drop dead from curiosity!"

"Come with me." Logan turned, trudging into his cramped living room.

On shaky legs, I followed, watching as he beelined it for the small desk set up by the window. He produced a small, metal box, popping the top open to retrieve a scrap of worn-looking paper.

He motioned to the couch, which I happily settled into, my head still throbbing.

"I found it a few years ago before I came to college. It was just there after I woke up one day." He pursed his lips.

"I don't remember a solid few weeks before that morning. It was like they were just gone."

Swallowing around the lump in my throat, I opened my hand, palm up, waiting for him to place the note there. He silently did, my eyes immediately dragging over the sloppy writing, the fragmented sentences all written in black marker, some of them overlapping.

TIME TRAVEL IS REAL. BUT ONLY IN YOUR OWN TIMELINE.

THE DREAMS ARE MEMORIES THAT CAN'T BE ERASED.

HARPER IS YOUR WIFE. NOT HIS. NEVER HIS.

FIND HER. DON'T LET HER RUN.

SHE'LL BE CONFUSED.

DON'T LET HIM KNOW IT'S YOU.

REMEMBER. YOU HAVE TO REMEMBER HER.

My hand trembled as I read—and reread, and read again—over and over, the note. My heart thudded heavily in my chest, my breathing short and shallow. I opened my mouth to speak, but nothing came out. I scrambled for an explanation, something, anything, but my mind was numb, my thoughts lost within the haphazard strokes of black on that piece of paper.

"I never told anyone," Logan rumbled. "But for some reason, I couldn't let it go." He plucked the note from my hand, his eyes darting over the sloppy script. "Then the dreams started."

"Dreams?" I croaked.

His gaze lifted to mine, holding me in their steel trap. "Yeah, about my life … with you."

"Me?" *Impossible, impossible, impossible.*

"I had these vivid dreams that were more than just—" He cleared his throat. "I dreamt about everyday things sometimes, too. Not just about us having sex."

"And when we met?"

"I thought, I don't know, you hear people talk about feeling like they knew someone before they met, but … but the—"

"The note had my name in it. It couldn't be pushed aside like the dreams." I didn't understand what it meant, not really, and yet what it implied was terrifying.

He grabbed my hand, crushing the note between our palms. "When you started talking about time travel last night—"

"You believed me."

His eyes blazed with fervor as he continued, "This is real, isn't it? Time travel. The note. The dreams. Fuck. The dreams."

Was that what I'd experienced before I woke up? The vivid sex dream that I'd assumed was either wishful thinking or a memory from the short time I'd spent with Logan in our never-to-be future. But when I stopped to reconsider, there were details I'd overlooked, such as Logan's age. He'd been older than he should have been, although I'd again chalked that up to dreamland distortion. But what if—what if …?

"I can see it written all over your face. What is it? What's wrong?"

My gaze flicked up to his once more. "I-I don't know. I don't have all the answers, but there's something in me, something that— Your wife?"

Those were the words that hung heavy in my heart. The devastating conclusion of Logan and my relationship was a few short years off. We'd never come close to making it down the aisle, even if I had entertained ideas of us one day being married, of us eventually growing old together. And then along came Ben, conveniently there to sweep me and the shattered pieces of my heart off the ground. But I'd always wondered … why? Why did Logan abandon me so suddenly? What happened and why did it always feel like I'd fallen into a nightmare not of my own making? And yet I'd been complacent as if I'd accepted my fate. Like I knew I couldn't escape the trap that had ensnared me so thoroughly.

No. This can't be real. It isn't. But … Occam's razor. There is no reason why Logan would make any of this up. How could he?

Underneath it all, the confusion, the hesitancy, and the hope was complete and utter terror. Had my life somehow been altered by someone other than me? Someone who wielded more control over the time travel process than I did? But how was any of that possible either?

"I don't feel so good." I clutched at my middle, bile rising up from my stomach, nothing left for my nerves to push around in my gut.

"Hold on." Logan rushed into his kitchen, reappearing a moment later with a small trash can.

"Logan, I—" Dark spots danced in front of my vision. "I think I'm going to pass out."

My eyes slid shut, and my body hit the escape hatch on reality, not wanting or being able to process what had just been revealed to me. The darkness took me, and I went willingly into the blissful oblivion.

Chapter 18

How could he? How could he abandon me like this without a word—a note—just nothing? His things, gone. Packed up quickly and efficiently while I was out with Sera for the day.

Numbness swept over me as I stood in the modest one-bedroom apartment in Shadyside. For an entire year, we'd cohabited in the space, our lives intermingling in new and interesting ways. It wasn't perfect, because nothing ever was, but I'd been happy ... and I thought he was, too.

Wrong. You were wrong. Completely and utterly wrong.

To leave, to slink away when I wasn't there without so much as an explanation in any form ... why? What did I do to make him think that was the only way? What did I miss? I didn't —couldn't—

Dropping to my knees, sudden and sharp pain twisted in my

chest, and a sob shoved up my throat, lodging there, a silent cry frozen like the rest of me.

What about all of our plans for the future? I couldn't picture my life without him. I thought ... I thought he felt the same.

Idiot. You're an idiot. A complete and utter idiot. You were never good enough for him and he finally figured it out.

I dragged myself to my feet once more, finding the cordless phone on its cradle near the kitchen. I called the only person I could, who I knew would be there for me.

"Hi, it's Sera. You know what to do."

Hearing her voicemail greeting broke the dam, and burning tears rolled down my cheeks, my face contorted with the effort to keep from screaming.

The doorbell rang, and hope flared. It was a mistake. All of it was a mistake.

I flung the door open, not to find Logan, a sheepish grin on his face, or even Sera, bringing with her the strength I needed in that moment. Instead, it was our upstairs neighbor, Ben.

"Hi, I was just wondering if you—"

Chest-wrenching sobs erupted from me, and I wailed, the sound almost inhuman as I slumped against the doorframe, clutching at it to stay upright.

Ben's cornflower blue eyes widened. "Harper, what's wrong? Tell me what happened."

There was nothing to say or rather nothing I was willing to tell him, and yet I couldn't stop. The floodgates hadn't merely been opened, they'd been torn free from the structure.

Ben shuffled forward, raising a hand towards me, and

letting it fall before he could make contact. "Should I call someone? A friend? The police? You're scaring the shit out of me right now, Harper. I don't know what to do."

I slid to the floor, a boneless pile of sorrow, words now a foreign entity to me.

"Okay, okay. Let's get you inside and then I can figure out what to do next." Ben scooped me up in his arms and carried me to the couch, and even though I wasn't thrilled by the act, I didn't have the willpower to stop him.

"Is there some way I can get a hold of Logan?"

At the mention of his name, I sobbed harder, curling into myself even more.

"Oh. Oooh. I saw him with some boxes today ..."

My head snapped up. "You saw him today? How long ago?" I swiped at the snot on my face, not giving two shits what I looked like. If I could find Logan, just talk to him. This had to be a mistake, all of it.

Pity swam across Ben's visage. "A few hours ago, I think. And he seemed in a hurry, now that I think about it."

"Did you talk to him? Was there anybody else with him? Please, tell me everything you saw." Ben's gaze flicked away, but not before I saw more pity. "What? What is it? Tell me!"

"I'm not sure I should, given your current state. It'll probably make things worse."

"Tell me!" I screeched, my heart thundering against my ribcage.

"Okay, but remember I don't know the context."

"Just tell me!" My chest heaved as I struggled to breathe. "Please!"

"He was with a girl. She was helping him load stuff into his car." He raised his hand over his head. "Tall, long, blonde hair. Really pretty."

He was with a girl. He was with a girl. He was with a girl. *Over and over the sentence spiraled through my brain. I couldn't—no, didn't want to process.* He was with a girl. He was with a girl.

And just like that, the sentence tore into me, forcing me to accept. It was the only explanation. The only reason for his cowardly behavior. He met someone else. Had picked someone else over me. Because of course, he could have any girl he wanted, it was just that I thought he wanted me—loved me.

But I was wrong. I was wrong about him. About me. About everything.

HALF AWAKE, but not conscious, I hovered in that in-between place of semi-awareness, my thoughts replaying one of the most traumatizing memories of my young adult life. The day when Logan Sharpe had packed up and left me with no explanations, no clues, and only the words of our next-door neighbor to offer any kind of insight as to why he did such a thing.

It was the not knowing that broke me. I never truly knew whether he cheated or not, whether he left me for someone else or not, although I did come to believe that was the case. I didn't just lose Logan that day, I lost the ability to trust myself and judgements of other people. I was left unsure from that moment on, wondering if I was perceiving something completely different than everyone else.

When Ben finally asked me out, despite my doubts, I decided to say yes, because he'd been there for me through everything. Helped me pick up the pieces of my shattered heart after Logan left. Ben was so patient and so forgiving, and he did everything right and said all the right things at all the right times. He was as close to perfect as any one man could be.

Until after we were married. Until after—

"Harper. Hey. I know you're not sleeping, and I think you should drink some more water and eat something." Logan's voice was barely above a whisper, and yet it rang through my entire body as if he was shouting at the top of his lungs.

Peeling my eyelids open, I took in the view from my prone position on his couch. I didn't know what to think, what to do. What Logan had presented to me was compelling, and yet, the memories I carried of him abandoning me, betraying me the way he did, I couldn't wipe those away easily.

"You hurt me. In your future, but in my past. You hurt me." The corners of my eyes burned, and I blinked back the inevitable. "I can't … I just … I don't know what you expect me to do."

Logan hesitantly sat beside me, his eyes warm despite their wariness. "I can't exactly wrap my mind around any of this, especially you telling me that you're upset about something I haven't done to you yet. And maybe won't."

I opened my mouth to respond, but he raised his hand. Normally, the gesture wouldn't have stopped me, but mental fatigue made me more compliant.

"But I do know what I feel for you is deeper than what I should feel for someone after the short amount of time we've spent together. It's like—" His gaze flicked away as he tried to gather his thoughts. "It's like there's a part of me that does remember you, just like that note says I should. Even if I don't have the memories to go with the feelings, you're imprinted on my heart." He rolled his eyes, and grumbled, "It sounds corny as fuck, even to me, but I don't know ... I feel this kind of desperation, this compulsion when it comes to you. And it's bigger than me, bigger than ... I don't know."

He huffed out a frustrated sigh. "Or maybe insanity is contagious, and we'll be neighbors at the asylum."

I sputtered on a laugh, despite the situation. "I'm actually impressed you had the nerve to tell me about the note, about any of this. I sure as shit didn't until I apparently blabbed when I was drunk."

"What do we do?"

The small amount of levity I'd drudged up for the situation drained instantly. What should we do? That was the billion-dollar question. But the information Logan had introduced into my personal timeline equation didn't add up. "I don't know what to do. I wish I did."

"Why don't we start with you explaining everything

you know to me, because it's a lot more than I have." He pointedly glanced at the small note in his hand, now slightly crumbled.

"You have a point." My stomach chose that moment to grumble.

Logan smirked. "Pizza will be here soon."

"I guess I could eat." My stomach grumbled again, and Logan quirked an eyebrow. "Fine. I'm starving."

He smirked. "That's what I thought."

My reactions to him were all over the place. I was attracted to him, and yet I wanted to hit him. I felt sorry for him, and I wanted to hit him. I suddenly wanted to give him a second chance, and I wanted to hit him. Okay, fine, I really wanted to hit him, but after that, all bets were off.

"You have a baffling look on your face. I'm not sure what to prepare for." Logan grimaced, his eyes twinkling with mirth.

It was just easy with him, to get comfortable, to slide back into old habits even I'd long forgotten. I dropped my face into my hands and silently screamed.

"I don't know how to act around you, Harper. What you told me last night, drunk or not, blew my world up."

I peeked at him from between my fingers. "And that little note didn't do the same to me?" I wasn't even going to let myself consider what he'd said about his feelings for me.

"You need to tell me more about how you got here."

Straightening up, I met his gaze again. "Oh, what? I

wasn't clear enough last night when I drunkenly babbled about time travel and who knows what else?"

He snorted. "There are a few holes that need filled in."

I was hungry, tired, and confused as fuck. He would be getting the abbreviated version. He could ask questions later if I even still remembered any of it later. Which brought me to—

Oh, shit! Maybe I should leave myself notes about stuff. Like the guy in Memento. I'd considered it before, but then I just didn't. Or maybe it was better to forget. To sink into the past to live my life with the second chance I'd been given. Although ...

"You most likely have time-traveled yourself, so I'll start with this. It seems like the more time you spend in your younger body, the more you revert. I'm starting to forget things already myself. Your note seems to confirm my theory that I'll eventually forget it all and become my younger self again, for lack of a better description."

"If I knew I was going to forget everything eventually, then why didn't I leave myself a detailed journal? Something more than a confusing scrap of paper?"

"Maybe you didn't know. I didn't. But for me, that's because we were still in the experimental process of time travel. I was never meant to come back this far. But with you, it seems like you came for a reason."

"I've dreamt about our wedding." He stared at me expectantly, like his revelation wasn't more of a bomb drop.

I gulped. Married to Logan. It was a concept I couldn't fathom, and wouldn't let myself attempt to at the moment.

"That didn't happen for me, which points at either an alternate timeline and multiverses existing or—"

"Someone already fucked with the timeline you existed in and maybe I came back to fix it?"

It made sense in a headache-inducing way. I thought time travel would be simple if I could avoid the obvious pitfalls, but as it turned out, I was quite possibly in an extremely volatile causal loop. Basically, the stuff of my nightmares.

"If there's someone else or multiple someone elses involved, we can't stay here and let time pass normally because we are at their mercy. They could come back and alter things without us even knowing. We could be puppets tethered to this causal loop, yanked in whatever direction these people choose."

Panic was beginning to spiral within me again, the sensation my constant companion lately.

"How do we get out then? Travel back to when we need to be?"

I wrapped my arms around my middle, hugging myself. "That's the problem. I don't know. It's why I'd basically given up and decided to stay here even though I know the potential issues my presence can cause."

Logan leaned forward, his eyes flinty. "But you decided to make a few changes regardless, didn't you?"

He asked the question, but it was meant as a statement and we both knew it. "Yes," I breathed. "I was determined to avoid what I considered the two biggest mistakes of my life …"

His brow furrowed as he continued to stare. He didn't need to say anything else, his expectations of an answer pressure enough.

My tongue lay thick and heavy in my mouth, protesting what I was about to say. "You. You and Ben."

Logan tensed, a myriad of emotions playing across his beautiful features. "Ben? Ben who?" His hands balled into fists on his thighs. "Explain."

I didn't know what he wanted me to tell him. Or the purpose for that matter. But I would, simply because I supposed there was no real reason not to anymore. "After you left me—cheated on me—Ben Wickham ... well, Ben and I— He's the only man I had a wedding with—in my timeline."

Logan's upper lip curled. "And it was a mistake?" His voice was calm, eerily so.

"Yeah, he just kind of swooped in after you left. Said all the right things and did all the right things. But after we were married ... I mean, it took years, but ..."

I didn't want to tell him the rest. I'd never told anyone, not even Sera, the way Ben got under my skin to lampoon my self-confidence, the way he tried to control everything I did, even how I wore my hair. The way he somehow said all the right things at all the right times to crush me instead of uplift like he once did. And I let him. I just let him, like a part of me had finally given up. I let Ben steal my joy, my essence, all because I'd lost hope at some point.

Logan grabbed my chin, forcing my gaze back up to his. "What did he do to you?"

Tears blurred my vision, turning my surroundings into watercolors. "Nothing …" My throat tightened as I choked on the next word. "Everything."

"I'm going to fucking kill him." Suddenly, I was surrounded by Logan, cradled to his chest as he gently stroked my hair, the gentleness he was showing me belying the rage vibrating within him.

Sinking into him, I absorbed his warmth, his strength, not wanting to ever leave his embrace to face what I knew I had to … eventually.

Chapter 19

"We don't know that it's Ben," I said around a mouthful of pizza, the cheesy goodness burning the roof of my mouth. Not that I cared. I was exponentially hungrier than I'd realized. I'd almost tackled the delivery guy when he showed up at Logan's door. I hadn't even made it back to the couch with the box before I had a slice out and was biting into it.

Logan's nostrils flared as he finished a mouthful of pizza himself, his eyes flashing with fresh anger. "Whether it is or not, he hurt you, so I'm going to hurt him back."

I rolled my eyes, wanting Logan to think the gesture was at him, but it was actually directed at my own folly of emotions. Logan's whole protective thing was getting me a bit hot and bothered. But despite all the revelations, I wasn't quite ready to give Logan another shot. Besides, we had more pressing matters at hand—matters my teenage hormones begged me to ignore.

"Ben hasn't done any of those things to me yet. And never will. You can't hurt him for things that haven't happened."

Logan's dark brows crept up his forehead. "Isn't that exactly what you were doing to me? Punishing me for things that haven't happened?"

"No." I tore off another big bite of pizza, using the time it took to chew to come up with a retort. I swallowed audibly, nearly choking on a clump of cheese.

"No? Then what would you call the way you—"

I waved my half-eaten slice of pizza at him. "I was preventing it from happening again. I refuse to go through any of that with either of you this time around."

"If it's Ben, then he'll find a way."

I shook my head fiercely. "No. We don't know that either. We have zero information pointing to him being involved or not. He could merely have been at the right place at the right time to do what comes naturally to a narcissist like him."

"We don't know that it's not him."

I sighed. "That note of yours is extremely unhelpful. You could have listed names and or dates. Something a bit less vague."

"I named you."

"But not my entire name. How do you know it doesn't mean another Harper?"

Logan dropped a crust of his pizza into the box and picked up a fresh slice. He gave me a pointed look before biting into it.

"Well, it could be a different Harper."

"Riiight. I have the wrong Harper. I just mistakenly feel an unexplainable connection to you that's beyond reason. Not to mention how I dreamt about our wedding before I even met you. My bad. You can go home, and I'll start searching for this other Harper then."

I itched to ask him questions about the wedding, and how he felt when he first laid eyes on me after having that dream. But I would resist—had to. It was pointless to know any of it. "Okay, fine. It's most likely me."

"You're in denial. You don't want to deal with the fact that someone fucked with your life. Our lives."

He was right. I wanted to bury my head in the sand and ignore what was certainly true. It didn't matter though because we didn't have the means to fix the problem. Why obsess over things that couldn't be changed?

"You're wrong," Logan said. "Something can always be done. Rolling over and playing dead isn't going to do anyone any good."

"I didn't say anything."

"You didn't have to. It's written all over your face."

The pizza turned into cardboard in my mouth, and I struggled to swallow my last bite. "Fine. Whatever. But I'm not playing dead. I'm being a realist. And the reality of the situation is that we have no way to deal with this particular time travel conundrum. We are stuck. Trapped. So I see no reason to dwell on it since it will only make things feel worse."

"I wouldn't have come back and left that note if there was no way."

"Then maybe you should have written the way down, dumbass. Instead of, I don't know, cryptic one-liners."

"Maybe I didn't write it down because I thought it would be obvious."

"Don't make excuses for your dumbassery."

"Dumbassery? I came back in time to salvage our relationship, and you're pissed because I didn't take good enough notes for you?"

"You cheated on me and then left without any kind of explanation! You just left!" My chest heaved as I sucked in shallow breaths, sweat dribbling down my spine, the room suddenly a thousand degrees.

And there it was. The fury for what he'd done no longer simmering on the back burner. It was in the front, bubbling over, about to explode in both of our faces.

I flipped the pizza box, spilling the remaining slices and crust onto the floor. "No matter what anyone did to the timeline, *you* did that to me! *You* made that decision! You! That's who you are to me! Someone who I loved with all of my heart, and you ripped it out of my chest for no reason!"

"No!" Logan roared, his gaze flashing dangerously. "I would never do that to you!"

Without a conscious effort to move, I found myself directly in front of him, my hands shoving at his chest. "You can say that you would never hurt me all you want, but you did. You did." The heat in me cooled, transforming my sweat to ice as it wove along my nape.

Tangling my hands into the fabric of his shirt to keep them from trembling, I spoke through gritted teeth. "And I hate myself because when I came back, I thought I could stay away from you. That it would all be so easy. But …"

His heart thrummed under my hands, the rhythm fast and strong, his chest rising and falling in short little bursts. "But what?" he rasped.

"You're my kryptonite." I squeezed my eyes shut, willing myself to disappear. And maybe if I concentrated hard enough I would.

"Tell me what happened exactly. Tell me how I left you."

I sucked in a shuddery breath, my eyes remaining shut as the images played through my mind like they happened yesterday. "We lived together, you and me, and one day when I got back from being out with Sera, you and all of your stuff was gone. Just like that. Gone."

"Why do you think—"

I twisted my fingers tighter in his shirt. "Let me finish."

His muscles tensed, but he remained silent.

"Shortly after I discovered you left, Ben showed up at our apartment. He was our upstairs neighbor, and you know, we were friendly with him. Saw him around, chatted, and went to the same social gatherings sometimes. I broke down sobbing when I saw him, and then he told me that he saw you packing up your stuff with another girl."

Logan swore under his breath. "And then what?"

I shrugged before pulling away from him. "Then nothing. I never saw or heard from you again. Ben and I grew close, and … well," I swiped at a few rogue tears, embarrassment settling over me, "the rest is history. Kind of. Since it hasn't and won't happen."

I shuffled back over to the couch, exhaustion taking hold once more.

"Yeah, okay, you still gonna claim Ben has nothing to do with this?"

My head snapped up to take in Logan's thunderous expression and rigid body. "Umm … again, no one made you leave with that girl."

"Did anyone see any of this happen aside from Ben?" he grated.

I blinked. "No. But—"

"And he just happens to show up with this information right after I leave?"

I blinked again. "Yes. But before—"

"It was a lie and you never questioned it!" Logan whirled, his booted foot connecting with the edge of the coffee table.

"Saying he saw you with another girl is one thing, but he didn't make you leave. You did not attempt to contact me in any way … ever again. It was obvious, even if there wasn't another girl, that you wanted nothing to do with me. Ever again."

"If we're dealing with someone who messed with our lives to the degree my note implies, who knows how far he was willing to go?"

I reared back, his words almost like a physical blow. Had I been that gullible? But to never have heard from Logan again? That part was difficult to digest. "He didn't murder you. Or put a gun to your head and force you to pack. Why did you go? Where did you go? And why did you never try to contact me ever again?"

Logan was pacing back and forth in the small space in between the TV and the now toppled coffee table. "I can't answer those questions. But I do know one thing." He was in front of me before I could process he'd even moved, his hands cupping the sides of my face. "I would never willingly leave you like that. I couldn't. Hell, you've been giving me fuckin' emotional whiplash the past few weeks and I haven't given up. After years together I wouldn't—"

He bit his lower lip, his gaze darting between my eyes. "I know I can't make you believe me. And I know I can't scrub those memories from your brain. But what if, what if we started over from this moment?"

I stiffened. "What, like a second chance?"

"From where I'm standing, it will feel like a first chance. But yeah, however you want to look at it."

I shirked out from under his touch, slouching back into the couch. "I don't know if I can do that. I don't want to get hurt like that again."

Even after everything that happened, somehow, what Logan did seemed so much worse than anything Ben had done. And maybe that was because Ben married a different person than the one who'd been with Logan. It was just the way of things, I supposed, and I always thought I was beyond lucky to find someone like Ben who knew that maybe, quite possibly I'd never be whole again.

Logan crowded into my space again, his callused thumb running over my lower lip. I snapped at it, causing him to withdraw, his pupils flaring nonetheless.

"What did you plan to do? Avoid me and Ben, but also avoid the potential for any kind of relationship pain ever again? You can't be one hundred percent in a relationship and not risk being hurt."

Turning my head away, I grimaced.

"Oh. So that was part of your plan, too? To not go all in when it came to any relationship ever again?"

"And what of it? Maybe I decided it was time to stop letting the male of our species ruin my life. Maybe I decided the chance of real and lasting love wasn't worth the risk. That the potential downside was way worse than the slim chance of reaching the potential upside."

"Harper," Logan rumbled.

Nibbling on the insides of my cheeks, I kept my focus on my nails, picking at the bright pink polish.

"Harper, look at me."

I continued to pick at my nails, wishing I had the power to disappear into the ether. I didn't know what I wanted and what I didn't want for that matter anymore. I'd been running on fear and anxiety for so long that I wasn't sure I was capable of making a decision without those two things being the deciding factors. Possibly the only factors.

"Harper," Logan growled. "Look at me. Now."

Unable to resist—because I was a weak fool—I lifted my gaze to meet Logan's, the blue in them clouded with guilt and anger. "I'm sorry you got hurt. But please, let me … just let me …"

He dropped to his knees in front of me, wrapping his arms around my middle, his head pressing into my chest. "Give me another chance. Please. I know you're scared, but fuck, so am I. This whole thing is terrifying as fuck. I'm out of my depth. Hell, I'm out of anyone's depth right now. All I know, all I can think about is that I want you. Want to be with you."

I raised a trembling hand, my fingers hesitantly threading into his dark locks. "What do I do if you wake up one day and decide you're done with me?"

He tightened his grip around me. "I'll never be done with you."

"You don't know that."

"I traveled through literal time to be with you. What more can I do to prove it to you?"

"You don't even remember doing that."

"And if you're right, soon you won't remember any of your other memories either. It'll be just us, here, again. We could start over again. Make it work this time."

"What if someone interferes?"

"We'll take precautions."

"Like what?"

He pulled away from me, one side of his mouth curling up. "We'll take better notes before it's too late."

I huffed out a laugh, smacking him lightly. "You're an idiot."

He grinned, pulling me down closer to him until our breath intermingled. "But I'm your idiot whether you want me or not."

The problem was, and always had been, that I did want him. And I was pretty sure that made me the idiot, not him.

Logan must have registered the acceptance in my eyes, because the next thing I knew, we were on the floor, me on my back, with his lips crashing into mine.

The air buzzed with frantic energy as we tore at each other's clothes. I wanted ... needed his skin against mine, his cock inside me—a promise made and sealed with our bodies.

There was nothing gentle about the way Logan took me, my hips angled up to meet each and every brutal thrust. Or the way he palmed my breasts, squeezing roughly every time he slammed home.

But I loved it, each and every moment of it, as Logan unleashed himself on me in a way that transcended the fledgling relationship we were supposed to have. Our feelings ran deep, deeper than even I understood. It was as if our bodies remembered things our minds had no concept of.

When I finally arched up, clawing at his arms and back with my release, he swore, groaning his own with wild, uneven strokes.

Collapsing in each other's arms, Logan rolled to cradle

me against his chest. He chuckled. "I think you have cheese in your hair." He tugged at my tangled strands. "Yep, cheese."

Silence again descended upon us, my thoughts whirling around everything that just happened between us. *I really hope I remembered to take my birth control. Because that would be an entirely different level of stupid.* I pushed those thoughts temporarily aside, not needing something else to stress over at the moment.

Logan shifted his fingers through my hair, the motion snagging periodically, probably catching on more cheese. I fidgeted, my body restless as I fought the urge to fall asleep. Not because I was tired, but because it simply felt right being there with him.

And yet ... I had doubts, so many doubts. And questions, a seemingly unlimited supply of those, too. Nothing had truly been sorted between me and Logan. We'd merely given in to the lust burning between us.

I tilted my chin up, nipping and then kissing the sensitive underside of his jaw. His pulse picked up speed underneath my ear.

"We should talk," I murmured.

"What you're doing right now isn't going to help me focus on anything but getting inside of you again."

Rolling my eyes, I huffed out a laugh. "You may be young, but you still need a little bit of recovery time."

I found myself on my back again, Logan looming over me. "True." He smirked. "But there are other things we can do in the meantime."

His gaze dipped down the line of my body, indicating exactly what he had in mind.

Okay, fine. The talk will have to wait.

Chapter 20

One of the follies of youth was being under the mistaken impression that all the time in the world exists to accomplish what you want and need to do. The seemingly endless amount of years laid out before you, thriving with possibilities. It causes a loss of focus, and the feeling of immortality, in a sense. And even though I knew better, and watched those years fall away like sand through an hourglass, I still found myself making the wrong choices ... again.

Logan and I needed to be planning, and preparing, for what would inevitably happen with my memories—therefore our memories. We should have been working diligently to avert another crisis. Instead, we spent the better part of the next day naked and entangled with each other.

I knew the world wouldn't wait because we wanted it to, but I pretended it would.

"Logan." Sliding my fingers into his silky locks, I pulled his head away from my breast.

He frowned, his eyes glittering in the low light. "I was busy."

"We need to figure out a plan."

He quirked an eyebrow. "Oh, I have a plan."

I yanked his hair harder, but he didn't so much as wince. "You know what I mean. We can't stay in here indefinitely, only stopping to eat and shower."

"You sore?"

"Yes, I'm fucking sore, but that's not the point."

Expelling a long breath, Logan flopped onto his back, gaze fixated on the ceiling. "Yeah, I know."

Propping myself up on my elbow, I studied his strong profile. The loss of his ministrations suddenly had my body screaming another tune. But I would resist. I had to. "There are a ton of things we need to figure out."

He rubbed his forehead absently. "Yeah, I know."

"Then we need to get started."

"My way was better."

I needed to remind myself that Logan was also in a young body, but without the tiny bit of guidance, my adult memories were giving me. He had his moments of mature clarity, as if it was indeed sourced from an older version of himself, but he also already faded into his past, lost to his not fully developed brain which was completely addled with hormones. Not that my hormones weren't driving me as well, and not the other way around.

"Yeah, your plan isn't bad." I wiggled my hips a bit,

replaying some of the things we'd just done. "But I don't exactly relish the idea of being caught off guard if someone tries to mess with our timeline again."

I still had a ton of questions, but I didn't think any of them would be sufficiently answered. One, for instance, was why did Logan have dreams about a future lost, like about our wedding, when I never had anything of the sort?

Dropping back onto the bed, I joined Logan in staring at the ceiling. "We need to make those notes ASAP. I don't know how much time I have left."

Logan sighed.

"And we need to go to class and stuff. If we're going to start over, so to speak, we need to make sure we don't flunk out of school or do anything else irreparable."

Logan sighed again.

"And we also need to—"

"You should move in with me."

"What?"

"Move in with me."

Of all the things I expected him to say, asking me to move in with him was not one of them. "I don't— I can't— It's too soon."

Logan rolled onto his side, and he rested his temple against a closed fist, his cool blue gaze locked with mine as a swath of dark hair tumbled across his forehead. "Is it though?"

"Yes," I sputtered, flapping my hands at him uselessly. "We just started ..."

He tilted his head.

"Well, we technically just started …"

His eyebrows lifted in challenge.

"We can't move in together. Not yet."

Our shared apartment flitted across my memory, and how it looked when all the spaces where his stuff had been were suddenly empty. My chest tightened, slowing the flow of air.

Logan cradled my face in his hands. "None of this is normal." He flashed a dimpled smile, making my middle warm. "So we should just do it."

I shook my head. "No."

He dipped his head to pepper my face with soft, sensual kisses. "Why not?"

Because we did it before and you left me. Because I won't be able to put myself back together if you leave me again. Because I'm absolutely terrified. "Because I said so."

"We're doing this though? Giving us a real shot?"

I nodded numbly.

"Then why not move in with me?"

Flicking my gaze away, I said, "You know why."

His fingers curled against my cheeks. "Then you know that's not a real reason. I was set up somehow. I would never leave you willingly. I know that in my soul."

My eyes slid shut against the burn of tears. "I want this. I want you. But I can't seem to … I can't move in with you. Not yet."

"I know you're focused on what happened with us— what hasn't happened yet, and I'm not trying to tell you that you shouldn't feel something about that. But we need to put it behind us. I want you near me. With me. I have this nagging feeling in my gut that you're going to slip away again."

Shame heated my ears and cheeks. I hadn't considered his insecurities in the matter of our rekindled relationship. He may not have his memories in the way that I currently did, but obviously, something was left behind by his future self.

As if reading my mind, he leaned in to whisper in my ear, "If we have any real chance at this, we need to work through your move-in issues before you forget everything and are left with an unexplainable mistrust of the situation. That's going to be worse because you're going to think it's your gut directing you to not trust me or some other bullshit."

I squeezed my eyes shut tighter. "You're right. I know you're right."

"But?" He pulled me into his side, curling an arm around my middle.

"But I can't seem to get past the overwhelming terror."

"I love you, too."

I was pretty sure my heart skipped several beats as I struggled to suck in oxygen. I never thought I'd hear those two words from Logan Sharpe again.

Belatedly, the word *too* registered with the other three. "Too? When did I say I loved you?" I pinched his nipple, causing him to jerk before laughing softly. "Because it doesn't count when you're inside me. Or right after we have sex either. Or right before. Or—"

"So what you're telling me is that when you tell me that you love me it doesn't count? Period."

"I didn't say that."

"You were about to."

"Was not."

Another laugh rumbled from his chest. "How am I supposed to know if you ever mean it? Should I request it in writing? Does it need notarized? How about witnesses? Do we need those?"

I slapped his chest. "Stop. You know what I mean."

"Do I? Because I just told you I loved you, and you fixated on the part where you think I implied that you said it first, or at all."

Rising above him, I snagged his mirth-filled gaze. He was so beautiful. Everything about him, from his dark hair and blue-eyed combination to the sharp cut of his jaw, to his full, supple lips, and the—

Am I really doing this? His appearance has no relevance in the end. So stop obsessing over it. Stupid teenage hormones. Ugh.

Did I love him in the here and now? Or did I merely remember loving him? What about all the pain that went with it? And did we actually stand a chance of making any of this work? Because it ultimately didn't matter if someone had stolen our relationship from us by messing with our timeline. We were both here now. It was what it was, and the only thing we could do was move forward. If I couldn't trust him with my heart, then we were doomed.

Logan ran a finger between my brows and down my nose, his lips turning slightly down at the corners. "I don't think I like where your head is right now."

"I need time to think about all of this … us."

His jaw clenched, the muscles feathering. "You've got to be fuckin' kidding me. After everything—"

Already on my feet, I scanned the room for my clothes. "Everything what? Sex? And more sex? Sure, we've got great chemistry. And also, yeah, you're a lot better at some of those things than you used to be so early in our relationship—"

He gaped at me.

I widened my eyes and crinkled my nose. "Please, like you don't know that younger guys have a tendency to need a bit of guidance when it comes to some sex stuff."

"Excuse you?"

I rolled my eyes as I pulled on my pants. "It's not limited to guys. We're lucky any of us enjoy sex the first few years with how confusing it can be. Especially since nobody wants to talk about it in the right way."

Logan stood before me completely naked, and utterly baffled. "I don't know what to say or do right now." He ran his hands through his hair, his gaze tracking my every movement. "You can't go. Not yet."

"I can and I'm going to. I need to check on Sera."

"She's probably with Derek."

That reminded me of a question I would now bother to ask. "You and Derek weren't friends before. Why are you now?"

He scratched his head. "Um, we've always been friends. We grew up together."

"Hmm …" I grunted. "But you weren't. And I would know since Sera and Derek got, or get, married. You weren't invited to their wedding."

He shrugged. "Maybe we grew apart."

"Maybe." I pulled on my shoes and coat, spurring Logan into action.

"Come on, Harper. Stay. We'll talk. Just talk. I promise."

"I need some time."

"What if we don't have time?"

"You'll remember everything I told you."

He grabbed me by the elbow, spinning back towards him. "And you'll believe me? If I come to you and tell you time travel is real and all the other stuff you told me—you're going to believe me?"

"We still have some time." I hoped. "I just need a day or so. To go check on Sera. To make sure she and Derek are back on track. And then we can talk." Also to make sure I was good on my birth control.

"And if you forget between now and then?" His steel gaze held mine, desperation simmering within.

"It's not like I'm going to forget you completely. I'm pretty sure I could never do that."

"And if your feelings from before seep into how you feel now but you don't know why?"

Pulling away from him, I clicked my tongue. "Hell, I couldn't even stay away from you when I remembered everything and there weren't any doubts in my mind about whether or not you cheated."

He rolled his bottom lip over his teeth and backed a step away from me. "If this is what you need."

I gave him a tight-lipped smile. "It is."

He nodded once, and turned, as if he couldn't stand the thought of watching me go, even if he would let it happen.

Careful not to glance back, in case my resolve crumbled, I hastily made my way out of his apartment and back out onto the street where he'd found me over twenty-four hours ago. I only hesitated another moment before I hurried in the direction of campus, and where I hoped I'd find Sera.

Good news. Good news. Please let her have some good news about her and Derek for me. Once that was settled, then I could turn my full attention to Logan and our ridiculous situation.

"SERA?"

The lights in our dorm room were all on, even the retina-burning overhead fluorescents, but there was no sign of my friend in the immediate space. I also noted that the bathroom door was open, and there were no other places to hide.

"Did you leave and forget to turn the lights off again?" I muttered to myself.

Her comforter rustled, what I initially assumed was a

pillow and a rumpled blanket wriggling in the middle of her bed.

"Sera? Are you in there?"

The movement stopped.

"Are you hiding in there?"

"No," came her muffled voice.

Marching over to her side of the room, I threw the covers off of her. Wide, rid-rimmed eyes met mine. "What are you doing in there?"

She sniffled. "Nothing. Taking a nap. Whatever." Her chin quivered.

My heart dropped into my stomach. "What happened?" *Please don't let it be Derek. Please don't let it be Derek. Please don't let it be—*

"It's Derek." Her face crumpled and then smoothed, before crumpling again. The battle to keep from crying a losing one.

Shit. Now what? I sat on the edge of her bed. "Tell me what happened."

"I don't know." She sniffled again. "I thought things were back on track, but then someone told him that I was stalking him or being crazy or … whatever." More sniffles. "I'm not exactly sure. But now he doesn't want to see me anymore." More sniffles. "And he doesn't even know about us going to his apartment."

Cringing, I tried not to think about that debacle. "No. Obviously, someone told him whatever it was to get in between you and it worked. We need to fix it."

Sera pulled the covers back over her head. "What's the

point? I mean, yeah, he's the hottest guy I've ever been with or seen, and he gets the job done in bed. Like seriously gets it done. And he's smart. And funny. And practically perfect in every way. But that's okay. I'm sure I'll find someone else much better than him one day. And not only better but with a magical connection that makes me want to—" She choked back a sob. "But it doesn't matter. I refuse to be the crazy girl he accused me of being."

Digging my nails into my thighs, I tried to find patience within myself, but upon inspection realized I never had any to begin with. "Don't let someone else ruin what you guys could have."

"It's too late. They win. Whoever they are."

"No. I refuse to accept that." If nothing else went right within my time travel disaster, I would ensure the happy ending with Derek that my best friend deserved. She was the best person I knew, and I would do everything in my power to guarantee her future with the man she loved.

Sera had emerged from under her covers again, tears tracking down the sides of her face into her ears. "I won't let myself look like an even bigger fool. If he doesn't want me then he doesn't want me."

"Anyone in love is going to look like a fool at some point. If you're worried about that then you might as well swear it off completely. So be the fool, do everything you can to go after love if you think it's the real thing. Or that it could be."

"Who are you right now?" Sera turned her head in my

direction. "You are always the cautious one when it comes to anything like this."

She was right. I usually was. Even when I got older. But something inside of me had shifted since learning what I did from Logan. It was a new kind of hope, the fragile bloom poking up within my once-jaded heart. And maybe there, within my advice to Sera, was the answer to whether or not I should try things again with Logan.

I shook my head. *The Logan situation is secondary to the Derek situation. Focus.* "I'm tired of worrying about what other people think, or how I seem to them. Crazy, not crazy, who the hell cares? You need to do what makes you happy. No holds barred."

"It's not like I broke it off with Derek this time. I can't force him to want to be with me."

"No, but you also— Wait!" I snapped my fingers. "Logan is friends with Derek this time around!"

Sera's nose crinkled. "This time around? What are you talking about?"

Ignoring her, I pushed forward. "I can explain everything to Logan and have him work on his friend for you." I still didn't understand how and why Logan and Derek were close now when they weren't before, but I would make it work for me regardless, and not look a gifted horse in the mouth.

Without waiting for Sera to respond, I headed to the bathroom, calling over my shoulder, "I'm going to take a quick shower and then I'm going talk to Logan about this."

I was met with silence, Sera already back under her pile of blankets and comforter. She might be resigned, but I wasn't. I could actually tell all of the details to Logan and get him to convince Derek to give Sera another chance. That, of course, meant I'd have to deal with Logan a lot sooner than I'd originally planned, but for Sera, I'd do it.

Humming under my breath, I smiled as the warm water sluiced over my skin. Hope. For the first time in a long time, I not only had some, but I let myself revel in it completely.

Maybe things will work out for both Logan and myself, and Sera and Derek. We could be ridiculously happy couple friends.

I hummed a little louder.

Maybe, just maybe ...

Chapter 21

S tanding at the threshold of Logan's apartment, staring up at his smug expression, I knew I'd made a mistake. I should have just called him. Although that would have been an issue in itself since I didn't seem to have his number in a place I remembered stashing it.

"Couldn't stay away?" He leaned on the doorframe, his arms above his head, wearing a faded T-shirt and low-slung jeans. My fingers itched to touch the sliver of skin exposed, to trail them lower ... lower ...

I bit the insides of my cheeks and notched my chin up. "I'm here for business not fun." *Did I really just say that? Ugh.*

Mirth danced within his gaze, warming the ice-blue contours. "Business, huh? Now this I've got to hear." He moved aside so I could enter.

Shuffling past him, I tried to nonchalantly inhale his

scent. I didn't even know why the overwhelming urge to do so was undeniable. It was as if I wanted to confirm the realness of him, the way he—

"Did you just sniff me?"

"What?" I turned wide eyes up at him.

His dimples made an appearance as his lips tucked in. "You did."

"What are you even talking about?" Why did I do that? It's not that hard to not sniff someone. I do it all day long. Walk by people and not sniff them. Why did Logan have to be the exception? And why did he have to notice?

Logan dragged his lower lip over his teeth. "I don't have a problem with you sniffing me, just so we're clear."

The words were innocent, and yet clearly they weren't meant that way. Heat bloomed in my middle, and I swallowed compulsively. "I didn't sniff you. Just so we're clear."

The door clicked shut behind me, the sound reminding me that I was now in Logan's apartment, alone with him … again. Had I even thought this scenario through when I'd come up with it? Or was I using it as an excuse to see him in person? To kill two birds with one stone by helping Sera and helping myself to Logan.

I groaned. "I really am here for a reason. And not a naked reason," I hurried to tack on. Even his lame innuendos were catnip for me. He could probably say nonsensical words in that sensual way of his and I'd be swooning in no time.

Logan snorted. "Yeah, all right."

"You're friends with Derek and I need you to convince him to give Sera another shot."

He moved towards me, herding me into his small living room. "Who Derek dates or doesn't date isn't something I get involved with."

Crossing my arms over my chest, I glared at Logan. "Maybe I didn't mention it, or maybe I didn't make it clear, but Sera and Derek are married, or they're supposed to be. And they are serious couple goals."

He quirked an eyebrow, before raking his gaze down my body, making it clear where his true thoughts were.

Ignoring my body's reaction to his not-so-subtle perusal of me, I said, "They're ridiculously happy. And I don't know what happened when I came back, but things aren't supposed to be this way. They can't be. Sera is a mess, like crying under the covers in her bed mess, and I don't know why any of this is happening."

"Derek goes through women faster than I do a box of tissues. I've seen this before, and it's like a light switches off in him. If Derek is done with her, I don't know what you think I can do about it."

"Did you not listen to a word I just said? They are supposed to be together. I broke something inadvertently when I came back. I need to fix it. And you need to help me."

Logan shifted to lean against the edge of the couch. "Huh. The Derek I know has never been in a long-term relationship of any kind. I can't even picture him being with someone like Sera beyond a hookup, let alone happy with her."

"Why are you being so stubborn about this?" I threw my hands up in the air in frustration. "You're willing to believe all the rest about time travel, but I say Sera and Derek are happy and need to be together and you what ... are suddenly sus?"

"Sus?"

"Suspicious. Duh." It was a wonder I didn't drop more future-type slang to confuse him. I wasn't big on that kind of stuff though, and never was. I couldn't help it if certain more popular phrases made it into my lexicon through audio osmosis.

Irritation played across his face as he frowned. "I didn't say I didn't believe you. I just was pointing out that there wasn't much I could do."

"You're his friend!"

"Guys barely talk about personal shit with each other, let alone give romantic advice. It would look weird if I suddenly started telling him who to date."

"Then look weird! I don't care what you have to do to get them back together the way they should be!" My heart thrashed against my ribcage, my breathing ragged.

Logan closed the distance between us in two strides, taking me into the warm embrace of his strong arms. "All right. If it's that important to you."

Wrapping my arms around his waist, I pressed my cheek into his chest. "Thank you."

"No promises though. I'll do my best, but I think you better start coming up with a backup plan."

"This is my backup plan," I muttered into the worn material of his T-shirt.

"What about us?" His hand came up to cup the back of my head, pressing me tighter against him. "Have you thought about things with us like you said you were going to?"

It was strange when Logan went from a swaggering nineteen-year-old, all smirks and smug expressions, to someone vulnerable with their thoughts and feelings. Not that the two couldn't co-exist under normal circumstances, but there was something more mature about Logan in those instances. It was like I was getting glimpses of the man he would become, or who he was, depending on how I looked at it. And that man curled my toes and melted my heart in a completely different way than the younger version set my body on fire for him.

"I haven't. Thought about us. As soon as I got back to my room, I found Sera …" My hands crept lower on his hips, completely of their own volition.

Logan's hand threaded in my hair, and he tugged my head back, our gazes clashing. "Tell me what to do to make things right between us. I'll do anything you want."

My heart kicked it up a notch as I stared at him, his visage etched with hope and fear. "I just don't know what to think or feel about you … us anymore. There are so many unanswered questions." I let loose a shaky breath.

"What if our situation is too complicated to unravel? What if we're doomed already?"

He ground his teeth together, a muscle jumping in his jaw. "No. I refuse to accept that. And I won't walk away from you if that's all you have for a reason not to do this."

I barked a harsh laugh. "I could walk away from you today and swear you off for eternity, but we both know the minute my memory of the future is gone I'm going to be right back here begging to be with you." One week. That's all it had taken for me when I'd blacked out, or lost myself to my younger self, to wind up right back with Logan. It would inevitably happen again.

He trailed a thumb down my neck, his hand stopping to cage in my throat. "I want you to choose me. Now. With everything you know. I want you to tell me that we'll figure out a way to fix what someone else broke between us. I want you to tell me that you'll fight for us no matter what happens."

How could I tell him that somewhere along the line I'd lost all my will to fight for such things? We talked about my marriage to Ben briefly, but not the full scope of things, or where I was emotionally because of it.

As if he plucked the thoughts right from my head, Logan's lips pressed into a tight line. "I won't let him hurt you again. And I won't let anyone take you from me again. Even you."

With my past—or future, whatever—that declaration should have set off every single alarm bell within me.

Logan was saying that despite my wishes, he wouldn't let me go. Nothing would make him let me go.

I guess what they say is true: It's only creepy if a guy you don't want says it. Therefore, my reaction to Logan pointed at exactly what I'd decided subconsciously, even if I didn't want to admit it quite yet.

The pragmatist in me wanted to rail against the entire concept. But truthfully, all sense of logic went out the window the second Logan turned his piercing gaze on me. Or spoke to me in that raspy voice of his. Or basically existed in my presence. It was pointless to fight something not worth fighting. To deny myself a chance with Logan just out of principle when he could make me happy. It was kind of like cutting my nose off to spite my face.

None of the rationales mattered, in the end. I wanted Logan, good idea or not. I'd done far stupider things in my life. Risked bigger things than a broken heart.

"Okay." I was going to regret this decision, I was sure of it. And I wasn't sure I cared all that much anymore. To have more time with Logan, even if it was finite, I would risk it. I had to.

"Hell, yes." Logan swept me up in his arms and spun me in a circle.

His joy was contagious. It couldn't be helped. I threw my head back and laughed; something inside of me was lighter, buoyant.

"I love you, Snow."

A chasm opened up in my chest, swallowing me whole.

Snow? Why did that sound … feel, so familiar, the echo of it a tearing a fresh gash into my patched-together heart?

"Snow?" I rasped. "What is that supposed to mean?" It was there, like something on the tip of my tongue, the knowledge of it just beyond my grasp, a shadow in my mind's eye.

Setting me on my feet, Logan regarded me, confusion swirling in his limpid blue eyes. "I don't know. It just came out." His brow furrowed as he considered it. "But it felt right. Somehow it just felt right."

I shook my head. "Why? I don't understand." Clouded images, out of focus and dizzying, filled my mind. But the more I focused on them, the further away they seemed.

"I don't know, I think it was a nickname I had for you. One that's in here somewhere." He tapped his temple. "But beyond my reach most of the time. I mean, it fits. Sort of." He motioned to me. "Short, dark hair, pale skin …" He shrugged. "And I vaguely remember it from some of my dreams."

There was no point in pushing him about it. He was suffering through the same thing that I was. If, and when, he recalled any other tidbits, I was confident he would share them with me. After all, he'd been more forthright with information than I had been since the time travel reveal. I was still hiding pieces of my other life.

Voices, mine and Ben's, swirled around my ears, an auditory memory of sorts.

"Why did you cut your hair?" Ben demanded. *"I told you I liked it long."*

"I don't know. I wanted something different. It was fine long, but this feels, I don't know, more like me."

"Grow it back. And get extensions in the meantime."

"No. I'll wear my hair any way I want. And I want it this way."

"You look like—"

"Like what?"

"Like someone trying to look like something she's not."

"What's that even supposed to mean? Why would you even say that? I look like me, but with a cuter, shorter haircut."

"I don't like it. That's not who you are anymore."

"I don't even understand what you're saying to me right now."

"Make the appointment for extensions."

"No."

The argument had gone on for longer than most would expect, most of Ben's points not making a whole lot of sense … until now.

"He hated my hair short," I whispered. "Like irrationally hated it." My gut twisted. "It's him. It has to be him."

Logan's icy gaze narrowed, dark lashes fanning down. "Who?"

"Ben. He hated my hair short. But for some reason that never made sense until this exact moment, when you called me Snow. It was like he didn't want me to look like someone else. It was always so strange, but—"

"He didn't want you to look like yourself from another

version of our timeline. The one where I called you Snow. When you were my wife and not his."

Logan and I discussed it. I'd seen the note. I believed him when he said he felt things and knew things that proved he also traveled through his own timeline as I had. But it was difficult to come to terms with someone sabotaging my life. To accepting that Logan and I were happily married in another time and place. Especially when just thinking about Logan had brought me nothing but pain for years.

"This is so surreal. All of it. Why would anyone want to interfere with our relationship? How is it possible? I don't have any of those dreams that you do. I never did." I brought my hand up to my mouth, nibbling on my nails.

"You forgot the most important question."

My hand stilled. "What?"

"How was someone in the position to interfere with our relationship? It has to be someone who had easy access to your work, or equipment. Someone who could get in and out unnoticed."

I went back to biting my nails. "It's going to be impossible to figure out since they screwed things up for us so thoroughly."

Logan grabbed my hand and tugged it away from my mouth. "Not thoroughly enough since we found our way back to each other."

"For how long though? And to what end? We could have done this hundreds, thousands of times before. Each cycle back convoluting things worse than before. The timeline could be so twisted by this point that there's no way to untangle it."

Definitions, solutions, equations, they were all slipping away. Soon, we'd be at the mercy of whoever separated us before, sitting ducks for them to do it again. And the worst part was I might never know the truth—about any of it. "I've seen so many movies, read so many books, where I'm yelling at the characters to remember, frustrated that they couldn't figure things out or when they forgot someone important to them in a time-loop, and here we are ..."

Logan grimaced. "I know."

"So what do we do?"

"We'll figure something out."

If only it was that easy. But then again ...

"Ben! If it is him, and we keep a close eye on him, then even if he jumps back into himself or is already here, then we know not to trust him or let him do stuff." Of course, it would be more complicated than simply keeping tabs on Ben, even if I wished it wasn't. But ...

"It's a start anyways." Or would be.

My mind began zipping around, struggling to consider all the variables—the ways that Ben could drop into himself from the future. The biggest problem was not knowing when the future him had originated.

"Come here." Logan swept me up in his arms again. "I can feel your panic."

"And I'm just getting started."

"Shhh ... calm that big brain of yours down." He kissed

the top of my head. "We'll figure this out together, I swear."

I bit my cheeks, choosing silence over a disagreement. I wasn't going to calm down because I knew the odds were stacked against us. It was partly why I'd been afraid to give Logan and our relationship another shot. He could be ripped away from me again, and the worst part would be not even knowing. What else had been stolen from me? And how much more would be taken?

"Sera. We need to fix Derek and Sera." I couldn't let my best friend's future fall through the cracks because I was about to have a nervous breakdown.

"Before we do that, we need to take some precautions. Putting them off can't wait anymore."

I nodded. "The notes. I need to write down everything about this, so I'll know when I lose my future self's memories." I still had doubts though. "Why did you believe that note? It was a scrap of paper with seemingly utter nonsense scribbled on it."

"It was the dreams that pushed me in the right direction, I guess."

I swallowed around the boulder in my throat. "But I don't have those."

Logan kissed the top of my head again. "Maybe not. But you have me. And there is something to be said about feeling like something is true when you hear it."

"What if I don't believe any of this? What if I run from you because I think you're a psycho?"

"Harper. Stop it. We'll get through this together."

Dread pooled in my stomach, an ocean of fear and regret. I didn't believe him, couldn't. Because that was the thing, I felt the lie. Knew that we were about to drown in a nightmare created by someone who was beyond our influence and control.

I didn't voice any of what I was thinking though. What good would it do to let Logan know that I saw our doom approaching? So instead, I said, "Okay. We'll get through this together."

Chapter 22

I'd fallen asleep entangled with Logan in his small, twin-sized bed. It wasn't a hardship though, being forced to stay close to him all night long. I'd let him sway me from interfering with Derek and Sera's relationship for one more night. Long enough for me to jot down some haphazard notes, signed by me, as if that would prove anything down the line, and then of course, we gave in to our barely contained desires.

Shifting in his sleep, Logan tightened his arm around my waist and pressed his face into the back of my neck. His breath was a warm breeze, pebbling my flesh. He groaned in annoyance when I moved, my half-hearted attempt to slide from our cocoon easily deterred.

But I couldn't hide in his arms forever. Getting a second chance at my life meant I had to live it, all of it, and not skip the downsides of being eighteen years old again in favor of simply focusing on the fun parts.

Flinging Logan's arm away from me, I rolled out of bed, awkwardly hitting the floor. In a flash, he was awake, peering down at me with rumpled hair and a furrowed brow. "What are you doing down there?" he rasped.

"I need to go."

He pursed his lips, regarding me with drowsy eyes, the pull of them almost undeniable. I wanted nothing more than to climb back into bed with him and languish the rest of the day away in his arms. Even if I was almost too sore to walk as it was.

"I need to go," I repeated, scanning the room for my clothes.

His face scrunched up as he ran a hand along his jaw, scratching the light scruff there. "Yeah, I guess."

"Don't give me that." I stood and pulled my clothes on aggressively, knowing I had to use annoyance as fuel to get me going. Otherwise, I'd fall prey to his allure, just like always.

Logan flopped back on the bed, propping his arms under his head, watching me get dressed with heat in his gaze. "Or you could just come back to bed." He wiggled his arm, drawing my eyes to the spot on his chest where I liked to rest my head. His nook, as I dubbed it.

"I need to check on Sera. And you need to get a move on your plan with Derek." I tossed a pair of jeans at him, which he snatched out of the air before they hit him in the face.

"Plan?" He snorted. "I don't have a plan. I'm just going to talk to him. But like I said," he rolled out of bed much more gracefully than I had, and pulled on the jeans, "I don't have any kind of sway when it comes to who he dates."

"You just need to convince him that she isn't some crazy stalker."

He quirked a brow before pulling a T-shirt over his head. "You two did break into his apartment. That says crazy stalker to me."

"Logan," I hissed, tossing a discarded shoe at him. He quickly ducked, the shoe thumping against the wall. "I told you what happened. Do not turn that into something it wasn't."

He raised his hands in surrender. "Okay. Stop throwing shit at me. It had to be said. Sera is a bit intense. That's all. And it might not be for everyone."

"She is for Derek. I told you how happy they are. Or will be."

He shrugged. "I'll do my best, but—"

I tossed a thick textbook in his direction. The heft of it caused it to hit the edge of the bed and topple to the floor in a heap.

"Hey. That book was expensive. I want to sell it back when I'm done, so how about not damaging it more than it already is, okay?"

Pivoting on my heels, I stomped into the living room. "Just convince Derek. And stop joking about it. It's serious. This is all serious. She is my best friend, and I won't be responsible for the ruination of her future."

Coming up behind me, Logan spun me to face him.

"Okay. I'm not trying to make light of the situation, I'm just— I don't want you to get your expectations too high, that's all. I'll do my best, but that's all I can do."

I heaved a sigh. "Fine." And if his best wasn't good enough, I'd have to come up with another option.

He leaned down to press a soft kiss to my lips, the intent to deepen it thrumming against my skin.

Smacking at his chest, I stumbled back, glaring at him. "I need to go."

Logan served me a faux innocent look. "I was just giving you a kiss good-bye. A small peck." He smirked. "It's not my fault if something so small is making you all—"

"That's it, I'm leaving." I hurried out the door, slamming it behind me.

I BURST into our dorm room, panting from the mad dash I'd taken to get there. I half expected Sera to not have moved at all since I'd last seen her.

Immediately I noticed that lack of décor on her side of the room. Gone were all the posters and pictures of celebrity guys she had crushes on that had been plastered along the wall. Gone was her bright, geometric-patterned comforter. No more piles of clothes on her chair. And no more leaning tower of books at the foot of her bed.

"What the hell is going on?" I muttered to myself.

A sharp knock at the door had me nearly jumping out

of my skin. Still eyeing the dramatic change on Sera's side of the room, hoping the Derek thing hadn't thrown her into some kind of existential crisis, I swung our door open.

"Harper," Ben purred, pushing past me.

The oily grin on his face sent claws of ice down my spine. "No one said you could come in," I hissed.

His grin grew impossibly wide, and I shuddered at the sight of it—the familiarity of it. "You're going to want to hear what I have to say."

Crossing my arms over my chest, I donned a false air of disinterest. "Probably not. But say whatever is it so you feel better and then get the hell out." *Is this it? Is this him from the future? Is he about to out himself as the time-traveling villain of my life?*

He perched himself on the end of my bed as if he had the right to be there, his possessive gaze sliding over me from head to toe. "I found you again."

I blinked, not entirely sure how to take his comment, or how to react to the situation. Feigning ignorance was the obvious way to go to remain on the safe side with little to no other options available. "What? I haven't gone anywhere."

His cornflower blue eyes flashed with familiar rage. "Don't play stupid with me. I know you traveled back again."

My heart quadrupled in time. *Keep feigning ignorance. Nothing good can come from him knowing that you and Logan suspect him of fucking with our lives.* "How did you …"

My lips were numb, unable to form the syllables needed. How did you know? How did you follow me back? What is your end game? Why the hell won't you leave me alone? Because the truth was, I didn't have any concrete proof of anything, only theories and suspicions.

Ben drummed his fingers idly over the rail of my bed, always impatient with me. "These are the times that frustrate the ever-living shit out of me." He sighed. "When you look at me with that big, dumb expression of yours. Sometimes I wonder why I still bother."

"Why do you then? Why don't you just leave me alone?"

His upper lip curled into a snarl. "Because you're mine. That's reason enough."

I took a step back, wanting to put space between us. "I don't belong to anyone but myself."

The harsh lines of his face softened. "I loved you once, you know that? I would have done anything to be with you. And I practically did." His lip curled again as he spat, "But time after mother fucking time you go to him—find him, refuse to fucking stay away from him."

"Logan?" I'm not sure why I asked when I already knew the answer.

"You're mine. Not his. Therefore, if I can't have you then no one else will either. Especially that prick."

Ben had the upper hand; I'd known it before he'd shown up. The only boon in the situation was he was now confirming himself as the one pulling the strings in the time travel game. Of course, that also meant he wasn't worried about me knowing that little tidbit either, which sent my panic spiraling.

Clutching my hands together tightly, I hid the way they were shaking, somehow keeping my voice calm. "What exactly do you want, Ben? Why are you here now?"

"I've decided to change tactics. Again." He stood, strolling over to study the CDs on my side of the room in their tower near the window. "At first I thought putting a rift between Derek and Sera would keep you occupied, but I was wrong." He pulled out a case and flipped it over, humming something under his breath.

"Just spit it out already. You're doing a whole movie villain thing right now." And frankly, my nerves couldn't take it. After years of dealing with Ben and his insidious dramatics and the way he drew things out to rattle me—I just wanted this interaction between us over and done with, no matter what that meant in the end. It was like waiting to be executed, but not knowing the method or when it would take place.

Ben straightened, turning dead eyes towards me. "I'm not the villain in this story. Logan is. For thinking he can have what I deserve. And you are, too. For making me ruin other people's lives to get you to comply."

Ever the narcissist, Ben was flipping the tables on me, trying to put the blame for what he was making a conscious decision to do, completely on me. It was nothing new, and yet every time he did it, surprise rose up in me. I simply couldn't wrap my brain around someone twisting the truth in such a manner, especially with the person that knew it was a lie.

"What did you do?" The how and why ceased to matter at this point.

He sat on my bed again, slouching into himself. "It's a shame really. I didn't want to go through all of this. But you won't stay away from him. I can't even blame Logan this time around since he's just a dumb kid who you're throwing yourself at. I can't expect him to say no to you." He winked, making my skin crawl. "I know how slutty you can be."

I dug my nails into my palms, using the pain to stay focused and steady. "We're not married anymore, Ben. None of that has technically happened. Please, just go away and leave me alone."

He sucked on his teeth, and then clicked his tongue. "Until death do us part. Neither one of us died, Harper."

I backed away another step, eyes wildly swinging around the room. What was I supposed to do in this situation? Ben was deranged, not just a run-of-the-mill narcissist as I'd previously thought. And he wielded the power of time travel in a way I didn't have or understand.

"How?" I squeaked. "How are you the one in control when it was me and my team that came up with and pioneered this manner of time travel?"

"I don't even know how many times I've had to explain this part as well." He sighed heavily and then groaned, like the weight of the world was on his shoulders. "Fine. It is enjoyable to see the look of utter defeat on your face every single time I explain it. Yeah." He grinned. "That part, at least, never gets old."

I swallowed, my throat seemingly filled with bits of glass, and my heart accelerating to another level of speed. I was slightly concerned about my blood pressure. But then again, if I suddenly keeled over maybe I'd finally have a way out of this mess. I swayed on my feet.

Ben's features pinched, and he waved at me. "Sit down. I'm not picking you up off the floor if you pass out. I'm done dealing with your dramatics."

Hesitantly, because I didn't know what else to do, I sat on Sera's bed, glancing again at the strange comforter beneath me. *Yellow and blue flowers. It's so unlike her. And where is she exactly?*

A dark laugh filled the space between us. "Ah, another priceless look on your face. Why is Sera's stuff gone all of a sudden?" he said in a mocking tone. "You can't quite put the pieces together, can you? Oops." He snapped his fingers. "Guess I forgot to tell you …" He paused, a Cheshire cat grin spreading his lips. "She's gone."

My heart jumped into my throat, lodging there as I gasped for breath. "What?" I croaked.

"That's right. Sera isn't your friend anymore."

"Sera would never leave—"

"You're right. Sera has staunchly stood by your side throughout all of this. She was your rock, the strength you relied on no matter what I did. I'm rather embarrassed to admit that it took me this long to figure out that I needed to take her away from you, too. That she was the real lynchpin in all of this."

He was lying. Had to be. It was another way he was using fear to steer me in the direction he wanted. He'd done it countless times before in our marriage, using my own weaknesses to get me to follow his orders promptly and precisely while missing things that should have been obvious. I wouldn't fall for it this time. "But I still remember her."

"Ah, but not for long." He chuckled, the sick bastard not even trying to hide how much he was enjoying my distress. "You see, you remember her now because you also remember the trip through time. But once you forget that, once your memories fade and blend into this new reality, you won't even know she exists."

"No." I couldn't accept it. Wouldn't. Losing Logan was one thing, but Sera ... she was my best friend, my sister, the one person who I needed above all else. Without her I couldn't— I wouldn't be me.

Ignoring me, Ben continued, "And once Sera ceases to exist to you, oh what fun I'll have." He leaned forward, a feral grin twisting his features. "You'll finally be mine in every way that I want."

"No," I repeated, the only word I seemed capable of uttering. I had to stop it. Somehow, I had to stop it all.

"And the best part is, I can sit here and tell you everything that I'm going to do, every little detail, and you won't remember any of it once your future melts into your past. You'll be a blank slate waiting for me to fill you up with whatever new truths I choose to give you."

My nails dug deeper into my palms, the pain not even registering anymore. "Lies, you mean. The truth will just be hidden from me."

Ben narrowed his eyes as he stabbed a finger in my direction. "You made me this way, Harper. You. I did my best. I tried to give you a good life. To love you. But my best wasn't good enough, and a man can only handle so much before he has to take matters into his own hands."

"I didn't do anything to you. I never have."

"Now that's a real lie. Ironic how the liar is so quick to throw out that accusation."

Yeah, isn't it?

"I gave you a good life. Took care of you, loved you. But you wouldn't let Logan go. Even when I made him leave you, over and over again." His gaze turned inward as he chuckled. "You know once I forced him to leave you days before your wedding? That was priceless. You were so broken you practically kissed my feet every time I did something nice for you."

My arms and legs tingled, adrenaline surging through my system. I needed to run, to escape, and yet I somehow managed to force myself to sit there and listen. The one line from the note Logan left himself springing to the forefront of my mind.

Don't let him know it's you.

Was it possible that Logan not completely forgetting, however he'd done it, was a way out of this? But how would Sera play into all of it? How could I get her back, too?

"Don't you even want to know what I did? To make him walk away?" Ben rested his chin on his hands, his fingers interlocked.

To think I used to consider him handsome. Now all I saw was an ugly soul shining through his eyes, and a snake wearing a realistic human skin. Staring at Ben blankly, I kept my features carefully neutral. I swallowed any retort or response I may have had, knowing it wouldn't make a difference. He wanted to talk, so he would. I wasn't sure I was even necessary for the conversation. He always did love the sound of his own voice that much.

Ben's eyes twinkled, reveling in the pain he was causing me. "But I won't tell you since you don't seem to care."

I wouldn't relent, wouldn't ask, even though he wanted me to. In the end, it didn't matter how he'd done it anyways, the results were the same. He'd ruined my relationship with Logan, more times than I was aware, he'd confirmed that much. Knowing the details of such events was pointless.

"Why? Why are you doing any of this?" When had his interest in me turned to obsession? I never led him on or did anything that would suggest I was interested in him more than a friend once we got to know each other. I only opened up to the true possibility of him after Logan was out of the picture.

"You do seem to love that question, too." He cleared his

throat and then said in a falsetto voice, "Why? Why are you doing this?" His voice dropped back to its normal level. "The number of times I've answered it countless now."

"Answer it one more time then." I'm not sure what I hoped to gain by knowing the reasoning behind his madness. It was just something I needed to know.

"Logan and I met you at the same time. Here at school. I thought I was being a gentleman, a nice guy by not pushing the line. I showed up where you were, flirted, and tried to be your friend, but waited to ask you out. Waited to build a bit of familiarity between us so you'd feel comfortable."

He dropped his hands, and his fists balled up at his sides. "But then Logan swept in. Took what I'd spent so much time cultivating. What rightfully belonged to me."

My mouth fell open, hanging there in shock at a level never felt before. And I was someone who'd time traveled. "I'm not a prize to be won. I didn't owe you anything because you seem to think you put time into cultivating a romantic relationship between us."

Speaking over me again, Ben continued, "I'd seen Logan in action around campus. He had quite a reputation as a player. I tried to tell you as much, that you needed to be careful, but you wouldn't listen."

"We fell in love."

"He took what should have been mine. All of this," he waved a hand through the air, "it's about me finally having the power to take what's mine and to punish people like him who think they can walk all over whoever they want."

Was Ben doing this because he was jealous of Logan, obsessed with having me, or both? Again, did it really matter?

"And do you know what the best part was?"

"I don't know because you keep saying a whole bunch of stuff is the best part. They can't all be the best parts." My surprise and horror were beginning to morph into anger.

Ben's lips pressed into a thin line. "Maybe they can."

I rolled my eyes, unable to help myself. I wavered between annoyance, anger, confusion, and hopelessness. What was going down between Ben and me in my dorm room was surreal on a multitude of levels.

"You're hurting Sera and Derek for no reason. They were happy together. At least leave them out of whatever this is."

Ben scowled. "Derek will be able to find someone else with no trouble."

"That's not the point. Just let them be together." I wasn't going to waste my breath trying to explain that I thought they were meant to be together, that they were soul mates. They were concepts that he didn't understand, or we wouldn't be where we were.

"I told you that all of this is your fault. It's too late for you to try to make a deal now."

"None of this is my fault!" Panic, rage, and grief for Sera bubbled up within me, shooting me to my feet. I rushed Ben, leaping at him with my hands outstretched like claws.

We fell back on my bed as I smacked and tore at him, nails and fists connecting wildly with any part of him as he rolled around frantically. He shoved at me, and I stumbled back, only redoubling my efforts when I was back on top of him.

Recovering from his surprise, Ben managed to encircle my wrists with his hands, wrenching my arms behind my back. I screamed, kicked, and bit, but his larger size and strength, combined with my lack of fighting skills, had me at his mercy.

Chest heaving, he spun me around, holding me hostage against him. "That was new. After all this time you're still keeping me on my toes." His hot breath fanned along my neck, and I shuddered with revulsion. "If you're this upset about Sera, then maybe I've finally found the right motivation for you." He rested his chin on my shoulder, and I jerked it up, connecting with the bone. He swore, twisting my wrists.

I gave a cry of pain, panting. "I'll find a way to hurt you just like you've hurt all of us."

"You mean Sera, don't you? Because I might be willing to make a deal now after witnessing this little display. You never did this for Logan."

How did I explain the difference between the man I loved and the woman who was like a sister to me? Romantic relationships can fall apart at any time, but with a sister, a best friend, you expect them to be with you forever. Losing either is unexplainable grief, but one you can move on from, and the other will fester for the rest of your existence. And even worse, is knowing that you are the one responsible for causing pain to a loved one.

"What do you want?" I'd do anything for Sera, even give up Logan if it came down to it.

"I want you to choose me over him."

Chapter 23

"What is that? A tattoo?" The dark ink peeked out from under Ben's shirt as he turned the steering wheel of his car to make a right. At a glance, it looked like a line of letters and numbers. Which in itself was odd, but it was especially so since Ben didn't have any tattoos. At least he didn't in the future. So if he had one now, he'd gotten it recently, and only in this loop.

Ben quickly tugged the sleeve of the shirt down over his forearm, meeting my gaze steadily. "It's none of your business."

I ground my teeth together. "Why do you even want to be with me at this point when you clearly can't stand to be near me?"

"It'll be different when you forget all of this."

"I forgot before, from what you're telling me, and you

still treated me like shit. Yes, I'm referring to our marriage."

"You were a brat. Expecting things like—"

"Like kindness? Respect? Basic human decency? How dare I expect any of those things? Especially from my husband. Sooo sorry about that."

"It's your attitude. How am I not supposed to be pissed off when this is how you always talk to me?"

"I talk to you like this because this is how I talk to assholes!"

Ben slammed his fist on top of the steering wheel, causing me to jump. "I don't know how it happened, but you're worse since you've come back here. I hope I don't have to break you again."

"Break me? I'm not a fucking horse!" I shot to the door, rattling the handle.

He lunged for my arm, yanking me towards him as the car came to a stop. "We're here. Now do what I told you or Sera will be the one to pay the price."

Trembling, I smacked at his hand. "Don't touch me."

He sneered. "I'll be doing a lot more than touching you once we get this situation ironed out again."

Bile surged up my esophagus at the thought of me willingly giving my body to him once I forgot. He could spin any number of lies and I would be clueless. "This is what you did to Logan to make him leave me, wasn't it? You forced him to abandon me."

Ben flung my arm away. "It wasn't hard."

"How do I know you're going to fix what you broke with Sera and Derek after I forget about her?"

"Guess you're just going to have to trust me." He slid out of the car, and rounded to my side, yanking the door open. "Come on, let's get this over with."

I glared up at him. "I'm going to need more than an empty promise. I need some sort of guarantee."

Ben spoke through clenched teeth, "How about this? You do a good enough job convincing Logan about us, and I will find a way to alleviate your concerns about Sera."

I sat there staring up at him, our gazes clashing in a battle of wills. I wanted to spit on him and tell him to fuck off, but I also realized he held all the trump cards in this game. I had to hope that if I made him happy, he'd reward me for my actions.

My throat burned. He'd done that in our marriage sometimes, given me something small for doing what he wanted. But Sera's future happiness wasn't a small thing, and I didn't know if I could do enough for Ben to follow through with his promise. I had to try though ... for Sera. For her, I was about to rip my own damn heart out—again—and promise myself to the bastard I'd been wanting to escape for years.

He offered me his hand, and I glared at it, choosing to exit the car on my own steam. We then trudged together along the sidewalk leading to Logan's apartment building.

Dread and panic combined in my gut, roiling. I moved forward on wobbly legs, my mind still scanning for options, coming up with none. There was something about Ben that terrified me on a level I couldn't quite grasp. Aside from the power he wielded, it was as if there was something deeply rooted in my psyche that told me to obey him, to listen, despite me rankling against it. After all I'd learned, I had to assume it was past conditioning I had no recollection of. Something in the caverns of my brain, hidden in the darkest recesses, that was reacting from experience, just like Logan knew to do with me.

"Hurry up," Ben snapped over his shoulder since I'd fallen behind a few steps, dragging my feet, quite literally.

"He might not be home," I muttered.

"If he's not, then we'll wait."

I swallowed several times, my throat dry despite the moisture in the air. Wrapping my arms around my middle, I forced myself to continue following Ben. He buzzed Logan's apartment, and I didn't bother to wonder how he knew which one was his without any names or labels next to the buttons.

"Yeah?" Logan's husky voice came over the intercom.

"It's me," I croaked. The door immediately buzzed, and Ben pulled it open, letting me walk ahead of him.

Logan jogged down the stairs to meet me, freezing when he spotted Ben. His gaze swung to my face, darkening. "What's going on?"

"I came to tell you something."

Ben chose that moment to take my clammy hand within his, a small smile tugging at his lips.

Logan's nostrils flared, rage seeping into his

expression as his gaze flicked down to where we were joined. He looked back up at me expectantly. "What is it?"

"I came to tell you that I'm with Ben." I bent my knees slightly to keep from swaying. "I choose him." Ben squeezed my hand hard, and I gritted my teeth. "I choose him over you."

Logan's upper lip curled. "Tell me what happened."

I knew he was fishing for information about whether or not Ben changed something in the timeline without his knowledge, and I forgot everything again, or if something else entirely was afoot.

Ben didn't know that Logan had any memories even in dream form. And he had no idea that he was also aware of the whole time-traveling thing at all. I wanted to keep it that way. I wasn't sure if it would make a difference or not, but I didn't want to risk it.

I shrugged. "I don't know what you want me to say. Nothing happened. I was seeing both of you and I decided I want Ben. He thought we should come and tell you together. Since Ben and I are to-together now. He didn't want there to be any confusion."

Logan's jaw muscles jumped as he continued to stare at me, his gaze darkening with violence. "Tell me what's really going on."

Tears welled in the corners of my eyes, burning, but I blinked them back. "I just did." *Sera needs you. You have to sell this for her.* "And I love him. I'm in love with Ben. Not you. I never had any real feelings for you. I was just trying to make Ben jealous." I gave Ben a sly smile as if to say my little jealousy ploy worked, and now the entire thing was a cute joke between us. "And much to his chagrin, he couldn't take seeing me with you. Even if my scheme was devious, he wants to be with me. And I want nothing more than to be with him."

"I don't believe you."

"What?" Ben said. "You can't believe she'd pick me over you? Maybe I'm just better in bed." He shoved his hand into my hair, and yanked me against him, his lips crashing down on mine brutally.

I whimpered but didn't pull away, letting him push his tongue into my mouth as his other hand roamed down to rest on my ass, squeezing roughly.

Internally I was screaming, fighting with all my might, but on the outside I made myself lean into his slimy embrace, even moaning a bit as if I'd forgotten we had an audience.

When Ben finally deemed it long enough to throw our physical relationship in Logan's face, he slowly pulled away, a smug grin adorning his face. I longed to scratch it off with my nails, to claw at his visage until it was nothing but a bloody mess.

Instead, I met Logan's stark gaze again. "Please don't try to contact me again."

Satisfied, Ben laced our fingers together and turned to leave.

"No," Logan growled. "I'm not going to let you do this to her again—to us."

Ben was torn away from me and thrown to the ground

before I comprehended what was happening. Logan's fist connected with his nose, and I gasped as blood spurted at the contact.

Ben rolled away, pushing to his feet. "You wanna go a few rounds, then let's do this." He shifted into what appeared to be some kind of fighting stance.

Logan flashed him a feral grin. "Sure, I'd love to make you bleed some more."

A vicious part of me mentally cheered, rallying for Logan to do just that, make Ben bleed. But it wouldn't help me with my objective of securing Sera's future happiness.

"Logan, no." Launching at him, I managed to drape myself along his back, my arms wrapped around his neck. "Please, don't hurt him just because I damaged your ego or something."

Logan stilled, his chest heaving under my grip. His voice cracked when he said, "He got to you again, didn't he? You don't remember any of it."

I didn't want him to say anything, to give himself away if he somehow managed to not already do so. My last chance to escape Ben possibly still laid with Logan and what little knowledge he contained. If the extent of what Logan knew was revealed to Ben, then it could all be erased. After all, Ben had taken Sera from my life, slicing her cleanly out of it like a surgeon. Nothing else seemingly changed except for her absence. It was another mystery I'd probably never solve. Therefore, any little scrap of a chance for our salvation needed to be protected at all costs.

"He took Sera from me. And I need to make sure she's going to be okay—that she can be happy one day wherever she is." It was all I could think to say, hoping it was enough to make Logan understand that I had to do this. And that him beating Ben to a bloody pulp wouldn't do either of us any good.

"Sera? Who's Sera?"

A wave of hopelessness rocked me. Logan didn't remember Sera. I don't know why I expected him to. It was nice to imagine I had someone who understood, who would know why I was doing what I was doing. Ben had managed to take that from me as well.

I let go, sliding from Logan's back. "Never mind. All you need to know is that you fighting Ben is useless. I chose him."

The more I considered Logan's reaction, I wasn't even sure he remembered anything about time travel or his dreams. Maybe his memory of time travel had been wiped right along with Sera. It was difficult to tell when the change in this reality solidified, and how it rippled into effect without me so much as noticing until it was done. Without that knowledge, I wasn't going to figure out the rest of the puzzle with a few coded words. And I didn't have time for anything else.

It was done. Ben had won.

Logan turned, his agony-filled gaze snagging mine. I

couldn't bear the weight of his stare, so I dropped my head, mumbling, "Just let me go."

Whether or not he remembered what I wanted and needed him to, I was hurting him regardless. I was breaking things off with the man I truly wanted to be with to enter into a relationship with the man who was manipulating time itself to control my life.

Whirling, I dashed from the building, whispering as I went, "Good-bye, Logan. This time for good."

Ben joined me at his car, dried blood cracking on his face as he smiled. "I may have a broken nose, but I think he's in worse shape than me." He chuckled. "What you did and said, not bad at all. I'm pleased."

"Good for you."

"Don't give me an attitude now." He opened my door, and as I got in the car, he glanced over his shoulder and kissed my cheek. "I bet he's still watching. I bet he's eating his guts out." He shut the door and came around to the driver's side, still grinning. "I bet he can't stop thinking about how I'm going to be fucking you from now on."

Bile burned its way up my throat. "I never agreed to have sex with you." It wouldn't be the first time with him, we were married in the future after all, but I didn't know what I knew now ... about everything.

Ben snorted. "You'll come to me willingly once you forget. Just like you did before." He leaned over to brush his thumb over my bottom lip.

I jerked back, smacking my head on the window. "Don't touch me."

He scowled in response but withdrew to his side of the car. "I'm really going to enjoy it when you're begging me to be inside of you."

I couldn't help the tears that sprung from my eyes, trailing their way down my face. I'd wanted a second chance at my life, a chance to make better choices, and I'd thought I finally found it. As it turned out, I would never even get the opportunity to make my own choices, let alone the right or wrong ones.

I silently cursed the day time travel had become a real possibility. Just because one can, doesn't mean one should. I would serve as a cautionary tale of why that was true ... if anyone, including myself, could remember any of it even happened.

Chapter 24

An explainable feeling of dread had seeped into my very bones, lingering without any signs of receding. There was no rhyme or reason as to why though. My life was in a good place. I was doing good in school, I had a good group of friends, and a boyfriend who loved me. Even delving deeper, into my home life and class choices, my plans for the future … good, good, good. Everything seemed good, and as it should be.

So why can't I shake this dread? This feeling that something is horribly wrong?

Maybe it was the dreams—the lucid dreams that felt like more than figments of my imagination. They'd begun about a week ago, some short and sweet, and others long and drawn out as if the entire night was consumed by them.

Even now his ice-blue eyes haunted me, having taken up permanent residence in my brain. If I wasn't actively thinking of him, then he was still there, casting a dark shadow over everything I did.

It has to be the dreams. There's no other explanation. But why—why am I having them and what do they mean?

"I need to go," I said, giving a half-hearted wiggle to get out of bed.

A solid mass of man slid in behind me. He wrapped an arm around my waist, pulling me snugly against his chest. I could feel the hard length of him pushing against my ass as his large, callused hand lazily moved down, down, down my abdomen, and past the barrier of my underwear.

"Stop. I don't have time for this."

Hot breath fanned along the side of my neck as he nipped at my tender flesh.

I shivered with delight, my traitorous body bowing into his ministrations. "I'm serious. I don't have time."

Suddenly I found myself flipped onto my back, those icy eyes blazing with lust as their owner loomed over me. One side of his mouth kicked up, his voice raspy and low. "You can make the time."

"No, I can't. Not today."

His lips found mine as his weight pressed into me, my legs involuntarily wrapping around his middle.

"Fine. Maybe I can spare five minutes," I murmured into his mouth.

Breaking the kiss and the hold my legs had him in, he moved down the length of my body, settling between my thighs. When he lifted his blazing eyes to meet mine, I frowned. "Okay, maybe fifteen."

Grinning smugly, he pulled my underwear aside to suck on my clit, causing my back to arch off the bed.

How? How does he get me so turned on so fast?

As if ravenous, he feasted on my flesh, all the while his gaze remained fixated on me, watching every little reaction, and lapping up my every moan and plea for more. More, more, more.

"Don't you have class?"

Startled back to reality, the memory of the dream scattered, causing shame and embarrassment to settle in its place. The mystery man was becoming more of a nightmare than a dream, his existence, although only in my mind, driving a wedge between me and my very real, flesh and blood boyfriend. Which was utterly ridiculous, and completely unfair. But then again … perhaps that was why I'd invented a fictional man in my sleep, to have something to hold against Ben when he was otherwise perfect in every single way. Of course, he couldn't live up to the ideals conjured by imagination. No one could.

What the hell is wrong with me? Why am I trying to sabotage myself? Could it be boredom? Do I just need some kind of manufactured drama? Ugh. Seriously … Why am I like this?

Grimacing, I turned to regard my roommate, Ashley. She was lounging on her bed with a book in her lap, a small, tentative smile gracing her mouth.

"Yeah, I do have class. I'm going to head out soon." I'd already skipped my morning lab, hating myself anew for picking such an early class. Clearly, I'd been over-ambitious when scheduling my semester.

She nodded, going back to reading her book without another word.

Ashley and I had a tense truce. Or maybe that was just on my part. It wasn't that I didn't like her, it was just that everything she did grated on my nerves. She was too short, too blonde, too tan, too ... Ashley. She'd done nothing wrong, and I reminded myself of that often, internally chastising myself for being such a mega bitch when it came to her. I would convince myself to be nicer, and then *boom*, she'd just be there, sitting on her bed, existing in my space, and I wanted to throw her out of the room along with all of her ridiculously flowered décor.

And again ... Why am I like this?

I had a rage inside of me, hiding beneath the dread, that couldn't be explained either. I didn't know when it had shown up, or where it came from, just that it sizzled inside of me, waiting to explode, a ticking time bomb with an already lit fuse.

Some days, it was like I didn't fit into this world, that I didn't belong in my life, and that didn't make any kind of sense either.

Sighing, I grabbed my shoulder bag, and skulked to the door, muttering a halfway polite good-bye to Ashley.

She grunted a response, the tone causing me to grind my teeth.

Shuffling out into the crisp afternoon, I unbuttoned my jacket, the heat of the sun causing me to sweat a bit. I tilted my head back to enjoy the warmer than normal afternoon for this time of year, while I attempted to focus my thoughts. It was exceedingly difficult to do so lately, another thing to add to my list of mental hangups that were new, unpleasant, and completely unexplainable.

"Hey, Harper!" a masculine voice echoed across Forbes Quad. "Wait up!"

I turned stiffly, swallowing back a grimace as my gaze caught on the tall, lanky kid jogging towards me.

"Hey, Evan," I said, plastering a welcoming smile on my face. It was brittle around the edges though, and I hoped he wouldn't notice.

Evan ran his slender fingers through his floppy auburn hair. "My friend's band is playing at Graffiti's tonight. You should come." He produced a small, rectangular flyer, offering it to me. "Bring your friends. And your boyfriend if you want."

Taking the bright blue paper from him gingerly, I stared at it a moment before responding. "Oh, uh, I mean …" The event didn't seem much like Ben's scene, but I could probably talk him into it if I wanted to go.

"Come on, it'll be fun. Plus, it's kind of a big deal that they got a showcase there. It would really help if we filled the place up."

"Sounds great." I forced my strained smile to widen. Maybe getting out and shaking things up a bit would do my mood some good.

Evan grinned, showcasing a crooked front tooth. That, combined with the smattering of freckles on every visible inch of pale skin made him seem endearing, in a younger brother sort of way. "All right, I'll see you there."

Waving at him feebly, I watched him retreat the way he came. As soon as he was out of sight, I returned my attention to the flyer crumpled between my sweaty fingers. *No Name*, which was apparently the band's name, was plastered across the top in a questionable font. Followed by Graffiti's logo, the address, along with the date and time.

I blinked repeatedly, reading and rereading the scant information presented to me on that scrap of paper. *No Name? That doesn't sound quite right.* Not that I'd ever heard of them before. But it seemed off. *Like maybe it should be ...*

I nibbled my bottom lip. *Nameless. Nameless has a better ring to it. But what do I know about band names?* Shrugging, I stuffed the flyer into my bag.

"Harper!" I turned as Ben loped across the quad, coming from the same direction Evan had just gone. He slid his arm around my waist and pulled me into his side, kissing my cheek.

I shirked out of his embrace, not particularly wanting to be touched by him. My mind flashed to my most recent dream, of an icy gaze blazing up at me from between my thighs, and suddenly even the thought of Ben gave me major ick factor. Suppressing a cringe at my complete and utter stupidity, I said, "Hey. I didn't expect to see you until later."

Ben frowned, annoyance flickering through his baby blues. "What's wrong?"

"What do you mean?" I started walking, keeping my gaze straight ahead. I wasn't capable of dealing with an emotional interrogation from Ben right now. There was no way telling him about my dreams would be helpful to our relationship in any way, shape, or form. Therefore, I needed to keep them a secret, and hopefully deal with them myself.

"You pulled away from me." As if to prove a point, he snagged my hand and interlaced our fingers.

Jerking slightly, I fought the urge to pull away again, revulsion roiling my gut. But I fought my instincts, both for me and for him. Plus, it would only serve to reinforce whatever he was attempting to prove and cause him to push harder for some kind of explanation. One that I refused to give. "It's just that it's hard to walk with you like that."

"Yeah, I guess," he muttered.

We walked in silence for a few minutes, both of us lost in our thoughts. Me, I was left to question my own sanity once again. I reminded myself that Ben was about as close to perfect as a boyfriend could get. Sure, we'd only officially been together a few weeks, but within that time he'd been nothing but caring and attentive. Plus, he was the kind of handsome that was usually reserved for the cover of magazines. And yet ...

And yet, sometimes when he touched me my skin scrawled. Today wasn't an anomaly when it came to that particular reaction. I had no rational explanation for it though. Because it wasn't always that way. I filed the entire phenomenon under the growing list of issues about my life that I couldn't explain. I had no one to talk to about it either since most of my female friends looked at me like I'd grown an extra head when I even started down the road of complaining about Ben.

Ultimately, I decided to give it time. Our relationship, my moods ... I would hate to throw away something good because I was going through some kind of existential crisis.

"Oh, hey, I was thinking about cutting my hair. What do you think?"

The angular planes of Ben's handsome face scrunched up. "Why would you want to? You have such beautiful long hair."

"I don't know, maybe I just need a change." It was possible the idea to change my hair was linked to my foul moods, and I was falling victim to the girly urge to alter my hair as a weird kind of trauma response to whatever had gotten under my skin.

"I love your hair long."

I ground my teeth together. "I asked your opinion, and it's noted."

Ben's hand tightened around mine. "You don't care what my opinion is. You just want me to agree with you to cut it. To encourage you—but I won't. Cutting your hair would be a mistake."

I halted abruptly, and someone swore at me as we barely avoided a collision. I ignored them and stared at Ben, his visage a mask of anger for some unknown reason. "You think I'll look bad with short hair? That's kind of mean since you're basically saying I'm not pretty enough to pull it off."

"Don't be ridiculous," Ben snapped. "Face shapes and all of that shit make a difference with hair. There are as many hairstyles as there are for a reason. We don't all look good with the same cut."

Fluffing my hair, I stuck out my lower lip in a pout, attempting to defuse the situation before it turned into a full-blown fight. "But I think my hair might be cute short. Plus, lower maintenance."

"No. Don't cut it."

My nostrils flared. Now I wanted to cut it even more. Instead of letting him know that little tidbit, and escalating the situation right there on the sidewalk in front of a bunch of strangers, I pulled the flyer for No Name out of my bag and waved it in his face.

"We should go to this."

He glanced at the flyer, eyes narrowing. "Why?"

"I don't know, because Evan asked us to, and he said it would help out his friend's band to fill the place."

Ben's gaze flicked from me to the flyer several times before he finally said, "Yeah, whatever. If you want to go, we can."

"Mmm … great." I stuffed the flyer back in my bag and started walking again.

Ben moved to grab my hand, but I pretended to fiddle with the sleeve of my jacket. I didn't want to hold it before, and I certainly didn't want to now after his attitude about my hair.

When we got to The Cathedral, I made a quick exit, waving at Ben. "I'll see you later."

He stood watching me, his hands in his pockets, and a scowl on his face.

But I didn't care. Not one little bit.

Chapter 25

"IDs," the supersized bouncer demanded.

My mind drifted, snagging on the fight Ben and I had on the way to Graffiti's.

"I can't believe you went and fucking cut your hair after I told you not to!"

"And I can't believe you thought you actually had a say in what I did with my hair! If you don't like it, if you think it makes me unattractive, then break up with me."

"It's always the hair with you. Every fucking time, it's how I know."

"What are you even talking about? This is the first time I've changed my hair since you've known me."

"Grow it the fuck back then."

"No."

"I hate it."

"Then break up with me."

"It's not going to be that easy for you."

"What?"

"Nothing. Just ... we'll talk about this more later."

"The fuck we will unless it's you apologizing."

"Harper," Ben snapped, his tone laced with annoyance. "Pay attention."

The tips of my ears heated. "Oh, yeah, right." After fishing around in my pocket, I produced my license, offering it to the bouncer with a slight tremble.

I shook my head, to dislodge the remnants of our fight, focusing back on my current situation.

The bouncer's eyes darted over the bit of plastic in his palm. "Give me your right hand."

Grabbing my wrist with more gentleness than I expected, he drew a large, black X across the top of my hand that went from knuckle to wrist. "If you get caught with an alcoholic drink in there, you'll get yourself kicked out and banned. You hear me?"

I nodded, and Ben grunted in affirmation.

He unhooked the rope and handed me back my ID. "Go on in."

Scurrying into the venue, the sound of the bouncer's curt, "Next!" was swallowed by a wall of music.

My nose, eyes, and throat caught fire, the burning sensation causing me to gasp for air as I swiped at my eyes.

Ben halted abruptly, peering at me with renewed annoyance. "What's wrong now?"

I waved my hand around in an attempt to clear the

cloud of smoke that was threatening to suffocate me. "I don't know why the smoke is bothering me. It normally doesn't."

He rolled his eyes and tugged me along by our joined hands. Even though he was still pissed, he continued to be incredibly touchy-feely with me. I was not a fan, but at the same time, I was resigned for some reason. Maybe I was just tired of fighting for the day. But somehow it felt like more than that, like I was soul-deep weary, and a part of me had given up completely. I was numb, and I wasn't sure I cared anymore about what happened around me or to me.

"Let's get some drinks," Ben muttered, steering me toward the bar.

My gaze snagged on a tall guy at the other end of the bar, my breath catching in my throat at the sight of him. He wasn't exactly the same, but similar—so similar to the guy from my dreams, younger maybe—or perhaps it was all in my imagination. He did have the dark hair and light-colored eye combo, but the shade was difficult to see from the distance. He was tall and lithely muscled from what I could tell, with features that were somehow pretty and masculine at the same time. Check, and check.

I was nearly overcome by the sudden urge to drop my boyfriend's hand, and to approach the stranger just to be near him. Even if he wasn't the guy from my dreams, because how could he be? This guy ... well, his raw sexual appeal was—

"What are you staring at?" Ben demanded.

I quickly turned away from the attractive stranger who had temporarily enthralled me. *This is merely proof of your self-sabotaging tendencies. That guy is nothing special. Just another hot guy at the bar. Ignore him and focus on fixing whatever problem that's festering in your relationship with Ben.* "Nothing in particular. Just checking out the crowd for anyone I might know."

"Spot anyone?"

"No." I gave him a small smile. "You know what, I need to go to the restroom real fast."

Not waiting for him to respond, I hurried around to the back wall, following it until I spotted a sign pointing me in the right direction. There was already a handful of girls waiting their turn outside of my would-be sanctuary, but I wasn't about to let that deter me. Dashing around the line, I blurted, "Don't have to pee, just need a sink."

"You better not be lying!" someone shouted as I burst into the restroom. "Because if I pee my pants, I will find you!"

The several girls next up for a stall eyed me with a mix of annoyance and hostility until they saw I did indeed head straight for the sink farthest from the door.

One of them called out, "She's cool! Just using the sink like she said!"

I pretended to fuss with my hair and makeup while my mind raced wildly. *What is it about this whole night that feels so off ... wrong? It's oddly familiar, and at the same time, it's like something is missing.*

Gritting my teeth, I stared my reflection down. My

hair looked good, not the huge mistake Ben was making it out to be. In fact, his aversion to me getting it cut had merely served as an added push to do it. *And it feels right. Like I'm more myself somehow. Fuck Ben. He'll either get over it or he won't. I'm not going to let him ruin my night either.*

Steeling myself once more, I hesitantly made my way back out into the main room and headed to the bar to find Ben. Inhaling a deep breath, I instantly regretted the burn of cigarette smoke as it resumed its torture of my lungs.

"Do I know you?" a deep, male voice rasped.

I whirled towards the owner of it, finding myself staring into the ice-blue eyes of the guy I'd been ogling just a few minutes earlier. The same eyes that had been haunting my dreams every night lately. "N-No," I stammered. "I don't think so." *How is this possible? I have to be losing my mind.*

"It's just—" He reached a hand up to skim his knuckles along the edge of my hair. "There's just something about you."

Does he feel it, too? Or—

No, don't be ridiculous. I knew his type, which was exactly why I was lucky to have someone like Ben. And the dreams ... I bet I probably saw this guy on campus at some point and invented him—the dream version of him — to sabotage my relationship with Ben because I was afraid. Yes, I was afraid deep inside. Of what I wasn't exactly sure, but admitting to the fear was half the battle. I hoped.

Now, to run this asshole off before I did something

irreversible. Snorting, I said, "There's just something about you. Does that line work for you a lot?"

He twisted a piece of my hair around his finger, his pupils flaring. "I don't need lines. And this isn't one."

Placing my hand against his chest, I gave a half-hearted shove. "I have a boyfriend."

He leaned in closer and licked his lips. "Tell me your name."

"Didn't you hear me? I just told you that I have a boyfriend."

One side of his mouth kicked up into a mocking smile. "Does that mean no one but him can know your name?"

"Don't be stupid." *Why aren't I pulling away? Ben will flip his shit if he sees you like this. And he has every right to. How would you feel if he was in a dark corner of a club, inches away from a hot girl?*

He tugged lightly on my hair. "So what is it then?"

I blinked. "What?"

His gaze darted along my features, taking every minute detail in, the thought making me squirm. "Your name. Tell me your name."

"Harper," I breathed. *And I still haven't pulled away. What the hell am I doing?*

He licked his lips again, and my eyes followed the movement unwillingly, as if I was caught in his thrall. "Harper. You don't seem like a Harper."

My mind had gone blank. The revving of my desire stealing every bit of power needed to think clearly. "Oh? What do I seem like then?"

He shook his head. "I don't know."

"You don't know?"

"Unh-uh."

The current band's set was over, and while the next performers prepped, someone had launched a playlist, and surprisingly for the venue, Cyndi Lauper's song "Time After Time" blared from the speakers above our heads.

Those lyrics, Cyndi's haunting, melancholy words, ripped open something in my chest, and I sucked in a ragged breath, desperate for something—something just out of my reach.

Suddenly, between one heartbeat and the next, his mouth was on mine, lips and teeth clashing as I launched myself enthusiastically into the kiss. A groan escaped him on an exhale, and I inhaled the sweet sound, transforming it into a moan on my next breath.

He broke away an instant later. "Come on," he rasped, tugging on my hand.

Wait. "What? I can't go anywhere with you." This was a mistake. A huge mistake. One that I couldn't believe I was making. I didn't cheat. I wasn't a cheater. And yet there I was making out with a stranger while my boyfriend waited for me at the bar. What was I thinking—or not thinking? What the hell had possessed me? Because that kiss—that kiss ...

"Come on," he repeated, his arm around my waist as he led me out a back exit door. Mentally, I continued to protest, but I remained physically pliant, following his lead.

Stop! What are you doing? You can't just go with this stranger!

Once out in the alley, I stared up at him, unable to force myself to leave, and yet utterly shocked that I'd gone so willingly … I couldn't understand why I was doing any of it. And why I was running headlong for the choices that would inevitably blow up my life.

And what about Ben?

Ben doesn't have to know.

Wait. What? I'm not that person. I could never … would never do such a horrible thing to someone. Cheat. I'm not a cheater. And yet, that kiss—I already did. I already cheated.

"What's your name?" I heard myself asking.

He smiled, showcasing dimples. "Logan."

My own answering grin stretched my mouth. "You seem like a Logan."

He twirled a piece of my hair around his finger, leaning closer. "Yeah?"

I pursed my lips and nodded. "Yeah."

His lips found mine again, his tongue pushing in to plunder my mouth with a fierce familiarity. His hands delved into my hair, angling my head back farther for better access, and I threw my leg over his hip, hooking it behind him as I rocked forward, moaning loudly at the feel of him.

What are you going to do? Have sex with a literal stranger in an alleyway? Who the hell are you right now? And what about Ben? Think about Ben. Don't hurt Ben like this.

"Harper?" As if I'd summoned him by thinking his name one too many times, I barely registered Ben's voice through my lust-filled haze.

Shoving at Logan, I whipped my head in Ben's direction. He stood by the back door, anger flushing his skin a lovely shade of red.

I glanced up at Logan, his gaze not wavering from my face, even with Ben's appearance. "Come home with me. Forget him," he murmured.

"Harper," Ben said again. "What the fuck?"

My face crumpled as the realization of what I'd done finally hit home. *Cheater, cheater, cheater.* "I'm sorry. I don't know what's wrong with me. I just don't—" I choked back a sob.

Logan grabbed my arm. "There's nothing wrong with you."

"Don't touch my girlfriend! Mine! Not yours!" Ben bellowed.

Pivoting, I dashed down the alleyway, running as fast as my wobbly legs could carry me, guilt nipping at my heels. But I couldn't outrun myself, and I couldn't outrun what I'd done.

I'm a shitty person. A horrible, shitty person. I hurt a good guy for no reason. Why? Why did I do that? Why?

Tears dripped down my face and blurred my vision, my chest heaving with each painful sob.

"Harper!" Ben called, his footsteps heavy behind mine.

A second set of footsteps echoed along my trail. "Wait!"

"Leave me alone!" I screeched. "Both of you leave me—"

Tires squealed, a bright light stole my vision completely. A loud thump. A brief instant of mind-boggling pain, and then ...

Nothing.

Chapter 26

A kaleidoscope of colors exploded, followed by a parade of images twisting and turning, spiraling before my eyes as if on the waves of time itself. They were scenes from my life—my first life—the original one before anything had been altered. And as they faded, as the concept of who I used to be, who I really was, settled into place, a lingering bit of audio played through my mind, the corresponding visual already faded. All that remained was my voice, and of course, Logan's.

"If you're going to be Snow White for Halloween, then who am I going to be?"

"Prince Charming of course."

Logan's low laugh. "There's nothing charming about me, baby."

"Stop. And you don't get a say in Halloween. It's my holiday. You'll wear what I tell you and you'll like it."

A grunt. "Can I at least see your costume?"

A door creaking, and then some rustling.

"Well, what do you think? Is it incentive enough to get you into that Prince Charming costume?"

"That's definitely not the Disney version." A dark chuckle. "Oh, yeah, I like it. You kind of look like her, too, especially with your hair. If Snow White was a porn star."

"Hey! I'm not sure how to take that."

"I'll give you something to take."

A squeal and then giggling. "Stop. I mean it. You're being a weird perv right now. And that line ..."

"You love it."

"Logan ..."

The sound of a zipper, and a moan.

"That's my good little, Snow."

The sound of a smack. "No. Absolutely not. I can tell where this is going, and I will not accept that nickname."

"Whatever you say, Snow."

I groaned. "It's going to stick, isn't it? Just like that?"

"That's how nicknames generally get started."

"I don't like it and I refuse to answer to it."

"We'll see."

It had stuck, the ridiculous nickname for an even more ridiculous reason. It was corny and stupid, and yet ... it was a part of who we were, part of who Logan and I were together. We'd shared silly moments, and dumb moments, and mundane moments, along with the special, magical ones. All of it wove together to form a tapestry of who we were as a couple, and what our lives were together. Each and every one important in its own way.

And Ben had ripped it away, leaving remnants, an echo of what we once were, pieces like my nickname to cling to —to associate with what was lost.

As even the last bit faded, and I swam in the space between life and death, between one second and the next, hovering in the unknown, I also understood that we couldn't get it back.

Because life was made up of choices, each leading to the next, and then the next, and so on … change one thing and the rest collapses like a house of cards. It couldn't be patched back together by fixing one choice. And it couldn't be replicated in exactly the same way either. Basically, time, life, all of it was too fragile to glue back together once broken. And our lives, mine and Logan's, what we'd shared, had been shattered by Ben's interference.

Hopelessness washed over me, pulling me under, deeper and deeper.

Ben had won. He'd won.

I let myself be swept away, a single soul drifting through all of time and space.

"HARPER, TAKE THE HEADSET OFF NO–"

My surroundings disappeared in a rush, a flash of white encompassing everything.

I blinked, once, twice, a third time, finding myself back in the leather chair, Sera next to me in the matching one.

327

"What happened?" I croaked.

"Oh, thank God!" Glorita tore the equipment off of me and yanked me out of the chair and into her arms. "I was so worried!"

The memories settled into my mind, the flurry of them hitting me all at once. From every single timeline, and alternate reality created by the time travel device I'd help create, there they all were coexisting within the folds of my brain, almost too much to perceive. Their presence expanding my reality in a nearly impossible way.

I swiped a hand down my face, my palm sweaty. "I died." Yes, that realization burned through me, causing adrenaline to surge. I'd died, been hit by a car or what felt like a friggin' bus, that part I wasn't positive about, but something had ended my life as I'd run from Ben and Logan out of that alleyway back in 1998.

"Death must have sent me back. A reset. It's the only explanation." It'd been pure, dumb luck. I sputtered on a hysterical laugh. I'd actually been lucky to be run down by that vehicle because it was the only way to start back at the beginning. Otherwise, I would have been lost forever.

"Death?" Logan moved around Glorita, grabbing me by the shoulders. His ice-blue eyes were wide with alarm as they bounced over my features, checking and assessing. "What are you talking about?"

Choking on a sob, I said, "Death sent me all the way to the beginning. To the very first experiment in any timeline. Before he got ahold of it. Before any of it went truly wrong." Before I'd lost both Logan and Sera, the two people who mattered the most to me in the world. My husband and my best friend.

Whirling, I pulled Sera out of her chair, her eyes already open. "What are you doing?" She stumbled forward, and Logan caught her.

"You remember that movie *Donnie Darko*?" I scanned the room, my gaze searching for what I needed.

"Yeah, it was—" Sera started, but I cut her off.

"It's kind of what happened to me. In a sense. Well, we both died. Which was the ending for Donnie, but the beginning for me. Or really the ending for me, and the beginning for him. Or, well, it's complicated."

Seeing the golf club in the corner of the room, the one Sera decided was a better option than a silly wooden bat if she needed to take a swing at someone, I scurried to secure it, raising it above my head.

"What the fuck, Harper?" Sera screeched.

Glorita cowered by the door, frozen like a deer in headlights. Wanting to flee, but unable to make herself. At least I knew she wouldn't try to stop me from doing what I was about to do.

I turned my head, and held Sera's gaze for a moment, nailing her in place, before locking gazes with Logan. "You guys need to trust me on this one. I'll explain everything later."

Letting the memories of being married to the wrong person, to letting him touch me, to him ripping away parts of me I didn't even know were missing, they fueled my fury as I swung as hard as I could, the rage buffering me from the reverberation ricocheting up my arms each time I connected. I wasn't merely destroying bits and pieces of machinery, I was ensuring Ben had no way to control me ever again. I was securing my freedom.

Screams rent the air, mine I think, that eventually turned to sobs as I continued to swing, swing, swing.

"Harper," Logan said softly, his front pressing into my back as he reached up to take the golf club from my grip.

Sagging into him, I let him pry it away, the weapon of destruction clattering to the ground a moment later.

I spun, burying my face in his shoulder, inhaling his scent, absorbing his warmth, wanting nothing more than to lose myself in his strong embrace. My husband, my love, the man who I couldn't let go of no matter what Ben had done.

Sobs wracked my body, my throat full of what felt like razor blades, their bite shifting to slice with each inhale and exhale. Logan's grip on me tightened, and I knew he would never let me go. No matter what happened, he would hold on to me forever, throughout all of time.

Ben hadn't won. I did. I'd won.

And yet I'd still lost. The only way to keep him from all of it, the only way to unravel the tangled loops of time, was to never let any of it happen. Not even the part where my team and I made time travel possible.

My life's work was gone. Not in an instant, but dissolved into infinity itself.

But it was done. It was finally done.

Epilogue

My time spent in the past, the various versions of the timelines as they were set, reset, and altered by Ben, his determination to have his life yield the results he wanted, no matter the cost to the world around him, faded away like a nightmare in the light of day. The fear and the trauma still lingered, but it didn't hold any true threat, not anymore.

"I know you're not sleeping. Tell me what you're thinking about," Logan's deep voice rumbled under my ear.

Shifting, I tilted my chin up so I could see half of his face from my position of being splayed across his chest. I traced his strong jaw with my index finger, still in awe that he was mine again. That this beautiful, kind, amazing man loved me and had refused to let me go. "You know what I'm thinking about."

His hand fisted at my lower back, and he grated out, "If I could kill that son of a bitch, I would."

Ignoring Logan's simmering anger, I mused over a few things I couldn't let go of, the riddle of them holding my attention, no matter how hard I tried. "I don't understand how Ben got involved—how he managed to take control. How he could travel back and forth and yet I couldn't. Something obviously happened in the future, in a future that can't happen now because I've destroyed the machines, but ... but how? And why for that matter? We haven't seen him in years."

Logan kissed my forehead tenderly. "You're hard to forget, Snow."

On a roll, I continued, "And there were so many weird, unexplainable things that I encountered in some of the timelines. For instance, in one, before our initial experiment, I went to this hotel to—"

"A hotel, why?"

I waved him off. "I mentioned it before, but it's not the important part of the story. Like I was saying, I went to the hotel and there was a guy who let me borrow his room, but in that room, there was all of my usual hair products and a note. I didn't even consider it before, but I think the note was for me, from you. I think the guy was you. But if you knew about the time travel thing, then why didn't you talk to me? Explain? Stop me from going back? I don't know, something—anything beyond leaving a cryptic note that still doesn't make sense."

Logan sighed. "I wish I knew. But that guy, and all the

other versions, I know they were—are me, at least technically, but they don't feel like it since I don't have any of those memories."

I shook my head. "Yeah, I know, I just wish I had the answers."

I'd gone over and over my experiences, sharing every last detail that I could think of, with both Logan and Sera, hoping to fill in the missing pieces … somehow. But the more I revisited the events, the more confused I became.

Logan wrapped his arms around me, sighing heavily into my hair. "I can't believe you were going to risk losing me to make sure Sera was happy."

"I wasn't going to lose either of you." Pulling away from him so I could get a better read on his expression, I frowned slightly. "Does it bother you? The part where I pretended to be with Ben, to choose him over you so that he would help Sera?"

Logan's icy gaze warmed, his lips curling up at the corners into a smug smile. "Nah. You knew I'd find a way to you again and didn't need help. Sera did. I get it. I'm just stronger-willed than her."

Smacking at his chest, I laughed. "Don't let Sera hear you say that you're stronger-willed than her."

"Tell me about it," he grumbled.

"I'm giving you exactly two minutes to get decent before I come in," Sera called through our closed bedroom door as if mentioning her had summoned my friend from thin air.

Logan was on his feet in a flash, pulling on pants. He

glared at the closed door. "I told you before that the key is for emergencies only, Sera. We could have been in the middle of something."

"I would have waited," Sera retorted.

I chuckled. The current tension between the two most important people in my life normally would have caused me some grief, but after my time traveling debacle ... well, I savored even this part of our chaos. Because it was chaos of my making, and no one else's.

"We'll be out in a minute," I said, watching my husband cover his sculpted body with clothes. It had been quite the interesting experience to relive being with the younger version of him, meet him all over again, time after time, but I much preferred him now, with the laugh lines from our shared life, and the—

"Hurry up!" Sera called.

"Yeah, yeah, yeah," I muttered through the cotton shirt I pulled over my head.

"Three, two, one—" The door banged open, Sera's silhouette illuminated by the hallway light.

"Seriously?" Logan grumbled, pushing past her. "I'll be downstairs." He quirked an eyebrow at me and then glared at the back of Sera's head.

"What's so important that you've again annoyed Logan? You know he's going to have Derek give you another talk about boundaries. And he's going to change the locks ... again."

Sera rolled her eyes. "Mmm hmmm ... and I'll again ignore it, and you'll just give me the new key. I don't know why he bothers. Besides, everything annoys Logan. He wants things his way all the time."

"Hi, Pot, meet Kettle."

She narrowed her eyes at me. "I'm going to let that one go for now because I have much more important things to discuss."

"Oh? My curiosity is officially piqued."

My friend switched on the overhead light and moved into the bedroom as I was left blinking away the black spots from my vision.

"Have a look at this. Hopefully, it'll say enough." She pushed up her sleeve, revealing a tattoo resembling the brief glimpse I'd gotten of the one on Ben's arm.

My mouth went slack. "Is that— It looks like—"

She nodded furiously. "It is. It's the way to travel back and forth. The time-traveling hack we discovered in the future."

I couldn't take my eyes off it. "But that means ..."

"Yep, you're not the only one who went on a wacky ride through time."

Dread roiled my gut, and I staggered back to sit on the bed. "But Ben—if I didn't destroy it then he could still—"

"Don't worry about Ben. I took care of him. Permanently."

My gaze shot to hers. "You didn't— Did you kill him?" If I could have gotten away with it—if it was the only way —I didn't want to say that I would, but I couldn't say that I wouldn't either. Would Sera do the same if backed into a corner?

She clicked her tongue. "Don't be ridiculous. But he's dead nonetheless. He messed with the wrong people, finally."

"Are you … are you the wrong people?"

She laughed.

My eyes widened. She wasn't denying it, and honestly, I wasn't sure I wanted confirmation either way. "If this isn't about him, then what's it about?"

"That should be obvious. We have the power of time travel now." A huge grin spread across her face. "It wasn't destroyed after all."

"B-But …" I didn't know what to make of any of it. This revelation seemed impossible, and yet, it had all seemed that way before we'd discovered the answers. I'd made peace with losing the technology, telling myself that it was for the best, that no one should hold that kind of power, but at the same time …

"So what's the plan?"

"Whatever it is, you're not going without me this time." Logan appeared behind Sera, his large frame leaning on the wall just outside the door, his arms crossed over his muscular chest.

"Mmm hmmm … yep, whatever," Sera said, waving a hand at him idly. "We can do what we set out to do—"

"Help people!" I squealed.

Sera nodded once. "Yes, that. But before we delve into it completely, we have to take care of one thing first."

My body was buzzing with excitement, and it was an effort not to bounce around the room doing a weird happy dance. My life's work hadn't been destroyed after all. I could have my cake and eat it, too.

"Jordan."

The name dropped in between us like a bomb, blanketing the room in a tense silence. I frowned. "Who's Jordan?"

Sera's brow furrowed. "Exactly."

"What are you talking about? Just tell me who Jordan is."

She glanced behind her at my husband, and then back to me. "He's my Logan."

Goosebumps erupted along my flesh as dread pooled in my gut. "No. Derek is your Logan."

"No. Something happened. Something went wrong."

"But my death threw me back to the beginning. If something went wrong according to you, then maybe you're not even from this timeline. Maybe ..." I shook my head. "None of that matters. You're here now, and you have always been with Derek. It's who you're supposed to be with. He's your soulmate."

"I'm not so sure anymore. Remember The Mandela Effect?"

"Umm ... yeah, but that's been proven to not be a—"

"Oh, no," Sera said, "The Mandela Effect is very real, and it's caused by the early reckless attempts at time travel. Basically, we caused that shit."

Even Logan appeared shell-shocked by the admission.

"B-But then we shouldn't do it anymore—time travel. I was right to destroy the equipment. We can't— And if everything was rebooted then all of that should have been, too." Of course Sera, with her tattoo and claims of coming from the future, threw that theory directly into the fire, the ashes of it making it hard to breathe.

"It wasn't rebooted, not all of it anyhow. So now we have to make sure we fix what we broke." Sera glanced from me to Logan, and then back again. "I'll explain everything I know, and then you can help me come up with a plan. Also, when I said we'd be helping people, that's what I meant, we need to set the timelines back to the way they're supposed to be."

Timelines. Plural. Confirming the theory of the multiverses once again. "Okay," I whispered. "We're listening.

My stomach twisted with nerves and excitement. We were about to embark on another adventure. The three of us, together. And, hopefully, together we'd be stronger, smarter—better than we'd been separately because the question wasn't *if* we'd get into some kind of trouble, it was: what kind of trouble would we get into? The possibilities were nearly endless.

But as long as I had Logan and Sera with me, I could weather whatever was thrown at me, in the past, in the present, or in the future. Home is where the heart is, and mine belonged with my husband, and my soul sister. For all eternity.

Acknowledgments

As an overthinker, acknowledgments are quite an arduous task for me. I wonder if I'm being lackluster or too intense with the thanks. Or did I forget someone? Possibly I gave too much credit to someone and therefore slighted someone else who actually did a ton. A part of me doesn't want to include these in my books at all because the people I appreciate should know it already ... or do they??? No matter how I look at it these damn acknowledgments make me friggin' sweat.

But here there are anyways since if I don't include them then people will probably think I'm ungrateful and weird. I mean, I am weird, but I don't want people to think that. I am grateful though, so I'll just go-ahead and make this uncomfortable for everyone. Heh.

Okay, here I go. Right now. Actual acknowledgments to follow. Hopefully, they represent an appropriate level of gratitude to all the people in my life that deserve it.

(And yep ... I have totally copy & pasted what comes next from my *Virtual Reality Bites* book acknowledgments. Maybe next time I'll come up with something better. Probably not. But stranger things have happened.)

My amazing Hubby! Words can't begin to explain how

supportive and truly amazing he is. Hmmm … I think I already used the word amazing. But unlike in books, when honestly applied to someone, the word amazing means something, well, amazing. And my hubby is all of the things that word implies. Romance heroes are nothing compared to him.

Lindsay Tiry … what would I do without you? I hope I never have to find out. From cover design to interior graphics to logos, you do it all. Your talent is awe-inspiring, and I hope one day everyone else will be able to appreciate how you shine.

Melissa Ringsted … my illustrious editor. Without you, this book probably would have gone straight into the trash. Thank you for giving me the confidence to publish when I convinced myself that I was the worst writer in the history of writers, and for fixing all the words.

Ren, Kristin, Shona, Ruty … my O.G. chicas … I wouldn't be here without you. I'm beyond lucky to know all of you.

And last, but certainly not least, thank you to everyone who has taken the time to read this book. Hopefully, you enjoyed it, but even if you didn't, I still appreciate the fact that with so many options out there today, you even gave my book a fleeting chance.

About the Author

Ava Wixx escaped into books at a young age and decided to stay there. It was only a matter of time before she was driven to create her own fantasy worlds from fear of running out of places to explore. Reader, writer, dreamer … Ava only toils in reality when absolutely necessary. She lives in North Carolina with her husband, and spoiled mini-poodle.

www.ingramcontent.com/pod-product-compliance
Lightning Source LLC
Chambersburg PA
CBHW020356260626
47156CB00007B/2138